Anna

Congratulations on
winning this copy
of:

CARLOS CROSSES THE LINE !

I hope you
enjoy it,

Ed Webster

ALSO BY EDWARD D. WEBSTER

Soul of Toledo (2016)
The Gentle Bomber's Melody (2013)
A Year of Sundays (2004)

Carlos Crosses the Line

A Tale of Immigration, Temptation and Betrayal in the Sixties

Edward D. Webster

Casa de los Sueños Publishing

CARLOS CROSSES THE LINE by Edward D. Webster

Published by Casa de los Sueños Publishing

First Edition, August 2020

Copyright © 2020 Edward D. Webster

Author Services by Pedernales Publishing, LLC.
www.pedernalespublishing.com

Cover by Kristin Bryant

Library of Congress Control Number: 2020905530

ISBN: 978-0-9970320-2-4 Paperback Edition
ISBN: 978-0-9970320-1-7 Hardcover Edition
ISBN: 978-0-9970320-3-1 Digital Edition

Printed in the United States of America

To people who choose compassion

CHAPTER ONE

Julie Booker, May 1968, outside Delano, California

G*oddamn it.*
Julie drove as fast as her headlights would allow along the deserted two-lane road. Where was the friggin' mailbox?

She'd screwed up, and now they'd taken Carlos.

Goddamn it.

The bartender had said to take a dirt road just past a big white mailbox .... *There.*

A beige pickup was coming out of the road. She slammed the brakes, staring into the other vehicle, hoping it would be them, hoping *he* was okay. No—some other man inside. She let the truck pull out, swung the Camaro to the right, and hit the accelerator.

Back at the bar, she'd been overwhelmed. Hadn't expected The Bastard to show up, hadn't imagined he'd come stomping in with a deputy sheriff in full uniform, the two of them like a couple of cowboys. They'd yanked Carlos from his chair and shouted, "Come with us, you wetback scum," as they dragged him to the exit.

The Bastard must have followed her there; that was the only way he could have found Carlos. Her fault!

She had watched like a helpless fool as they took him, watched along with a dozen other bar patrons. At the door, the deputy turned back and called out, "Don't worry, folks. This man's a thief who needs setting straight." But anyone could have seen the brutal way he had Carlos's arm bent up behind him, his dear mouth twisted in pain.

By the time she'd recovered, they were gone. And her only clue was what the deputy said next: "After we have a little talk we'll just take him home." Which could have been total BS.

If the barman's directions were right, Carlos's place should be coming up. A couple of mobile homes out in the fields ... She spotted the lights of the first one now, through the light evening mist—the one where Carlos lived.

Only one car out front—nothing fancy like The Bastard drove, no sheriff's car either. She skidded to a stop and jumped out of the Camaro

A woman opened the door of the mobile home a crack and peeked out, then threw it wide open. She was tall and voluptuous, with long black hair. She waved her arms and screamed something Julie didn't catch, then covered her face with her hands.

Julie shot up the stairs and tore the woman's hands from her face. "Are you María?" she asked in Spanish.

Tears streamed through black smudges under the woman's eyes. "They're going to kill him! That's what the pig, Hiram Booker, shouted. He came with police, made Carlos kneel in the dirt *como un matón* and smashed his head with a gun."

Julie flinched, releasing her hold on the woman. "Booker is my friggin' father. Did Carlos move after that?"

"No ... maybe. Yes. They broke our window and threatened us. I thought they were going to take me, but they just threw Carlos back in the car and drove off."

"Which way?"

María pointed down the road.

"What's out there?"

"Cotton fields. Miles of them."

"Come with me." Julie gestured to her car.

María backed up a step, eyeing her.

"Help me save him," Julie demanded.

The woman nodded, but she kept backing inside. With the door almost shut, she spoke through a crack. "That crazy *pendejo*, Booker. I want nothing to do with him. Please."

"Fuck you." Julie ran to her car.

A minute later she was racing down the rutted road, a red reflection in her mirror, billowing dust lit by her taillights. Ahead, the dirt road in the tunnel of the headlights, stubby cotton plants close on either side. No side roads, no sign of where they'd taken Carlos.

What had she done? Carlos had a wife and family in Mexico. What would happen to them if The Bastard killed him?

A flicker off to the left and a track that ran between the plants. She skidded and turned in. A clearing. A car with headlights shining on two men, no, three; one was kneeling on the ground. The two standing men turned toward her—her father and the one in the tan deputy's uniform.

She slammed the car into park and jumped out. She saw blood on the kneeling man's face—Carlos's dear face.

April 1994, Santa Lucia, California

Julie shook her head to clear it. That memory of the night in the cotton fields had been vivid this time. No question why; she'd just sent Lilia to find Carlos in Mexico. Now the memories, good and bad, flooded in. She had to focus on the best times with Carlos

3

and put the horrors out of her head. But horrors had a way of creeping in, and the sleeping pill she'd taken didn't help. *Don't dream about it*, she told herself. *Dream about Lilia meeting Carlos.*

CHAPTER TWO

"For Californians who work hard, pay taxes, and obey the law... I am working to deny state services to illegal immigrants."
Pete Wilson, California Governor, Supporting Proposition 187, 1994

"The governor's office is not a place for blamers, it's a place for builders. ... Proposition 187 would punish the children and turn teachers into police officers."
President Bill Clinton, 1994

Carlos Montoya, April 1994, Michoacán State, Mexico

Carlos sat on a barstool at the cantina, nursing his second beer, struggling to follow one of his wife's last requests: "You're a good man, *querido*," said Isabel. "When I'm gone, don't lose yourself in drink like those *miserables* at the cantina." *Miserables* was a good description of the regulars here, and Carlos feared becoming like them. So, he only came once a week now—Sunday evenings, to watch the nine o'clock sports show on the big TV. Beer and highlights of the week's *fútbol* matches distracted him, but, when the news came on, he would disappear into the night.

Finishing his beer, he ordered a shot of tequila.

Sorry to say, but he looked forward to these pathetic Sunday evenings almost as much as he did to the meals he shared with his daughters, Rita and Anita. The rest of the time, when he wasn't talking to his sheep or trimming fruit trees at his *ranchito*, he watched mindless comedy shows on TV—he'd finally given in and bought one. Small comforts to take up the lonely hours. Anything to avoid drinking.

He glimpsed his image in the mirror behind the bar. Well-shaven; he made sure every day. Lonely as hell, but not *miserable*, not like those first weeks after Isabel died. It took a silent conversation with Isabel's picture to convince him. "You shame me, *querido*," she'd said.

The bar was dark, the men familiar, but not one of them a friend. His friends, his cousins, were up north this time of year. These men were just loud, happy voices, cheering for one team or another on the TV screen.

The sports show ended, and a preview of the news began, showing a California politician denouncing illegal immigration. "They rob good Americans of jobs and gobble our tax dollars for medical care. Their children suck up space in our classrooms while we pay the tab."

Why didn't Carlos leave? Why stay to see the painful images of protesters marching in California and police with helmets and batons strapped to their belts, glaring at the crowd, like back in the 1960s. Those hateful *policía del Norte* triggered memories he'd pushed down deep.

Don't think about it. Get out.

Carlos gulped the tequila and took his solitary walk four times around town before ambling back to his empty house. A pause outside the front door. *No more cantina tonight*, he told himself. *Keep your dignity. You owe it to Isabel.*

In bed, the usual questions nagged at him. Why go to the cantina every week? Was he that desperate to be in the presence of others who were not friends? And why Sunday? That one was easy—his senseless rebellion against God.

Late the next afternoon in his kitchen, Carlos resisted the urge to drink a beer and turned to his breakfast dishes in the sink. He thought of Isabel, quietly singing to herself as she cleaned the dishes. Sweet songs—he wished he could remember them all— but one was the old favorite:

"Ay, ay, ay, ay, Canta y no llores ..."

He would sneak up from behind, wrap his arms around her, and she would laugh as he murmured *"Cielito lindo, mi corazón."* He could hear her even now in his empty kitchen—not her words, but that delighted, carefree laugh.

He ran a sponge over the plate, rinsed the coffee cup, and set them both on the counter. He left the frying pan in the sink. It would soon be cooking his dinner.

A knock on the front door.

As Carlos opened it, his stomach upended. The attractive woman on his front step looked so much like María—the María of all those years ago. But this one in khaki pants and a blousy red shirt was under forty and willowy.

She watched him as she spoke carefully in Spanish, "Excuse me. I'm looking for Señor Carlos Montoya."

"You've arrived."

"Great!" she said in English. And then Spanish again. "I've come from California, the United States, to find you."

The woman had Mexican blood, no doubt, and her Spanish was fluent, but she couldn't have been raised here. She'd referred to that all-consuming country up north as the "United States" instead of "the other side," a place you would enter in desperation, seeking morsels for your family—a place where they'd persecute a man without cause.

Besides those dark brown eyes and long black hair, she didn't resemble María so much, did she? But the idea of María upset him.

He realized he was staring. "Why me?"

"Julie Booker sent me."

Julie, after all these years! He brightened at the thought and led the woman inside, where he gestured toward the pale green armchair near the door, the one with no coffee stain. "Would you like tea? Lemonade? Ice water?"

Rather than sit, she stepped toward the side table, focusing on a photograph of Carlos with Isabel. "Lemonade, if it's no trouble."

He hadn't wanted company, and her arrival reminded him again of those repulsive news stories from the North: helmeted police, angry Latinos. And now she followed him to the kitchen. As he opened the refrigerator, he asked, "Did they drive you out of your country, those Anglos in California? They revile us now. I see pictures on the news."

"There's no problem there, Señor Montoya."

Lying about California. Why?

Carlos poured from the jug, hoping she wouldn't notice his awkward right arm, the fingers that refused to straighten all the way.

Julie.

He noticed the way the woman's eyes scanned his kitchen— judging him for the dirty pan in his sink? Fidgeting a bit, but not doing badly for one who'd invited herself into a strange man's home.

Back in the living room, she settled into the armchair, Carlos on the sofa. "My name is Lilia Gomez. I'm a kindergarten teacher. On weekends, I work for Julie." She gave him an enticing smile, the way María used to do. Ha! "I've come to Mexico for two weeks to learn from some of your teachers."

"Excellent, Señorita Gomez. There's much to learn here in Mexico that you wouldn't discover in that land of ignorance up north."

Lilia tensed. "It's obvious you dislike the United States. Maybe you have reason. But Julie hopes you don't resent her."

"I could never."

"Good. She sent this note for you."

Lilia handed him a sealed envelope.

Inside Carlos found a letter written in neat cursive Spanish.

Dear Carlos,

It's been over 25 years since we saw each other, but I think of you every day.

I was sad to hear you'd lost Isabel. My heart goes out to you. My life is screwed up now, too. Do you remember those English words I taught you? We really educated each other, didn't we?

I've sent my friend Lilia to ask a favor of you. But first, please spend some time with her. I'm sure you'll enjoy her company. Tell her about our days in Santa Lucia back in 1967. The Summer of Love. Remember? As you think back to our passionate Wednesdays, maybe you'll forgive the pain I caused, and then you will agree to grant me this favor. It's very important, or I wouldn't ask.

Con mucho cariño,
Julie

Carlos seldom thought about the three women who'd changed his life all those years ago—avoided the memories intentionally. Now two of them were reaching out: Julie, whose fingertips would have touched this letter, and María, in the dark eyes and delicate hands that delivered it.

CHAPTER THREE

L ilia held her glass in front of her, the brim obscuring her chin. "So, tell me about those days in Santa Lucia."

The North invaded Carlos's life every day. Townspeople would speak of a son who crossed the border to work in a factory. He would hear of the way ranchers up there cheated Mexicans out of their wages; of people who'd been arrested at the border or even after they'd begun to work in North American cities. Now that despicable proposed law in California and the protests against it. "Please. Tell me what Julie wants from me."

She shook her head, black hair brushing her shoulders. "I can't. Not yet."

"And what's happened to her? Her letter said …"

"I can't speak of that."

"You say nothing, and yet you ask for …?"

"Quite a bit. I know." She gave a little smile, those dark eyes coaxing. "It's what Julie wants. Tell me what happened between the two of you."

Pretty smile, ugly question. "My memories of that place are better left asleep."

"Julie told me they treated you badly."

He snorted. "It's a cruel place."

"There's so much that's good. I'm sorry you didn't see it." She paused, and said, "I'm proud of my country."

Carlos's heartbeat kicked up. All right, since she demanded it, he would give her a dose of truth. "Proud? *Norteamericanos* are bloated with arrogant pride. We Mexicans are far more welcoming. In our culture, we open our homes to strangers."

Lilia's smile vanished as she sipped her lemonade.

"I can tell you how I was welcomed at the ranch of Julie's father with my cousin Rafael," he continued "Do you care to hear?"

She slid back in her chair, looking uneasy. "I'm listening."

"A foreman—his name was Ruiz—he told us to wait in the dirt outside the big white house while he summoned his *patrón*. You know him? Señor Hiram Booker."

"Julie's father. We never met. He died years ago."

Carlos found images coming back, bitter feelings, and he told her.

April 1967, Santa Lucia

Señor Booker came halfway down the stairs and looked over Carlos and Rafael with haughty gray eyes, his mouth working as though he were chewing a bitter root. Booker was tall, about fifty, his sun-dried face creased like a squashed prune. Instinctively Carlos whipped off his hat, but Rafael gave Carlos a slow, ironic glance before removing his own.

After years of coming north for work, Carlos was used to getting surly looks, although his gut never failed to clench in response. Would there be work this time? If not, would this *patrón* sneer and insult them or wish them well before sending them off?

Booker said something to Ruiz, who pointed to Rafael's *sombrero de vaquero*, and told him to, "Toss it on the ground."

Bewildered, Rafael dropped the hat. Booker marched down the remaining steps and stomped on it. The hat was made of stiff cane, and it crunched as the *patrón* ground it under his heavy boots— right and left, right and left, all the time staring at Rafael.

"Put it on," Booker said in English. Rafael was shaking, and Carlos didn't know if it was from anger or fear, or whether his cousin might lash out and put them both in danger. Rafael grimaced and picked up the filthy *sombrero*. He crammed his fist into it to put it back in shape and stuck it on his head, dirt flaking onto his face.

"Next time don't be slow to show respect," Booker said. "You want a job?"

"Yes, sir," Rafael said.

He looked at Carlos. "You?"

"Yes, I do."

Later that evening, Rafael said, "It doesn't bother me. He's just displaying his big *cojones* for Ruiz, like the purple feathers of a prancing peacock." But Carlos saw the way Rafael's eyes narrowed whenever the *patrón* came around. He felt his cousin's shame as well as his own for failing to object to their treatment, and for groveling to secure work.

Carlos carried that humiliation in his heart as Ruiz showed them the bunkhouse. Before leaving, Ruiz said, in his coarse Spanish, "You're lucky to have these bunks close by the latrine. And those fine lumpy mattresses ... *Gracias a Dios*." Then in English, "Welcome to America."

"So that was our welcome to the Booker Ranch, and it wasn't the first time I'd been treated that way during six years coming to your country," he told Lilia.

13

Carlos felt the tension in his jaw and saw Lilia sitting rigid. He lowered his voice. "So, when I speak of the *Norte's* disdain for us, I speak not just about the television news."

She frowned but didn't turn away. "Not everyone in the United States is kind, and not everyone's cruel. Mexicans can be mean, too. If you believe so deeply in hospitality, does it bother you that you're making me uncomfortable?"

He felt a twinge of guilt. This young woman was no weakling. She hadn't deserved an angry lecture. And truthfully, some of his *patrones* in the North had been cordial, if not generous. "I'm sorry … truly." Lilia's arrival had caught him by surprise, but why had her defense of the North made him so angry? "What can I do to make you feel better?"

"Tell me about your time with Julie."

He shook his head. "I apologize. My daughter expects me for dinner."

"Oh," Lilia said. "I would have called, but I couldn't find your phone number."

"Of course, I have none."

"Can I come again?" She gave him a smile he didn't deserve after his rudeness. So, she was insincere—first her assurances about California, and now this fake smile.

"Are you sure you want to see *me* again?" he asked.

She turned serious. "I'm doing this for Julie, and maybe you could, too."

Okay, that was honest. Maybe he owed Julie something, but he needed time to think it over. If he put her off and she went away, that would be fine. "I'm busy until Wednesday."

She looked into his eyes and said, "I'll be working in the daytime, but we could meet for dinner."

Empty flirtation, no doubt, but that look lit a little spark in him. Damn. He was about to give in to his loneliness, and he knew it. "All right. I'll make my famous enchiladas."

She seemed to relax, letting herself sink into the armchair. "Great. Now tell me one thing about you and Julie before I go."

How much would Julie really want him to say? The letter mentioned things that happened in Santa Lucia, which definitely excluded that night near Delano.

"Well … at first, I thought she and her mother were crazy."

"Why?" Lilia focused on him, acting fascinated. *Acting.*

"The two of them, Julie and her mother, had all of us workers compete in a beauty contest."

"I'll bet you won, Carlos. Am I right?"

"You asked me for one thing, and I've given two. It's your turn. What's Julie's request?"

"No. No. No. You read her letter. First, you'll tell me all about 1967." She paused, looked him straight on, and said, "And if you don't bite my head off, maybe I'll tell you something I like about my country."

He blew out a skeptical puff of air and led her to the door. As he reached for the doorknob, Lilia touched his arm for just a moment, looking up into his eyes.

It felt good—better than he wanted it to feel—but this was calculated, wasn't it? A pretty woman knowing how to get her way. Manipulative.

As she drove off he shook his head, confused—tempted to give in to Lilia's charms, angry at Julie for sending her. But Julie had been so good to him.

Back in the living room, he saw that his picture with Isabel lay face down on the table. Lilia? It must have been. But how? She'd never left his sight. And why?

CHAPTER FOUR

April 1994, Santa Lucia

Julie gazed out the window at the avocado grove and mountains. She was half listening to her book on tape and half absorbed in rambling thoughts—two incompatible halves. She'd lost track of the book's plot.

Lilia had been in Mexico a week now, working not far from Carlos's home on a project for her school. Had she met him yet? Did she like him? Did he find her beautiful? Why hadn't she called? Oh, yeah, Julie had told her not to worry about keeping in touch.

A tear of frustration trickled down her cheek. She longed to be there.

The phone rang, and a moment later, Felicia entered, still wearing her white apron. "It's Lilia, just what you've been waiting for." The maid gave Julie a knowing smile before turning off her tape player, hitting the "speaker" button on the phone and heading back toward the kitchen.

"Hi," Julie said. "You've seen him?"

"This afternoon."

Julie felt her heartbeat kick up a notch. "He's really nice, isn't he?"

"Not so much. I showed up unannounced, and I think it ticked him off."

"He used to like surprises from pretty women."

"He knows about the demonstrations in California," Lilia said. "And he hates the US. He lectured me about your father and the Booker ranch."

"Yeah, that was hard on Carlos, which is why I asked my gorgeous friend to charm him."

"He kind of hurt my feelings."

"Sorry." A fly buzzed by Julie's face. She blew a puff of air to drive it away. "How's he doing physically? Any signs of injury?"

"There's something wrong with his arm. He tried to hide it."

"Oh." Julie swallowed a flutter of guilt and said, "He's gotta be the most handsome man you've seen lately."

"He *is* good looking … for an old dude."

Carlos was a bit older than Julie—forty-nine? Fifty? Julie chuckled. "Too old to appreciate? I don't think so. Is he pissed at me?"

"Not at you, Julie, but he wants to know your request."

"Too soon for that. What else did he say about me?"

"He mentioned a crazy beauty contest."

"Right." Julie sighed, remembering Carlos's confusion that day. "One of my favorite memories."

"I think he was touched by your letter," Lilia said. "That's hopeful."

"Good. When are you going to see him again?"

"On Wednesday."

The crappy fly landed on her ear. She turned her head, and it buzzed off. "Why not tomorrow?"

"He's not the most cooperative guy." Lilia sounded perplexed.

"You're up to the task, Lilia. I know you are."

"Julie, when he got angry, it brought bad memories."

"Steer him to happy thoughts, like you do with the kiddies

in your classroom. And don't talk about the lousy California proposition."

"You haven't said why you want this so much."

Julie laughed. "Talk to Carlos. He knows sooo many of my secrets."

Lilia made a *pfft* sound. "I touched him before I left, just a quick one. I did it for you."

"Good girl! Well …? Did he like it?"

"He scowled and sent me out the door."

"Next time, try a hug, okay? That'll do the trick."

Lilia laughed, and hung up.

The phone droned out an annoying dial tone. Felicia came in and shut it off.

So things weren't going well down in Mexico. But they would; Julie had to believe it. In Carlos, Lilia would find something she needed. And the young woman would entice him to offer Julie what she craved.

CHAPTER FIVE

Benito Ortega, April 1994, San Francisco

Benito wasn't a baby, for God's sake, but here he was sitting at his mother's kitchen table with the usual iced tea, staring down at the stained linoleum floor to avoid eye contact as he put up with another of her *talks*, because—because he loved her, because he needed her support.

A pan simmered on the gas burner, the familiar smell of beef fat and onions making him hungry. His mother stood at the kitchen counter, chopping lettuce for tacos. She glanced over her shoulder at him. "I can't afford this," she said for the third time.

"I'm working, Mom," he said. "I'm also a student. I need a little help getting by."

"A twenty-five-year-old shouldn't still be a student. You wouldn't be if you weren't wasting your time printing leaflets and planning protests."

How many times did he have to explain? "I do this because of you, because of our people. They want to take our rights, *your* rights. They keep us ignorant and poor and break our backs picking perfect vegetables for their fancy banquets."

He could see that her tears were about to fall. "I *am* ignorant," she said. "But I try. I speak English with you, don't I? I've sacrificed for your education, which goes on without end. *Dios mío!* Graduate and get a job. Have a career, like I never did. Then they won't be able to put you down low, like they did your father."

So there it was, the reference to his revered father, the man he'd never met. And, yes, the tears.

He stood and set his glass down hard, splashing tea onto the table. "I fight for people like him. No one should have to sneak across the border, hide from *la migra* and plead for a pathetic job that pays crap."

She dropped the knife and faced him with one of those what's-wrong-with-you looks. "Your father, my Luis, would have wanted better for you. He would not approve your fighting someone else's battles."

"Be realistic, Mom. If they pass this proposition, it will screw our people worse than ever. They'll kick our children out of school."

"The illegals are my people, not yours." She swiped at her eyes, one then the other, with the back of her hand. "You were born here. They're not even my people anymore. I'm a citizen, remember? Fight for yourself as hard as you do for them. Earn your way and let your mother work herself out of poverty. Look at this place." She glanced around the room. "We both deserve better. We must earn this for ourselves."

Okay, it was true; he hadn't contributed, hadn't given up even a few hours to paint these dingy gray walls a brighter color, but his work was important. His work was for humanity. He couldn't give in. "*Illegals*? Do you hear yourself? When our ancestors came, this land was beautiful, unpolluted by their machines, their diesel fumes. The Anglos stole it. So, who's illegal, Mother, the men who stole the land or those who sneak across a phony border to make a living?"

"Your father was a good man, but he had a weakness. His

ideas were in the clouds, instead of finding practical ways to improve our lives. Like you, Benito, he made idle talk about history, even complaining of the padres who brought Jesus and the Holy Mother." She stopped abruptly and turned to look out the window.

Benito craved more but tried to act casual about it. "What did he say about them?"

"Nothing. Ay, you make me so angry. You know it hurts me to talk about him." She wiped at the tears and turned back to the frying pan.

Rats. No matter how he asked his questions, she always shut him down. Still, he had to try. "When I was young, you told me about him. The way he defied the rich ranchers and stood up for workers' rights. But you don't talk about him anymore. Those stories are important to me. You can't even tell me if he's alive or dead."

"I won't discuss this, *mijo*." She swiped one hand across the other in a "that's that" gesture. "Finish school. Finish now. Look to the future for answers, not the past." She filled three taco shells and set a plate in front of him on the table.

After a few more tries, Benito gave up. Except for the information about his father's interest in history, this argument was stale. In the end, he agreed to take two classes in the summer term at Berkeley and log enough hours at the 7-Eleven to pay his living expenses. By taking a full load in the fall, he'd graduate in January.

His mother hugged him and said she'd find a way to cover his tuition as long as he earned the rent.

Walking to the bus, he thought, *Alive or dead, he was a hero. I need to know about him.*

CHAPTER SIX

Sometimes at night Carlos reached out to Isabel in half-sleep, wrapped his arm around her waist, pressed his lips to her cheek, only to wake embracing a pillow.

Now another torment, María, who hadn't invaded his dreams for years, not until Lilia Gomez appeared with those seductive María eyes.

But why resent Lilia for resembling María, and then for defending her own country? He'd been irritable lately, hadn't he? Not just for a week or a month; for years, since he'd broken off relations with God, the God who'd callously taken Isabel.

María. He'd seen her as a gift back then, imagining that opportunities God offered were meant to be accepted. He'd taken her into his arms without hesitation—the present with a rattle on its tail and a venomous bite. It was María who'd forced him to stop trusting in God's gifts.

Bad memories. Pretty soon, that night with the deputy would come into it …. No! No, no, no. He and Julie had vowed to forget all about that.

Julie had understood him. She'd led him to examine his doubts about God. But now she'd sent Lilia, whose eyes tempted him to imagine ridiculous things and, foolish again, as God had made him, he'd invited her to dinner. *Damn it, Julie, why did you send her?*

When Lilia came, he'd find out what Julie wanted and be done with her. "Go back north," he would say. "And pray they never attack you for a crime *you* didn't commit."

It was only Wednesday, not Sunday, but he made an exception to his rule, drinking a shot of tequila as he prepared dinner. He poured a second, then dumped it back into the bottle. Poured it again and allowed himself to sip.

Lilia arrived in khaki shorts and a yellow blouse, handing him a bunch of yellow roses as she stepped inside.

Did she think a few flowers and that hopeful smile would coax him to tell her all about himself? Foolish man that he was, as the tequila had warmed him earlier, he'd looked forward to seeing that smile again.

Carlos laid the flowers on the kitchen counter, poured iced tea for two, and gazed at the tequila bottle for one long moment before slipping it into a cabinet under the sink and retrieving a glass vase.

"Mmm … it smells good in here." She lifted the lid on a pot of beans, sniffed, and reached for the vase. As she leaned over the sink to fill it, Carlos stole glances at the graceful sweep of her calves, the way her blouse draped over her chest, her black hair spilling down to her waist.

He served chicken enchiladas from a pan as she spooned pinto beans and rice onto plates. They carried the plates and the iced tea to the kitchen table and sat.

Her presence didn't feel like an invasion, like it had the other day, but he was still uncomfortable. Why? She was a stranger. She wanted something she wouldn't divulge. And because, for no good reason, he was tempted to tell her whatever she asked. Better to admit it—being miserable was losing its appeal and the tequila was melting his resistance to this pretty woman.

She leaned forward to click glasses with him. "To Julie."

"To telling me what she wants."

Lilia looked down and took a bite of her food. Then another bite. "Hey, you can really cook."

He could see she wasn't going to budge. Might as well make conversation. "You said you have a project here in Mexico."

"Yes, my school gave me two weeks off to come."

"Paying you to spend time here?"

"They are. We have many immigrant farm workers in Santa Lucia. These days, some bring their families. We teach their children every day."

The evil law they want to pass in California would end that, Carlos thought. Better not to mention it and insult the country she seemed to cherish. "Still, I don't understand about this project."

Lilia sipped tea and said, "Our kids attend schools down here before coming north. We want to find out what they know and learn techniques from your teachers."

"And they chose you because?"

"I'm single, I speak Spanish, and I wanted to get away. I teach kindergarten, but I'm finding information for first-, second- and third-grade teachers, too."

She looked so serious that Carlos was tempted to grin. "Commendable."

"It is," she said. "I doubt it's half as interesting as what you have to tell me."

Carlos ate a forkful of rice and a bite of enchilada. He sipped his tea. If he held out longer, maybe she'd give in and tell him Julie's request.

"I know what you're waiting for," she said. "But I can't tell you what she's asking, not yet." Lilia let out a breath. "Tell me something good that happened. Tell me what it was like back then."

She seemed sincere (at this moment), this young woman. Determined, too. Probably a good person, a teacher, dedicated to her students. "And after that, you'll answer my question?"

"When Julie allows it."

"You are a tough señorita." He savored her smile, thinking how nice it was to have a woman's company for a change. "In the early sixties, I was a *bracero* for several years, a seasonal agricultural worker. I came north legally then, under your government's Bracero Program. But in '64, your leaders decided they no longer wanted us. That didn't end our need, though, so thousands snuck across the border like mice nosing through cracks in a granary wall. It wasn't difficult to cross, and work was available for men willing to dirty their hands."

She watched him as he remembered it all: Booker Ranch with its avocado orchards and wild hillsides; another rich *patrón*'s orange grove just to the east. He'd thought rich people like Señor Booker and his neighbor owned the whole world.

"Back then I was a serious fellow," he told Lilia. "In your country that spring and summer—1967—craziness fell out of the sky like a net dropping on fish. There were lunatic people here in Mexico—witches, men who dared scorpions to bite them. There were drunks and men who kept two or three wives, all open and unashamed. With Anglos, I'd seen meanness, but never such peculiarity." He hesitated. "You're Julie's friend, but as I said, I wondered if she was mad. Wondered even more about her mother."

Lilia, listening as she ate, seemed enthralled, her dark eyes radiant. How weak he was, how malleable—desiring nothing more than her smile.

So he told her about the hot summer nights: the meager enchiladas with just a little cheese and onion; the workers drinking beer and arguing politics; *ranchera* music that made him homesick; sleeping in the bunkhouse with twenty sweaty, snoring men.

"The *patrón* charged us half our pay for those thin mattresses and sparse meals. The mosquitos took a peso's worth of blood for tax."

Lilia gave him a crooked smile. "And the day you met Julie—there was a beauty contest?"

April 1967, Santa Lucia

So many years ago, that day when Carlos had met Julie at the end of the workday. The foreman, Ruiz, shouted to summon the men. "No beer. Wipe the salsa off your chins. Don't swear, you stinking *pendejos*."

Carlos and Rafael, both in their early twenties, leaned against a fat eucalyptus. Off to the side stood the bunkhouse and cookhouse, stucco walls the color of dry mud, white window frames flaking paint like dandruff. The windows stood open, screens torn and useless.

Rafael said, "I'll wager the *patrón*'s coming to offer us five dollars an hour and free beer."

"Sure," Carlos said. "They'll drive us to the ocean for a swim on Saturday instead of sweating our asses off in that field."

"Ruiz is a son of a whore," Rafael said.

"Or God's messenger, here to teach us humility."

Rafael cackled. "The angel Gabriel with a lard belly and the breath of a dying dog."

"You, men," Ruiz called. "Line up."

Carlos saw two blonde women coming their way. He stepped forward, trying to see between the twenty men all moving toward the bunkhouse, and finally got a good look as the line formed. The women wore dark sunglasses—expensive-looking, with large round lenses.

"Pay attention," Ruiz shouted. "Mrs. Booker and her daughter have something to say."

The daughter—named Julie, he soon learned—looked about twenty and was almost as tall as Ruiz. When she smiled, her mouth seemed wider than Carlos expected, which made her less intimidating. But her mother was formidable—in her forties and trim, in a pale blue dress that showed tanned skin running down between her breasts. She balanced in her high heels like a dancer, her stance both challenging and graceful.

The daughter spoke. "I'm Julie Booker. My family has owned this ranch for fifty years. You all work very hard, and we thank you."

Julie Booker spoke better Spanish than any gringo Carlos had heard—more formal Spanish than any ranch hand. And she was thanking them!

"My mother, Amy Booker, will select one man for a special job with some extra pay." Julie smiled. "I promise you, this will be even more fun than what you normally do twelve hours a day."

The men laughed. Mrs. Booker paraded past them, examining each man. Carlos dropped his gaze and looked back up after she'd passed, but there was the daughter observing, her lips turned up in a half-grin. Carlos looked down and up again, found her still watching.

Mother and daughter took off their sunglasses and scrutinized one man and then another. Their eyes lingered on Carlos. He thought about the money and forced himself to return their gazes.

Mrs. Booker took her daughter by the arm and came close. His knees wanted to abandon him to the dirt.

"Tell him."

Julie blushed. "Look my mother over. All of her—her body and her face."

He felt Ruiz watching, but he couldn't refuse the *patrona's* command.

He glanced at Julie, who shook her head. "Not me. Stare at Mother. Act like she's your lover."

Dios Santo. His heart like a piston hammering, he looked at the *patrón's* wife. Her beauty took his breath—striking cheekbones, the sculpted lips of an American movie star, and dazzling blue eyes. He'd never seen such eyes, not in a real woman, not so close.

He trembled with nervousness but also helpless attraction as he followed the low cut of her blue dress, past her breasts, down to her tummy and legs.

"If you want extra money, win her over," Julie said. "Act like she's the most beautiful woman in the world."

Shaking a little, he smiled into Mrs. Booker's eyes, thinking that she might be the most beautiful.

"Good, I choose you," she said at last. "Do you speak English?"

What English he knew was hiding in the cellar of his brain. "*Sí*, yes, missus. I speak … little."

"Look at me again," she said. "You'll come to the house after lunch tomorrow. You *comprende*?"

"Yes, señora." He wanted to ask about this new work, but Ruiz was glaring. He wanted to sink into the earth, and disappear. He wanted to pick celery, and forget about these two strange women. But if he wasn't willing to take chances for money, why had he come?

Her mother spoke to Ruiz as Julie Booker said, "She's telling him to drive you to the house tomorrow before noon. Our cook will feed you, and then you'll work for Mother. You'll see her this way every Wednesday, as long as she keeps you."

Keeps me! The distaste in Ruiz's eyes churned Carlos's bowels.

"Don't worry," Julie Booker whispered in her eloquent Spanish. "You're under my mother's protection."

That night in bed, Carlos couldn't shake his fear. What could the *patrón's* wife want? He was a married man! She was the wife of the cold sonofabitch who held Carlos's life like a bug between his fingers. *Stop worrying*, he told himself. *Be grateful for this chance to earn more* plata.

Carlos enjoyed the way Lilia laughed and nodded, sympathized, those dark eyes never leaving him as she finished her meal, set her fork on her plate, and wiped her lips with the napkin.

"So, there she was—Julie—just come into my life," he said.

"And you won the contest, but angered your foreman."

Carlos poured more iced tea for them—not the tequila he wanted—and quickly ate the last of his enchilada. "You know, Lilia, I feared those powerful men—*capataces, patrones, policía, la migra*. I worked long hours, but I'd never done anything different from the others. So, I hadn't been beaten, abused more than normal, accused of a crime, or deported. I'd also never made enough *dinero* to hold my head up. And here I had a chance to make more." He took the empty plates to the sink.

She followed with the glasses. "I see why you thought Julie and her mom were nuts."

He smiled. "Julie also seemed very kind."

Lilia stood leaning against the counter, so attractive, but did she realize it? "You must have needed the money," she said.

29

He nodded. "We lived with my mother-in-law, and the house was crowded with Isabel, me, and the two girls. Hoping for more. We had no land, no way to progress. Now God provided an opportunity. That's the way I thought back then."

She laughed. "Tell me everything."

Carlos was tempted to spend another hour doing whatever she asked. Still, something about that laughter seemed insincere. She wanted *everything*.

No, damn it. She was just another seductive brown-eyed woman. "Your turn to tell."

"I can't."

"It's a simple request."

"And a simple answer: *No.*"

"I've told you I'm not angry with Julie. That's enough."

She shook her head. "I know you're frustrated, but all I can say is, it's very important to Julie."

He sighed and gave up. "I have to get up early to work."

She pouted for a second and then smiled. "Are you tired of me, or may I visit again?"

Before he could answer, she came a step closer, arms spread, like she was about to hug him. "Thanks for telling me all of that."

Instinctively, he went to wrap his arms around her, but she stopped short and blocked him with both hands. She backed up a step, looking wary.

"I'm sorry," he said, feeling empty and ashamed, confused and resentful. He hadn't done anything wrong, had he?

Her look softened. "Not your fault, Carlos." She put on that smile again, the one he didn't trust. "I'm a little mixed up lately. I'm busy tomorrow and Friday. How about Saturday?"

The question surprised him. She was an odd, mixed-up señorita, and her confusion played tricks with his good sense.

"You're probably angry," she said. "I shouldn't …"

He looked her over for a moment, deciding. "I'll be picking plums that morning."

"I could help."

"I start around eight."

Lilia's smile lingered with him well after she'd departed. "No, damn it," he said—aloud this time.

CHAPTER SEVEN

April 1994, Berkeley, California

Back at his apartment, Benito found his roommate, Marcos, staring out the living room window at the traffic on their busy street. Marcos was slender, five inches shorter than Benito. He wore a thin black mustache, too slick for Benito's taste. Marcos never spoke at rallies but worked the background, gathering information, preparing speeches. "New numbers," he said. "The *Times* poll says the shitty proposition scores 70 percent approval."

"Crap, it's getting worse. And now the jerks are starting to call it the 'Save our State' proposition, like we're wrecking it."

"We've got to keep it off the ballot."

"No chance," Benito said. "With petition hawkers outside every supermarket, millions will sign on. There's got to be big money behind this."

Marcos settled on the worn brown sofa and snorted. "What kind of person donates a million bucks to spread hate?"

The door popped open and Juan Hernandez entered. Juan was clean-shaven, almost as tall as Benito, three years younger, and brilliant. He wore round wire-frame glasses, like in the old pictures of John Lennon, and he carried two six-packs of Corona.

Within minutes, the three were seated—Benito on the ratty armchair, separated from his friends on the sofa by the three-legged wooden coffee table that already held six empty beer bottles—engaged in their usual pastime: ranting about the lies pitched to support the proposition, phony crap about the cost of services to "illegal immigrants," rampant Mexican gang crime, and the lies that immigrants took jobs from deserving American workers who would be eager for them. By midnight, they'd gone through the dozen bottles of beer.

"We do every crappy piece of work they're too dainty to touch," Juan said.

Marcos chimed in: "With politicians screaming, 'Get the illegals out,' mothers are afraid to drop their kids off at school for fear of being reported and deported."

"Nice rhyme, Marcos." Benito chuckled. "You two said the same words last week. Only you were sitting there, and you were on your way to the toilet. Then I added my piece about asshole California citizens voting to turn this place into Nazi Germany with every teacher and every doctor as Gestapo agents."

Juan stood, adding his empty bottle to the collection on the table "And here I go again to take a piss. You're right, Benito. It does no good to shout slogans at each other. So, we march. When we lose this election, we'll fight in the courts. But our future—our future—I'll tell you what I think in a minute. Right now I've gotta go." He went into the bathroom, shutting the door behind him.

"You've already told us," Marcos said, speaking to the bathroom door. "If we lose this time, we'll register Latinos who'll vote in elections five, ten, and twenty years from now."

Marcos rummaged in the refrigerator and produced three more beers. He uncapped one and handed it to Benito.

Juan returned to claim his bottle and settled onto his end of the sofa. "You know, Benito, I appreciate your work organizing rallies and making pamphlets, but I'd like you on the stage with

33

me." He twisted off the cap and tossed it at Benito. "You'd be a good speaker, *amigo*. You should step up."

Benito felt proud that Juan would say so. "Which part of the talk would I do?"

"Not my speech," Juan said. "Something personal. You're passionate, but you never say why. What makes you so strong? What drives you? Share your heart and inspire people."

Benito yawned. "Maybe I'll give a lecture about Sociology 420. I have a test in the morning."

Later Benito tried to study, but his mind kept returning to Juan's request. Juan had relatives who weren't here legally, according to the US fascist government, so his reasons for fighting the proposition were clear. For Benito, it came down to those stories his mother had told when he was little, the ones about his father, the hero, struggling for justice, for farm workers' dignity. He'd been beaten and defeated by the Anglos' paranoid, brutal system. Benito grew up not talking to his friends about it because of scorn for "illegal immigrants," and because the stories had wounded his heart. Years ago, his mom stopped talking about it, only able to cry when he asked for details. Her tears added to his sense of shame and isolation. Why refuse a boy his past?

CHAPTER EIGHT

Carlos found himself thinking often of the lovely kindergarten teacher. He pictured her in a classroom, helping tiny children stack colored blocks, teaching the names for "brown," "blue" and "red" in English.

He'd resigned himself to the fact that she wouldn't reveal Julie's request until she was ready. Why should she? Lilia saw the way her smile affected him and, like a rancher who knows that a man must have work, she had no reason to compromise.

On Friday evening, Carlos set a bottle of tequila on the end table in the living room and sat in front of the television, not really watching the show. Not drinking the liquor either—he wouldn't let himself. He had to respect himself because Isabel deserved it.

For so long, Carlos had banished those memories of the 1960s. But much of his time with Julie *had* been special. Why not share those good parts? Tomorrow he would tell Lilia what she wanted to know. If telling his past got to be too hard, if he came too close to the ragged wound, he'd stop and send her away.

But do I really want her to go?

As he waited for her on Saturday morning, he thought about the uncomfortable issue he'd avoided the other night—the hatred spewing from politicians in the North. He'd been cautious, not wanting to offend, but he couldn't let it go.

He heard her drive up and stepped outside.

She strode toward him, wearing an olive green T-shirt, beige shorts, and sandals. "Ready for work."

"Is that little red car yours?"

She shook her head. "Rented at the Guadalajara airport."

"It has no dents. People here think smooth bumpers mean *new and expensive*. Red cars are for young—"

"Young loose women?" She laughed, and it made Carlos foolishly happy. "It didn't cost much to rent, and my school's paying."

"Not loose." Carlos searched for the words in English and blushed. "A *sexy* young lady."

She looked away, suddenly sullen. "I used to think I was … sexy. Not so much now."

After a quick meal of tortillas and eggs they climbed into his old black pickup. She gestured toward the horizon as he drove. "Those dark hills are pretty."

"They're volcanic, some not so old. In 1943, one pushed up in an empty field south of here, like a mushroom from manure." He gestured to the old Spanish church and municipal offices on the square. "Our finest buildings."

"I like it here," she said.

He glanced at her. "It's the only home I want, but I think you're being kind." She couldn't have missed the junk trucks in the side lots, the mules waiting to cart their loads, the woman hauling a bucket from the city well. "As you see, we're far from prosperous."

"It's charming."

A motor scooter cut out of a side street, and Carlos swerved to avoid it. Lilia looked at him and shrugged as he gestured at the speeding cycle. "We have our irritations, but it's mostly peaceful. The people are genuine. Some of the old ones speak only the ancient Purépecha tongue."

"Colorful." She pointed to a row of houses, two with banners—the Virgin on one porch, *The Last Supper* on the other—and the next with an outdoor produce stand, fruits spilling from shelves.

As he drove, Carlos glanced over every few seconds, unable to resist quick views of her. "*The Last Supper* banner outside, charms against evil spirits in a bedroom. Old women pray to the Virgin of Guadalupe at church, and to the volcano demons with another circle of believers. For sick babies, witches cast spells using bat wings and spider toes."

"You made that up." She laughed, and her grin delighted him—he couldn't help it.

"I'm not sure about the spider parts."

"Do they have toes?" She reached across and touched his arm.

"A good question." Carlos felt buoyant as he turned south along the highway, until he remembered to be suspicious of those endearing ways.

"We live simply. But you see those homes with wrought iron gates and tile work? The owners spend most of the year in factories or packing houses up North, earning to pay their gardeners and maids." Carlos bent forward and looked up through the windshield. "Our most successful coyote has the finest house, way up there—with stone walls like a Spanish castle."

"So it pays well, smuggling people."

"You see, even our rich criminals, who could reside in your land, prefer it here."

She gave him a suspicious look which broke the spell, and he decided it was time to bring up his question.

Turning down a dirt road, headed for open country, he swallowed and said, "I avoided this at dinner on Wednesday because you seem so proud of your country, but I must mention it. The way *Norteamericanos* resent foreigners ... it must be hard for a young woman like you."

"I told you, it isn't."

And I didn't believe you. "It's cruel for them to pass a law against the workers who till their fields."

She sat back in her seat, staring at the road ahead. "Politicians like to shout about 'law and order.' They're just scaring people for votes."

Her casual words struck him in the chest, and he stopped the truck, thinking of those politicians on television screaming about "illegals" crowding hospitals and schools with unhealthy, illiterate children. These ideas *Nortes* believed, words that destroyed lives. Was she callous, after all—this señorita who taught little kids? "The law will hurt children," he blurted. "How could you not understand?"

She blanched, pressing herself back into the seat, a crease appearing between her brows.

He took a breath and lowered his voice. "The people hate us so much, they'd deny schooling and medical care to our little ones. That's what the proposition says."

Lilia's mouth dropped open. "Oh. I didn't mean ... I was just trying to let you know it's safe for Mexicans there." She shook her head. "The proposition is horrible. It asks teachers to become police. But law or no law, we'll find a way to educate them. Our teachers love those kids. We won't let them down." He saw tears welling in her eyes. She wiped them away with the back of a hand.

He'd meant to stay calm, but his anger had risen like one of the volcanoes destroying a farmer's field. There was just a little more he had to get out. "On the television, I see *policía* with helmets shoving our people and waving clubs. I was there in 1968. There were riots and—" Images darted through his mind as a twinge of pain pinched his forearm—a hundred big city police advancing, that brutal clubbing that had stolen his strength, his spirit, his courage. He shook his head to bring himself back.

She leveled a hand at him. "This isn't the sixties. We Mexican-Americans march to protest, but we won't burn Los Angeles down. Police are keeping order, not attacking us. I said I'd tell you something I like about my country, so here's one thing: People can protest in the US and not fear the police."

He could argue the point, but he'd already upset her.

She took a breath and then touched his arm again. "I don't want you to think it's dangerous in California. It's not."

He let her touch calm him, thinking that maybe, finally, he was seeing the real Lilia. "I had to speak of it because you're a teacher and you seemed … unsympathetic."

"Don't hate my country," she said. "I couldn't stand it if you did."

Her words surprised and touched him. "I know there are good Anglos, like Julie."

Lilia kept her eyes on him. "She told me you were lovers, so you don't have to worry about divulging secrets."

He wanted to protest that they hadn't actually been *lovers*, but let it go. "I'm glad she told you. I've been wondering how much to say."

"You can't embarrass me, so don't hold back." Lilia's smile was catlike and comical, but somehow her eyes never seemed completely happy. "Julie doesn't say much about her mother, but I've seen one of the pictures she drew of you."

He felt himself blush. "Julie's mother still has those humiliating pictures?"

"She died last year, but Julie would never give it away."

Holy God, which one? And how much was I wearing?

CHAPTER NINE

Carlos turned the truck down the gravel drive and gestured. "My humble farm—two rows of plum trees, two of peaches, over there mangos, and beyond the fence, my shed and a corral with two dozen sheep. If you came last month, we could have wrestled the beasts down and sheared them."

She laughed. "Fruit picking's more my style. I'll work hard if you'll tell me about 1967." She reached for the door handle, but Carlos had more to say.

"You know, Lilia, when I was a boy, Padre Miguel told me God gave gifts to special people. I thought I could be that lucky person. I'd take what He offered, and it would make me happy. Life contradicted my innocence with hard lessons. My sister succumbed to a fever, my father a farm accident. I stopped believing all of the *padre*'s words, but I clung to bits of naive faith. So here I had Julie and her mother, with wonderful blue eyes that spoke of the beauty God created."

"Your plum trees and sheep came from Him," Lilia said. "Better to be skeptical of two blue-eyed tarts."

And skeptical of you, señorita.

They climbed out and walked to the back of the truck. Taking the weight mostly with his left arm, Carlos slid the ladder from the truck bed. He brought out two leather harvesting packs. "First the plums go in here, and later into the baskets. Strap this over your shoulder and rest the bag against your hip, like this. The plums are our babies. We treat them gently and then send them into the world."

She watched intently, fascinated. With him? No, she was just a flirtatious woman and he a lonely fellow.

He set the ladder by a tree and climbed.

"While we work, you can tell me about Julie and Mrs. Booker … and Ruiz, too."

The limbs, laden with dark purple fruit, flexed like a rod challenging a prize bass. He reached under the netting that kept the birds from devouring the crop and began.

April 1967

The morning after Julie's mother chose him for her special project, the men worked a lettuce field, stooping low, gouging weeds from the soil with the *cortito*, the short hoe. Each man tilled a row, beginning side by side, but as some worked faster, they spread out. At the end of the first row, Ruiz waited with the water bucket. When he was happy, his grin was like a wild coyote's, but it could turn sour—a coyote sucking a lemon. Carlos's stomach clenched as Ruiz gave him that sour look.

Ruiz dipped his ladle and held it out. When Carlos reached for it, Ruiz dumped the water onto the dirt. "The *patrona* gives you an afternoon off and it robs me of your labor. You're going to give it back. You want water? Work faster than these other *pendejos*. Go slow, and you'll be dried-up horseshit in the sun."

Carlos moved quickly through the next row and finished first. Another foreman, Conteveras, dipped a ladle of water, waited for the next man to finish, and handed it to him. As that fellow drank, Conteveras said, "He beat you, Montoya. Back to work."

Carlos turned to the next line, gritting his teeth as he worked. Feeling weaker now, he finished behind some of the others. Ruiz sneered. "Pitiful. No drink for you."

Carlos stood fast, trembling from anger. "The lady wanted me alive at noon."

Ruiz spat in the dirt. "What do I care?"

Carlos braced for a blow. "Instead of weeding, I'll walk to the big house and ask Mrs. Booker for a drink."

Ruiz spit again and waited, but Carlos didn't budge.

"I'd let the sun bake the shit out of you, but the *patrón* told me to treat you nice." He granted Carlos a drink.

At noon, Conteveras drove him to the big house. The cook gave Carlos a sandwich which he ate sitting on the steps outside the kitchen door. He jumped up when Julie Booker approached. She led him to a cottage painted green like the avocado trees; inside, a bright room with cabinets, stools and an artist's easel. "Take a shower and put these on." She gestured to some clothing on a stool and to a door that led to a bathroom. "Your dirty clothes go on the porch so Rosa can clean them." She looked into his eyes, and he stopped breathing. She screwed her mouth into a funny look, and Carlos thought, *She's uncomfortable, too.*

"Mother's a strange duck," she said. "That's an American expression. You'll pose, and she'll draw you. Act like you're in love with her. Explore her body with your eyes, like yesterday. I know this seems *loco. Loco* for me, too. When Mother releases you, walk up through the grove. I'll meet you by the dirt road and explain."

Santo Dios.

He showered and began dressing, anxious and wary. The white gauze shirt he'd been provided was open halfway down his chest, the pants linen with a drawstring tie.

The door latch clacked, and he jumped. Amy Booker entered, acting calm—how could she be? She took his arm and led him, as if they were going to dance together. "Stand over here." She put her hand on his chest and turned him the way she wanted. Could she feel his heart going wild? His trembling? Sense his fear?

"Good. Smile at me," she said.

He did, and Señora Booker gave him a hot, sexy look that stole his breath. His hand wanted to reach.

No, his head shouted. He felt blood rush to his face and other parts. She was so beautiful, so close.

She ran her gaze down his body, nodded, and moved behind her easel. "Good. Stay like that." As she drew, she said things like, "Look at my body. Love me with your eyes." She spoke mostly in English, with a little Spanish and some gestures, but he understood well enough.

At one point, she bent to pick up a pencil, and her blouse dipped down. She caught him looking and glared. "*Stop it*. Only look when I tell you."

He looked away, feeling his heart hammering, but then she walked over, smiling in that sexy way, and ran her hand up the inside of his thigh. His body responded; he couldn't help it. She drew again, coaxed him, drew. Finally, she looked the picture over and pointed to the outside door. "Get your clothes."

He obeyed, then came back inside, carrying his freshly laundered clothing. She jabbed a finger toward the bathroom. "Get dressed and leave." She dropped an American fifty-dollar bill on the stool, twice what he received for a week of hard labor. "Be here next Wednesday by 12:30."

43

Stung by the tone of her voice, he entered the bathroom to put his clothes on. When he came out, she was gone. He took the money.

Flee, his thoughts screamed. *Run back to Mexico!* But the fifty shouted louder: *Return next week and meet my brother.*

Picking plums with Lilia, he finished the story. He'd told her everything except the way Amy Booker had touched him, and his body's response. He blushed at the thought of it.

"My God," Lilia said.

"That day Julie's mother drew the first of those pictures, like the one you saw at Julie's house."

Lilia walked to the truck with him, watching as he carefully emptied their bags into one of the baskets.

"That was bizarre," she said. "And Julie's mom sounds mean. Still, you must have been excited to be alone with a beautiful American woman."

He walked ahead as they moved back toward the plum trees. "I can't deny it. You see why I thought Mrs. Booker was some crazy witch."

"Did you go to Julie afterward?" Lilia stretched to reach into the branches, the fabric of her blouse outlining her breasts. Small, as he'd thought, but enticing. Why were men so fascinated with breasts? The answer couldn't be denied; it was men's nature.

He climbed the ladder and resumed picking. "Curiosity overpowered my fear. I wanted Julie to explain about her mother."

Below him, Lilia kept gazing up, plucking fruit slowly.

"You know," he said. "Imaginary lines separate people from one another—some thin, others broad; between strangers, perhaps a meter wide. Inside a Mexican family, the lines disappear.

We touch and hug and kiss cheeks. We lean against a cousin or a brother or aunt on the sofa. But there are still boundaries. We get to know someone and lines narrow—friends wrap arms around each other, lovers caress. But chasms gape between a worker and his *patrón*, which only the master crosses, maybe to strike you. The *patrón*'s wife might touch a domestic, but the servant senses cruelty etched in the hard rock of even the most benevolent mistress. With Julie, I expected that. I expected never to see her alone, never to come close."

He swallowed, remembering. That day, on the other side of the avocado grove, he'd found Julie leaning against a large oak.

April 1967

Julie was smiling. It reassured him, but only a little.

"The land below belongs to my parents." She gestured to the expanse below the road, stretching west to east. "So let's walk up here." She took his hand and it touched him.

Julie led him between bushes to a small clearing, out of sight of the road. They settled on the ground, side by side, leaning back against two boulders.

"When I spoke about how hard the men work, I meant it," she said. "You leave everything behind in Mexico. Is that how it is for you, Carlos?"

She took his hand again. He was alone with her, the *patrón*'s daughter, in this foreign place. A vehicle passed slowly on the road. He couldn't see it, but it felt so close it might roll over his feet. He wanted to jump and run.

She stroked his forearm. "Don't worry. They drive by every hour to scare off avocado thieves."

God. What if they'd come when I was crossing the road? "I should leave."

"Please. There are things I want to explain. I talk to my father about fair work hours, and he sneers. I can't help all of you workers, but maybe I can make your life a little better."

"But if the *patrón* should find us …"

"We'll be careful. I promise." She smiled with the same blue eyes of her mother, confident eyes that said she'd keep him safe. So very close to him. She was innocent, he thought; she didn't understand the way a man would take this openness.

She gazed across the valley. "That's Spring Mountain. If we walked further up, we'd see the Pacific out there." She pointed. "But you already know my country. How about your home? Do you have a large family?"

She was trying to distract him from his fears and partly succeeding. He relaxed a little as he praised Isabel and raved over Rita and Anita, describing how Rita played with the little one and how hard it was to leave them. His smile came sometimes as he spoke, but he was also close to tears.

"Lucky man," Julie said. "You have pictures?"

He brought his wallet out and showed her photos—Rita in a red dress and pigtails; Anita, sweet in her leopard pajamas; Isabel, with her curly black hair and lovely, wide nose. In the picture, she wore a white blouse that contrasted so well with her dark skin. Julie stared. "Your wife is …"

She seemed reluctant, so he confirmed. "Her father was black. He was a sailor. Her mother met him in the port of Veracruz."

"That's wonderful," Julie said. "If only everyone could be that accepting. That's what we're striving for in America, young people denouncing our parents' bigotry. People are marching in

Alabama, being beaten, even getting killed, trying to force the bastards to back off."

"It's hard for Isabel in our small village. Many people without your high ideals."

"Like my father," Julie said. "He rants about sending blacks back to Africa. Down South, they bomb black churches. A governor blocks a doorway to keep fine people from being educated. The bombers are my father. The haters are my father. But we'll change that. When my generation takes charge, we won't tolerate hate speech. Blacks and Mexicans—all people—will find respect and justice." She paused and said, "You're not a racist. You married her."

"I didn't hate her for being different. And I wed her because … she captured me."

Julie laughed and waited for him to explain.

"As you see from the picture, Isabel's skin is no darker than mine, a lovely shade with some cream in the coffee. But it was her eyes—amber mixed into chestnut. She held me with them and never released me. Always when I come home to Mexico, it's like that. She offers her heart and soul that way, and we shower each other with kisses."

She squeezed his hand. "Bravo, Carlos."

Julie told him about the two-year college she attended, all the Spanish language classes she'd taken. In turn, he spoke about his town—the pretty church, his priest, who'd been such an influence on his early life, but no longer.

He described the dirt streets, adobe houses with leaky roofs, Sunday markets where old women sold produce and hand-knit clothing. "I've installed running water in my mother-in-law's home using money I earned here. An inside bathroom, too," he said. "But with two children and surely more to bless us—a boy for sure—we should have a separate place."

"They deserve it," Julie said. She looked at her watch and sighed. "Your *compadres* are coming in from the fields."

He'd grown almost comfortable, but now fear struck. He jumped up.

She stood, too. "You'll pose for my mother again next week?"

Thinking of the fifty-dollar bill, he nodded.

"Come see me here afterwards?"

He looked at the ground, hardly able to breathe.

"When you get close to the road, just listen for the patrol truck." She touched his cheek, and he looked at her. "Come as a favor to me?"

With her smiling into his eyes, he could only agree.

"Now return through our neighbor's orange grove, and I'll go that way."

As Carlos glanced where she was pointing, she wrapped her arms around him, hugging with her whole body, like a girlfriend, so their thighs touched and her chest was full against him. He expected her to step back, but she kept him close. He felt her hair against his cheek and looked down to savor the red-blond color of it cascading over her shoulder. He felt embarrassed and excited, still more embarrassed at the way his body responded, and he wrapped his arms around her. She whispered, "A good man like you shouldn't be alone so far from home."

That chasm between them had dissolved. He was drunk with disbelief. *What's a poor Mexican doing with his arms around the blue-eyed daughter of a rich Anglo?* That feeling—the shock and the sheer pleasure of it—would come back often, every time they were alone, every time they touched.

As he walked down through the groves, he tried to decide if Julie Booker was an amazing, free, enchanting girl, or if she and her mother were two crazy magpies who'd get him beaten and killed. It was natural to think that way, powerless in a strange land, where others could pay him or not for his labor, where they could beat him or make him disappear like a cat falling into a well.

As he neared the bunkhouse, he realized Julie had never done what she'd promised: She'd never told him why her mother wanted him to leer at her as she drew his portrait.

With Lilia, he'd minimized his description of that long, intimate hug. But telling his tale had brought it back to him, and with it, a flood of warmth for Julie.

"You see, she was asking favors even then," he said. Glancing down, he caught a touch of sorrow on Lilia's face. Not the first time he'd seen it.

Not so happy, is she?

CHAPTER TEN

After unloading more plums, Carlos moved the ladder to another part of the tree. Lilia stepped close and ran a finger along his scar, from wrist to elbow. A chill darted through him.

"You don't have to hide it," she said.

The scar had faded over the years to a pale, crooked line. No one besides Isabel and a few doctors had touched it, and it surprised him, this little intimacy. "I know it's ugly."

She wrapped her hand around his forearm. "It doesn't spoil anything. We all have scars."

Lilia turned and quickly climbed the ladder. He thought of protesting that the man should take that perilous task, but he liked watching from below as she reached for the plums. And the way she'd touched him had made him start to doubt his cynical opinion of her.

April 1967

Amy and Julie Booker had dropped so many boundaries, but the line separating Carlos from his *compadres* swelled, like a balloon going to burst. In the bunkhouse, his cousin Rafael and the others asked about his afternoon with the *patrón*'s wife. He couldn't tell them about posing that way, having her touch him and boss him around. "You're ugly goats," he said. "The Bookers choose handsome guys even to move furniture and touch up peeling paint."

In the fields, Ruiz glowered when he returned, but he said only five words: "Lazy son of a whore."

The second week, Amy Booker drew with colored pencils, and when she finished, she said, "Get dressed and get out." Her command struck like a blow, but another fifty-dollar bill had him imagining he could send three hundred home that month. Grateful for the money but resentful, he told himself, *You're doing nothing wrong, like the men posing for magazine pictures.*

Leaving the studio, thoughts of Julie's intimate hug the week before lured him. He strolled, trying to look like a casual fellow, heading east into the neighbor's orange grove. He hunkered under a tree by the dirt road, listening—no patrol truck coming—then rushed across. By the boulders where he and Julie had hugged, he scanned for danger. Hearing a sound, he whirled to find her near. She took his hand again, sending a tickle like a furry caterpillar scurrying up his spine. "I'll show you my favorite place," she said.

They followed a side trail that ended in a thicket. She released his hand and stepped to one rock and then another, bending to pass beneath a fallen tree, then down to a protected hideaway surrounded by palms. It was floored in sand with a hammock strung between trees on one side, a thick, half-buried log laid across another—a pretty spot that felt almost safe.

He heard a truck pass along that road, farther away now, and tried to hide his fear.

Julie stood close watching him for a moment. "What did my mother have you do today? Nothing too embarrassing?"

"Embarrassing? Crazy! You never explained why."

"Mother's not dangerous, just pathetic. Last week she set your picture on a chair in our dining room, right opposite my father. She's a good artist, and your machismo showed in the front of your pants."

Carlos could hardly breathe. "My God."

Julie grimaced. "He shot my mother a sick, mean sneer that turned my stomach, then calmly ate his pork chops and his chocolate pudding, ten feet from your hot body. It's a game they're playing; a sad, fucking, stupid game. And I'm caught in it."

"I'm sorry," Carlos said, but he thought, *I'm trapped now, too, aren't I?* He glanced at the palm trees all around. What if Ruiz were lurking behind them ... or Booker? "I have to leave. Can you help me?"

Julie grasped his wrist. "My father *won't* act against you. It would show weakness."

She was so close, he thought she might hug him again. What had pleased him last week scared him now. This whole crazy ranch terrified him. "I don't understand. Why would your mother ...?"

"Father has a Mexican mistress. He brags about her sexual appetite and runs Mother down. He acts like he doesn't care about Mom, to make himself feel superior. You see? He can't touch you, Carlos. Really."

"They hate each other?"

"Mother loves the pig, or she wouldn't try to make him jealous. Father relishes their pathetic contest." Julie stroked the back of his hand. "My father goes to church to worship his perversion of Christianity. God disdains the poor and rewards the worthy. The church is a joke, but my parents follow like it's some kind of holy perfection. They sent me to parochial school until I was thirteen for a good brainwash. I wanted to keep believing in God and Jesus and the United States of America, but I found out better." She looked sad for a moment, but then she laughed. "I called my priest a dickhead to escape their crappy Christian school."

Carlos thought of his arguments with Padre Miguel back home as he realized Julie was beginning to distract him from his fear. She was funny and irreverent. "Why not leave?"

"My sister, Ivy, has adventures. What I have is Mother, who begs me to stay and keep her company, and my father, who threatens to cut off my inheritance. When I'm twenty-five, I'll inherit a trust that will free me, but only if I obey."

Julie retrieved towels from a canvas bag and spread them on the sand. Carlos hesitated and then lay beside her, feeling awkward, nervous, and yes, intrigued.

"Don't worry," she said.

Listen to the birds. Think of the beauty, not the danger, not the temptation.

Julie went on casually. "This isn't just about my father. The government, the businesses, the universities are corrupt. They poison the rivers, enslave people, and send our boys to die for profit. Have you heard about this?"

"I know your blacks are rebelling ... and there's a war of aggression in Vietnam."

"You're a victim, too, Carlos. You cross the border to pick the fruit our lousy president eats in the White House and the olives that fat-cat businessmen nibble from their martinis. Because so many work cheap, they don't have to raise anyone's wages."

He'd felt lucky coming north to earn. But was he an accomplice in a crime against his fellow laborers?

They lay still for a minute, and then she said, "I told you I'd like to make your life more tolerable." She slipped her hand onto his thigh.

His heart beat like a boy running from a bull. How should he respond, a married man of twenty-two, lonely? A natural man, as God made him … *No! This isn't sex, just a little comfort in a lonely place.*

She rolled on her side facing him. "Is this okay?"

Uncomfortable, suddenly ashamed of his work here, afraid of the *patrón*, thinking he should flee this spot and this ranch but not wanting to anger the *patrón*'s daughter or to lose out on the first real money he'd made… and her hand, gently stroking his thigh, so enticing.

"There's a union," she said, as if touching him were nothing unusual. "César Chávez and his people strike for better conditions. Crop dusters dump poison down …there's little pay, no toilets in the fields. Female workers can't piss in private.…"

Julie's words about oppressed people faded as Carlos's thoughts followed her fingers edging closer to intimate territory. He would stop her, but she was the *patrón*'s daughter. *Not sex, just comfort.* "They oppress women, too," she said. "Disrespect us, harness us in bras to hide our femininity. We twenty-year-olds defy their tyranny. Young men refuse the military. Students seize university buildings. Women burn their bras."

Carlos was half listening while thinking he should find an excuse and leave, but then Julie sat up and pulled her shirt over her head, revealing her bare chest.

Lilia gaped at him. "Wow. She just whipped herself out like that?"

Carlos hadn't meant to tell her that detail, but there was no taking it back. "I was amazed."

She shook her head. "I think if things were different she'd still be that free spirit."

Carlos wondered what Lilia meant, but she was climbing down from the ladder. "Time to empty these plums."

He looked into his sack, surprised to see it full. He'd been intent on memories, his hands working without instruction.

Lilia headed for the truck. "You mentioned God bringing you gifts."

"That's the way I thought back then—that God presented opportunities—but I've lost faith in that notion."

"Still, you believe God brought your wife to you?"

He poured his fruit into the basket and retrieved another from the back of the truck. "I used to."

"And you were lucky with her?"

"At first, but not forever. My Isabel was ill for a long time and died two years ago."

"She's with God, then." Lilia's look seemed sincere and kind.

"I'd like to think that."

She shifted the sack into position to dump her fruit. "You should hold on to that belief."

Normally, Carlos only talked about Isabel with his daughters, discussions that ended with too many tears—Rita lamenting her mother's death, resenting the burden of worry she bore for Carlos's well-being.

Needing a diversion, he looked down at his sweaty shirt and lifted the hem, letting cool air in. "Okay if I …?"

"Sure, take it off." She smirked. "I've already seen your picture."

Carlos pulled the shirt off, wondering again how much he was wearing in that portrait. "You look a little damp yourself."

"No way. Mine's staying on."

April 1967

"They're wonderful." The words shot out of Carlos's mouth without thought. He looked from Julie's breasts to her eyes, and her eyes invited him. *My God, she flew so fast from outrage to seduction*, he thought. Then he realized that he no longer had any wish to leave. He retrieved the hand that had been drifting toward her, thinking he might need to sit on it.

"It's all right," she said. "They make us ashamed of our bodies. The damned preachers and our parents want to keep us sexless. Then they seduce their parishioners, or each other, or pretty much anyone. My father screams if I go braless, and Mother gets hysterical, so I wear the worthless thing." She blew out a breath. "Father claims that Jesus demands modesty and chastity. If a person was tempted to believe in Jesus, knowing my father would kill the urge." She pointed a finger at him. "And didn't he make friends with a prostitute—I mean Jesus—*a hooker*? That's a good English word for you to learn."

Her rage distressed him, as the bitterness for her father made him sad, even as he tried not to look where his eyes demanded to go.

"My dad wasn't like that," he said.

"Past tense?"

"He died in a farm accident when I was eight. I've questioned God since then."

"I'm sorry. He was good to you?"

Carlos tried to picture his father, but what he saw was one of the photos his mother kept. "He taught me to play *fútbol* and told me stories." Julie's bare chest quickly recaptured his vision.

"No yelling?"

"He was tired when he came home from work, but not

angry. Sometimes a stern word if I misbehaved." Carlos's voice quavered.

"He didn't spout commandments from God?"

"Just said to be a good boy, listen to Padre Miguel, and don't cause trouble for my mom."

Julie settled back on her towel in the sand. "Lay your head on my shoulder. Close your eyes and pretend I'm Isabel."

Amazed at this situation, heart pounding and mind churning with doubts, he did as she asked. "I miss her and the girls so much," he whispered. All of a sudden, tears ran from his eyes.

Julie caressed his shoulder. "It's all right, Carlos. I'm here, touching you with her love."

He felt her ribs with his fingers, confused by so much, but longing for Isabel and home. Despite his arousal, he fell asleep. When he woke, Julie was sitting beside him on the towel wearing a serene smile, as if she were altogether comfortable being half naked with a foreign man. His gaze skimmed from her thighs to her chest.

"You like them?" she said.

"Your eyes *and* your.... In my country they say that tragedies come in threes and delights in doubles."

She laughed. "Do you think it would be wrong for us to—?"

"I'm married."

"You took vows in a church?"

"I did."

"And you're Catholic?"

"Not anymore," he said. "But it's still wrong."

Julie shook her head. "What my father does is wrong. It hurts my mother, but you touching my body will hurt no one. Your wife could never know."

God will know, he thought. But wasn't it God who'd brought him to this place with curiosity and with this woman? God who had planted this desire? God seemed more and more like a part-time *patrón* who appeared, gave out gems, and drifted back to heaven to drink a Corona with his angel pals.

"You wouldn't be foolish enough to tell her, would you?" Julie asked. "If you're not still Catholic, why do you think it's immoral?"

"But ..." He searched for reasons. "I wouldn't want to hurt you, Julie."

She laughed. "I couldn't fall for you."

He opened his mouth, feeling a little hurt, not knowing what to say.

She touched his cheek. "Don't be upset. I won't fall in love with anyone. It does a person no good. You're married, so you'd better not fall for me either. Promise."

He had doubted so much he'd been taught by the church—having gone through the commandments one-by-one and dismissed the ones about taking God's name in vain and graven images as priestly inventions. Actions that caused destruction or hurt people were wrong—thou shalt not steal or kill (of course), honor thy parents; those were fine. But adultery ... why hadn't he questioned this commandment? It was only wrong if you believed someone else's moral code, like Padre Miguel's—or because it would hurt Isabel.

Isabel was two thousand miles away. She would never know.

Thinking about it in the bunkhouse that night, he realized he was attracted to Julie for more than the obvious reasons. Like no one before, she'd coaxed him to explore his religious doubts. She was free and joyful, but also serious and thoughtful, sometimes angry, too, which unnerved him, but maybe she had reason, with a hostile father and a country at war with itself.

CHAPTER ELEVEN

As most men are fettered by bonds of tradition, and by imitating ways followed by their fathers ... everyone continues, without investigating their arguments and reasons, to follow the religion in which he was born and educated, thus excluding himself from the possibility of ascertaining the truth, which is the noblest aim of the human intellect.

Letter from Akbar, Mughal emperor of India to King Phillip II of Spain, 1582.

Padre Miguel, October 1962, Michoacán.
Four and a half years before Carlos met Julie

Miguel was cleaning candlesticks after mass in the church's narrow back room. He looked up and saw a young man standing in the doorway. Lean and handsome, as before, but more manly now, darkened by work in the sun. Carlos Montoya.

They hugged, and Miguel said, "I've worried about you."

"No need, Padre."

Miguel took a bottle of apple juice from the only shelf not crammed with books or linens, poured glasses, and handed one to Carlos as they settled on stools.

"You're doing well, Padre?"

"More weddings than funerals. Enough baptisms to buoy my spirits." Miguel saw that the new, lankier Carlos had a man's grin, more challenging than the boy who'd gone to California eight months ago as a *bracero*. "And what of you, young man? What adventures has life handed you?"

"Adventures." Carlos snorted. "Abuses. They disinfected me like a sheep and shouted orders while I worked like a mule. I bribed them for the privilege of joining this wonderful Bracero Program, approved by the *Norte* government. They promised money and didn't mention I'd pay half back as rent for my mattress in a chicken coop."

"You'll remember that I urged you to—"

"I know, to join the seminary. But my family needs my income. And your seminary would no longer want me."

"It's harder now that you're older. Eighteen?"

"Seventeen, but that's not the reason."

"Oh?"

Carlos finished his juice and wedged the glass between his thighs. "You know I've always had questions, and you've helped by sharing books. You're generous, Padre."

"A good spirit and fine mind must be cultivated."

"The way they treat me in the North—the way they treat us all—is that what God intends? Is that the life He offers? And who's to say what this Lord wants? Who's to say there is a Lord? You, Padre, you're supposed to know."

Carlos's tone stung Miguel, but he had answers. "God sent the Word, and the church has followed, from Peter down to Pius, and soon a new pope. We must keep faith."

Carlos stood and looked out the window. "If I don't?"

"Surely you accept God."

Carlos blew out a breath. "Hard to give up the notion."

"*Santo Tomás* offers proof of God's existence and many insights about the Lord Jesus." Miguel spotted the book on its shelf and dusted it off with a cloth. "Here, the priests have revised the saint's words for better clarity." Miguel grasped Carlos's arm. "Will you pray with me?"

They knelt together on the tile floor and bowed to God.

July 1953

How could a priest explain the inexplicable, a child losing a parent? But this time was worse. This time it wounded Miguel's heart. Eight years ago, the day Miguel had arrived in this parish, he'd assisted Padre Ricardo in the holy baptism of Carlos Montoya. Miguel held the babe wrapped in white linen as Padre Ricardo anointed him with holy water. Miguel dried the baby cheeks with the cloth and looked into the infant's eyes, embracing the sweet innocence, the miracle, the full life awaiting this child. He sensed at that moment the wonder of creation.

Now, eight years later, this. He heard the knock on his cottage door and there was Señora Montoya with the boy, on his front step. Her face etched with grief but also those hopeful eyes, the look of a woman who expected miracles from her priest. "I know you'll help Carlos, Padre. I'll wait in the church." She turned and walked away.

Miguel led the boy to one of his brown armchairs. Should he offer something? Candy? No. Carlos was bright for his age, also miserable. Candy would be an insult. Miguel slid the other armchair opposite Carlos, held his little boy's hand. How to begin?

"Mom says you'll explain everything." Carlos, so solemn, his jaw clenched for a moment. Then he began to sob. He stood and leapt into Miguel's arms.

"Oh my boy. My dear Carlos." Miguel pulled the boy onto his lap.

"Mom said *Papá* can't come back to see us, but I know he will."

"You'll miss him, son. I know. But in the next life—"

"He will come back, won't he?"

"You won't be with him any time soon. I'm sorry."

"Why? Why would God allow this?"

Miguel absorbed the boy's misery as Carlos sobbed against his chest. "We can't know God's reasons, but as long as we trust Him, He'll take us to heaven when we die."

Sobbing still— "And I'll see *Papá* there. *Mamá* says."

Miguel patted Carlos's head. "You will." And he thought of an offer, far better than candy. "You're a special boy, Carlos, intelligent and good. I'll teach you about Jesus and Mother Mary."

Carlos wiped his eyes with the backs of his hands. "To help me understand about my *Papá?*"

"Yes, son. I have books that the priests have written to help boys like you. You'll learn about God's love and about the holy mission of His church."

Carlos watched him, like he expected something more.

"We don't understand everything, but we know God's intentions for us. That's most important."

Carlos was nodding but looking confused, tears still running down his cheeks. Miguel longed to dab them away as he had the baptismal water eight years before.

"You do, don't you?" Miguel asked. "You believe in God's goodness?"

"Of course, Padre. But it doesn't make sense to take *Papá*"

"That's why we have faith, Carlos. That's why Jesus came, to give us hope and truth and love. You must kneel in the church and talk with Jesus. And, if your mother agrees, I want to make you an altar boy."

Carlos's eyes opened wide. "You mean I wear the white robe like Diego?"

"Yes. You will serve God, and God will comfort you—you'll see. The best thing is, you can spend private time in the church, conversing with *Madre María.*"

Over the next few months, Miguel often saw Carlos praying before one or another of the holy statues. And then Miguel and the boy would reminisce about his father and discuss the holy saints and the missionaries who brought faith to the people.

Now Carlos challenged Miguel again, and Miguel prayed he was up to the task.

November 1962

The seventeen-year-old Carlos Montoya hadn't attended mass in the past month, and Miguel prayed for the boy. Now, as he entered the back of the church, he found Carlos standing in the storage room, looking out the window, the volume of *Santo Tomás* beside him on a stool.

"Pomegranate juice?" Miguel poured two glasses. He glanced toward the book. "What did you think of Saint Tomás?"

Carlos gave Miguel an affectionate smile and shook his head. "I tried to make sense of it. His 'proof' of God's existence isn't much. He begins by assuming there is a being that created it all. Then he uses his assumption to prove what he already pretends to know. Does that make sense?"

Miguel tried to hide his disappointment. "Can you imagine this glorious world came about from nothing?"

"I never needed proof of that. But the God you told us about and the God who resides with us—they're not the same. There might be beauty, but what of justice and compassion? Padre, what I really want to believe is that He cares about us."

"Then do, son."

Carlos picked up the book, then set it back down. "This *Santo Tomás*, he leaps to the idea that there has to be a 'most perfect being,' and this God he's imagined is it. How could he claim that, seeing this world?"

"Well, then ..." Miguel swallowed, feeling blood rise in his face. This was Carlos, this special boy, the one Miguel had practically raised, so patiently instructed and nurtured, now questioning everything.

"What about cancer? Starvation? Families killed in floods?"

"We priests have explanations."

"I didn't mention this the last time I came." Carlos paused. His eyes welled with tears, and his voice cracked as he said, "The way God killed my father."

Miguel felt his chest tighten. He stepped close and laid a hand on the boy's shoulder. "Tragic. You were young, but we prayed together, and your faith helped you through."

Carlos backed away, bumping into a bookcase. "I'm not eight. I need an adult explanation."

"Some would say suffering is deserved, that man does evil and God punishes. As Saint Augustin taught, all men are sinners. It's part of our makeup, passed down from Adam and Eve and unavoidable." Miguel saw that Carlos was about to object but pressed on. "Still I don't believe in a vindictive God. He gave his son to redeem us from our sins. You must remember—this is the God of kindness and love."

Carlos's mouth twisted in a skeptical grin, but he let Miguel finish.

"God alone understands why He sent your father to heaven early. We can't comprehend, but we believe He's good and has a worthy purpose for everything. In heaven, perhaps we'll learn why."

"Back to Aquinas and his empty reasoning," Carlos said. "You hide behind the saints' robes and their seven-hundred-year-old logic, while I'm trying to *understand*. Why presume He's good—and for what reason only one God—and why believe in Jesus at all? Because a *priest* said so from the time I was three?"

The way he said "priest" wounded Miguel. "If you see a flaw in *Santo Tomás*, he won't convince you. But you've heard Jesus's words, and you have a good soul. How could you not believe in their rightness?"

"Virtuous," Carlos said. "But true?"

Miguel searched for the right argument. "What if Jesus hadn't come and preached goodness, nor Moses laid out commandments? Wouldn't men seek after their neighbors' wives, steal their livestock, and attack one another for gain?"

Carlos snorted. "Which they do every day, even murdering in the name of the church. Now you're saying the commandments make men ignore their evil hearts? Shouldn't a person see what's right and do it without threats of damnation?"

"If you're naturally virtuous, you're blessed, but not all people…

Carlos tilted his head to one side and studied Miguel. "So a parish priest would lead children to worship lies?"

Miguel suppressed a spark of anger. "That's not me, Carlos. I believe with all my heart."

Carlos clapped Miguel on the shoulder. "The perplexing

thing is, I can't completely give up this God of yours. I like the idea of heaven, even if it can't be proven. And every once in a while, God pops up like a magician. He gave me you, Padre, and your illuminating books. What should I borrow next?"

Miguel let out a long breath. "Perhaps a different view of God. Gandhi the pacifist, or Martin Luther the crusading rebel."

Later, after Carlos had hugged him and departed with two books, Miguel poured a glass of wine and sat, old questions murmuring inside his head. It was natural for young people to question their elders, as Miguel had in those early days at seminary. His brother priests had helped him through it. But questions never completely disappeared.

God offered many paths. Once one was chosen, best not reconsider.

CHAPTER TWELVE

L ilia stood on the ladder, two plums in one hand, watching him. "You've stopped working. It must be time for a rest," Carlos said.

"Your story about Julie exposing herself distracted me."

"All of it true, I assure you."

At the truck, he poured cups of lemonade and gave Lilia a foil-wrapped snack. He brought out a tarp and laid it at the edge of his orchard, where the hillside provided a comfortable hollow for sitting. He settled, but she stood over him, hesitating.

"You're not used to sitting on dirty cloth?" he said.

She knelt and then sat close beside him. "Not lately. You miss Isabel very much. I can tell when you speak about her. But still—"

"I know. Still, I was willing to have sex with Julie. I *am* a man, the way God made me."

Lilia crossed her arms, looking away. "Your argument about God making you that way—it's self-serving. My God gave me a brain and the strength to restrain urges."

There had been other reasons that should have restrained Carlos back then—he was realizing that now—but none had to do with religion. "What if it's not God but the priests who say you must?"

"He gave man a mind and a conscience and marriage vows that you pledge in His church."

Carlos watched a hawk soaring in the sky over the next hill. He'd avoided thinking about those days up north until Lilia brought it up. Maybe he hadn't wanted to let his conscience examine past actions, maybe he still didn't. "God has not provided a clear message, then. Why did He create men and rabbits one way, and apparently make geese differently? And that mind you speak of ... God constructed it so irrationally, with lust and greed for trivial things and—"

"If you pretend to know God's intentions, you might decide all sorts of ridiculous things. Like, maybe because women are weaker, they should be servants." She shook a finger at him. "Do you believe that? Because if you do, I'm not picking any more stupid plums."

"Ha. What I've seen of women and men, like Isabel and me, both have strong and weak, crazy and sane, all mixed up like a fruit salad."

She shook her head. "You don't believe it was right to be with Julie. Your soul knows better."

"Priests don't own my soul."

"You were married."

"And my wife far out of reach."

"You loved her, and now you miss her terribly. Tell me you regret all of this."

Talk of God's wishes was interesting; talk of missing Isabel, not so much. "If I admit I was reckless with Julie, can we speak of something else? You grew up in Santa Lucia?"

She narrowed her eyes. "I'll let you avoid the issue for now. My father was foreman on a ranch there, in the country illegally until the amnesty in '86—that's something good my country did, by the way."

Lilia seemed intent on defending the North. Maybe she was

really happy there, but Carlos wasn't sure he believed it. "His name wasn't Ruiz?"

"Gomez. He was good to his workers. When I was eight and nine, I spent the summers in Mexico with my grandparents—the year my aunt died and the next. They had me 'work' in my grandfather's bodega in a village like yours and pretended I was useful."

"I don't know how you were then, but you're an excellent fruit picker."

"Thank you, señor." She paused and said, "I hope you don't mind having a sweaty girl close."

She looked deep into his eyes—just for an instant—and a tingle of desire ran through him. He wanted to reach for her, but then she drew back and settled a little farther away. "You're a beautiful señorita, but confusing. Did Julie ask you to flirt with me?"

She tensed. "Why would you think so?"

"Sometimes you distract me. You're so lovely," he said.

"I'm not lovely, and calling me that could piss me off."

"Sorry." He sat, silent, but then he heard a vehicle grinding along his driveway. He stood, and seeing the white Ford approaching, his jaw tightened. *Mierda.* "You're about to meet my oldest daughter," he said, heading toward the car with Lilia following.

Rita stepped out of the car and slammed the door. She wore faded blue jeans and a tan short-sleeved shirt, hair tied in a horse-tail.

Sometimes he wondered where this daughter had come from, darker than Isabel, with more of Carlos's native features but none of his easygoing nature. Like her mother, her waist had all but disappeared after the birth of her second child. She was how old—thirty? Lilia, several years older, possessed so much more spirit.

Rita halted a step away, her stance like a coyote demanding payment for last year's foray across the Rio Grande. "Are you the woman with the spicy red car?"

Lilia opened her mouth, but Rita kept on. "Parked at my father's house even now, for all the town to see. Who visited him last week and again at dinnertime Wednesday?"

"Yes. Is there—"

"Now, here, sitting together, cuddly-cozy. Señorita that my neighbors mock behind my back. 'Making a fool of him,' they say." She turned on Carlos. "I went to the church early this morning to help the new padre clean. My friend, Ana, came. She'd seen that car and asked if the 'pretty-pants' girl was sleeping with you, *Papá*."

Carlos glanced at Lilia, who was standing with her legs in shorts, not pants.

"Rita, this is my friend, Lilia. She's helping me pick plums."

"*Your* plums or the ones from the trees? That's what everyone wants to know."

"Daughter, you'll embarrass her." He glanced over to see if Lilia was upset, but she seemed to be stifling a grin.

Rita blew out a harsh breath. "You're sure she's not from a Mexico City whorehouse?"

Carlos reached for his daughter's arm, but she pulled away. "*Rita*," he said. "Would you feel better if I said she's my girlfriend?"

Lilia blew out a breath. "No chance. I'm not sure I even like him."

"I was teasing, teasing you both. Look, daughter, Lilia's a good woman, a kindergarten teacher, who knows one of my friends on the other side."

"Friends? They tortured you there!"

"Go home, daughter. Let us finish picking fruit."

"She goes, not me." He saw the rigid stance and Rita's hard eyes. There'd be no winning.

"All right. She goes." Carlos led Lilia to the pickup. They climbed in, and he drove off, leaving Rita staring after them.

"I apologize for Rita," Carlos said. "When she gets this way, I try to tease her out of it, but today she's a stubborn bull."

"She thinks she's protecting you."

I might need it with you so pretty, he thought.

CHAPTER THIRTEEN

Carlos drove toward town, thinking about why he'd told Lilia so much. Her beauty had drawn him in, and his craving for closeness, because … because he'd felt no tenderness for so long.

Lilia seemed pensive, too. "Before, when I sat so close to you—"

"That was nice."

"I shouldn't have." She kept her eyes on the road ahead. "I don't mean it was wrong, but I shouldn't give you ideas. I could see by the way you looked at me."

"I was obvious?"

She frowned. "It's just very soon, for many reasons. Sorry. Sometimes I imagine I'm braver than I truly am."

Finally, he felt, she was being genuine, exposing something of herself rather than luring him to reveal his past.

At the cooperative, Carlos and the men unloaded the plums. When he jumped back into the the truck, Lilia seemed more cheerful. "Your daughter called me a whore, didn't she? I should be angry as hell." But she mostly looked amused.

"I know how to strike back at her. I'll buy beer, and we'll drink together."

She hesitated, so he added, "Not at the cantina, where people might stare. We'll go to my house."

"Your daughter will take an ax to my car."

"Don't worry, it's rented."

"I still have to drive it."

"We can't let her intimidate us."

Lilia slapped the dashboard. "Why not? Let's show your snotty daughter we have spunk. But first I want to call Julie."

"When I need a phone, I use Rita's."

She laughed. "At a phone booth."

"There's only one—behind the vegetables in our little market."

"Is it private?"

"It's enclosed in windows. The local women will pretend to shop for produce while their eyes peep at the new pretty face. Some will claim they read your lips."

He bought beer while she made her call. It was only Saturday, not the day he usually allowed himself to drink.

But this time, I won't be drinking from loneliness.

CHAPTER FOURTEEN

Sitting on his living room sofa, Carlos watched the graceful way Lilia raised the beer to drink: the cord in her neck that stood out as she turned her head, the fabric of her T-shirt that revealed enticing hints of her contours. There was God again, pulling his puppet strings, but his strings were quite content.

"What did you and Julie talk about?" he asked.

"I told her she was some wild girl back in the sixties."

"And?"

"She said it was the happiest she's ever been."

"Wild and pretty," Carlos said.

Lilia shook her head. "I said what you did together was wrong. You were married. She called me puritanical."

"Julie hated religious rules." He went to the kitchen and came back with two more bottles, twisting off the caps. He took a breath, deciding—resolving—to only drink as fast as Lilia did.

"The Puritans were creepy." Lilia accepted the beer and took a swig, then looked at him. "There's something I want to mention. I had a serious boyfriend. We were going to be married, but it didn't happen."

"He must be crazy to let such a lovely one escape."

"I'm *not* lovely."

"I'm surprised to learn that's an insult."

"I'm plain and uninteresting."

He touched her hand for just a moment. "You're beautiful. And you seem mostly nice."

"He broke my heart, and it hasn't quite mended. I haven't seen him in months, and that's enough to say." She stood, and he saw her eyes welling with tears. "I'm off to the bathroom." She glanced at the picture of Isabel on the shelf across the room as she left. He got up and turned it toward the wall.

When she returned, he patted the cushion beside him.

She glanced at the picture, nodded, and faced him. "I'm not used to drinking, so it doesn't take much. But this is important. I have to say it before I have another. I'd like to sit near you. I'd *really* like to sit near you, but you mustn't think we're going to—"

"I have no expectations," Carlos said. But desires and expectations were different beasts.

"After another beer, I won't be able to drive to my hotel."

"There's no lock on the guest room door, but I can give you chairs to pile against it. Or stay with my daughter, if you enjoy murderous glances."

She stood over him, teetering a little, amusing him with that subtle grin of hers. "Or a murderous knife through my heart. I'm already worried she'll go after my car."

"Not likely, but possible."

She settled with her back against his side, head resting by his cheek. "I'm not afraid of you. I know karate." She giggled.

"Not sure I believe you." He wrapped an arm around her waist.

She snatched it off. Giggling again and slicing her flattened hand through the air. "I could smash your balls with one precise blow."

The thought made him wince. "I'll give you no reason to

emasculate me. I've told you about my life with Julie, and you've unburdened yourself a little. Now tell me what Julie wishes."

"Oh, no." She waved her hand like a butterfly flitting. "There's more to your story, I'm sure. I'm feeling pretty free here. Julie said I could trust you. I'll have another beer as long as you promise …"

Carlos was feeling pretty free, too. Some of his distrust toward her had melted away. And he didn't feel lonely! "I do. I understand."

"You haven't even mentioned your other girlfriend back then," Lilia said.

Another surprise. "Julie told you too damned much."

"What was her name?" Lilia turned her head, and Carlos pressed his lips against her temple. His hand slid up her side.

Lilia pushed herself away and stood. "You're mourning your wife, and I'm getting over my boyfriend. We could have a nice evening … or end it *now*."

"I apologize."

"I'd like to be close, but maybe you aren't able, or maybe you don't want to. Maybe you should take a cold shower."

He gave her a moment and said, "You can drink all you'd like, and we won't do anything you don't want. We could both use a shower—separate showers—after our day in the orchard. You can trust me. I promise."

She wiped her eyes and looked at him. "I'd need a robe and a shirt."

Carlos led her down the hall, pointing out the guest room along the way and retrieving clothes from his room.

"How about a washing machine?" she asked.

"I have a modern home. Flush toilets, too, thanks to money from the other side." He opened the hall closet and showed her the machine.

"Close your eyes," she commanded. When he opened them again, she was on her way to the bathroom, wearing the robe and carrying the shirt, calling over her shoulder, "Your clothes can join mine in the washer."

After his shower, he found Lilia under the sheets in the guest-room bed, back propped on pillows against the carved mahogany headboard. She saluted him with a bottle of beer. "This is a nice soft shirt," she said. "Sit with me if you like."

Carlos grabbed pillows from his bedroom and another beer from the kitchen and settled beside her. "You're a surprising woman."

She grinned. "It's a special moment, isn't it? And spending this time in Mexico feels a little like coming home. I hope you like being with me. We could both enjoy it, and it would make Julie happy." She laid her hand on his thigh, and he pressed his hand onto hers. She didn't flinch or pull away. "I like this more than I want to like it. Does that make sense?" she asked.

"It's been a long time for me." He took a breath and realized he was moving dangerously close to talking about Isabel, so he veered in another direction.

"A few weeks after I became Mrs. Booker's model, I was with the men, weeding strawberry plants, when I saw the *patrón* and the two foremen watching me. The master wore a white felt hat, what North Americans call cowboy hats, and the two foremen wore straw sombreros, the style from Sinaloa. I wondered if I should shrug at the *patrón*, as if to say, 'I'm only doing what your wife commands,' or shake my head indicating, 'I have no lustful intentions,' or say something—I didn't know what. But I saw Ruiz's grimace and the master's disagreeable smirk. Perhaps I imagined it, but his gaze seemed to linger below my belt.

"At the far end of the row, the *patrón* waited alone. I whipped off my hat, hoping he wouldn't trample it. He looked me hard in the eyes. 'You're a lowly Mexican,' he said in Spanish. 'Do what my wife tells you and don't try to think. Put your hat back on. The sun's fucking hot.' He climbed into his pickup and drove away. When I reached the other end of the row, Ruiz slammed his fist into my stomach and said, 'How long do you think he'll put up with you?' I crumpled to the ground, thinking, *very good question*. After that, Ruiz hardly spoke to me, but whenever I came close, if he had the ladle in hand, he'd give me a drink and then whack me in the ass with it."

Lilia lifted his hand and kissed it. "I'm sorry they treated you that way."

He savored the kiss. "So Julie told you to trust me. Did she say more?"

"Yeah. To stop at three beers."

"After beer, tequila settles the stomach."

She laughed in a charming, lighthearted way, like a girl or a younger woman who'd consumed the perfect amount of alcohol. "Are you trying to kill me? Do you have limes?"

"Is this Mexico?" He returned with the tequila and lime wedges, poured a small shot for her and a larger one for himself. They clicked glasses.

Swirling the tequila in his glass, he asked, "You'll want me to go to my bedroom soon?"

"Maybe not, if you follow some rules."

Pleased by the new, relaxed Lilia, he waited.

"I'll be under this sheet, and you'll stay outside it. You'll wear pajamas *and* underwear. Put them on backwards."

He went to his room and then returned in the required clothing and settled on top of the sheet with his chin touching her shoulder.

She stroked his arm. "This is nice." He waited a minute, then slid his hand across her stomach. "Too nice," she said, and started to sit up.

He retreated. "Okay. I'll take it easy."

After a moment, she said. "I *really* want you to stay. I'll hold your hand to make it behave."

CHAPTER FIFTEEN

April 1994, Santa Lucia

Julie waited in bed as Felicia poured a glass of water.

"Here it is, Miss Julie." Felicia popped a sleeping pill into Julie's mouth and gave her a drink.

She swallowed, already worrying over the dreams and visions it might bring. "I need a new prescription. These are giving me nightmares."

Felicia patted her cheek. "Rest gentle, sweet Julie."

The maid left, and Julie closed her eyes, waiting.

But it wasn't the medication that was causing trouble. Horrible thoughts had invaded her sleep because she'd sent Lilia to see Carlos.

She breathed deeply, trying to think about happy memories. But as she drifted off, there she was in 1968, her car headed down that dirt road toward Carlos's mobile home outside Delano.

It's because of me. The Bastard found Carlos—my fault.

She skidded to a stop outside Carlos's home. A woman banged the door open and sprang onto the porch.

María.

Julie climbed the stairs and grabbed the woman's arm.

"They're going to kill him!" the woman shrieked in Spanish between gasps and sobs. "It's that pig, Hiram Booker, and the police. Oh, my Carlos!"

Julie grabbed her arm. "Where are they?"

"They threw Carlos into the car and …" María pointed down the road.

"What's out there?"

"Cotton fields. Miles of them."

Julie knew what was coming next. "You won't help, so fuck you." Julie ran to her car.

Racing down the rutted road, dark as hell, like something in a horror movie, stubby cotton plants close by either side whizzing past in her headlights. María's words ran through her head. *They're going to kill him… going to kill him … kill him…*

A flicker off to the left. She skidded into a clearing. A car with headlights shining on two standing men, another kneeling. Her father and the deputy turned toward her—eerie, malevolent leers on their faces.

She jumped out, seeing blood streaming down Carlos's face.

The Bastard came toward her. "Now, honey, you can't be here." His gaze felt like an invasion, his voice like a recording played too slow.

"Out of my way, prick."

"Go on, now. Go home, doggone it. It's none of your business."

Behind the deputy, she saw Carlos crawling toward the cotton plants. She had to keep their attention, give him time to hide. "You can't beat him to death. I won't let you."

"He's a thief who needs to learn how to act," her father said. He glanced over his shoulder at the deputy. "Watch out, McDougall. He's getting away."

Julie slipped past The Bastard and ran for the cop—Deputy McDougall—who dragged Carlos up by the belt as if he were a puppet. Carlos wriggled and almost broke free. The deputy raised his baton high over his head. Still running, Julie saw the gun holster at his waist. The weapon … the gun was all that mattered.…

McDougall somehow saw her coming. She tried to get past—get to Carlos. She shoved the cop, but he didn't budge. He held her effortlessly with one hand, like she was a child. That couldn't happen. It really couldn't.

She had to get the gun.

McDougall tapped her on the forehead, and she fell backwards onto the dirt. He leaned over her, grinning, his face huge and freakish in the headlight beams.

"You can't do this," she screamed.

He leaned even closer, his terrible mocking eyes paralyzing her. "You just wait here while I go back to beat him to death."

The deputy turned toward Carlos, and Julie saw his gun holster again. She struggled to get up but couldn't move. "No! It didn't happen like this."

She felt The Bastard come up behind her, his breath warm on her ear. "You're dreaming, darlin'. If you don't like it this way, try again."

It's a dream. It has to be, and if it is, I can start over.

… She was back in her car again, heading for his mobile home. María on the porch, yelling at her, driving again, into the clearing … and there was McDougall knocking her to the ground and raising his billy club to slam Carlos.

NO.

"Start this dream over, darlin'," The Bastard said again.

CHAPTER SIXTEEN

Lying beside Lilia, Carlos listened to her breathing, memories washing past. He hadn't spoken of Julie in all these years, and now he was spouting like a broken irrigation pipe, revealing so much about Julie and her mother. Why hold back the rest, when Lilia accepted it all with so little judgment? Why not tell her about María?

He woke in the morning alone in bed. She'd been there with him, hadn't she?—Lilia—and then gone around sunrise. He found her in the kitchen, wearing her clothes from the day before, slicing bread for breakfast.

Carlos heated the fry pan and diced onions, peppers, and potatoes. "How do you feel after last night?"

She beamed at him. "Did you think three beers would do me in?"

"You've forgotten the shots of tequila?"

"You're the one who would be too *borracho* to remember." She put slices of bread on a cookie sheet and started the oven heating.

He'd promised himself he wouldn't drink more than her, but he'd failed. Still, he hadn't been drinking to cover pain this time. "Then you recall that I told you all about Julie and the other woman from back then, and Ruiz, and Amy Booker, everything there is to know about my wonderful Isabel."

A smile started at the corners of her mouth and rose to her eyes. "I do remember it all, so I know you're lying." The smile evaporated in the opposite sequence. "I have today free, and—I didn't mention this before—tomorrow, too."

"I thought you were working this week."

"Monday's a school holiday." She pursed her lips. "I didn't tell you, because I wasn't sure I wanted to."

"Sensible. I wasn't nice to you at first. We have two full days…and then?"

"And then, if we're still getting along, next Saturday evening. I head home next Sunday."

"It's time to tell me Julie's favor." He paused, deciding if he dared say it: "And agree to take a shower with me before you go."

She gave him a look halfway between a grin and a scowl. "I don't know why Julie likes you. Before we discuss favors, tell me your other lover's name."

"It's 'Lilia.' You're my *otra amante*."

"I'm just someone who shared your bed with a modest sheet between. Your other lover from 1967."

"You resemble her," he said. "That startled me at first—those brown eyes, so dark I can't tell where the iris meets the pupil. María was her name. I met her at a dance one Saturday. When I saw her across the room, her eyes ignited something in me. Like yours, Lilia—same eyes, same long black hair."

Lilia blushed but didn't turn away. "You said your wife captured you with hers."

The potatoes were sizzling in the pan, and he turned down the heat. "I admit it. Eyes can render me helpless, and now yours are taking me over. Don't feign innocence."

Lilia didn't look away, but she stopped smiling. "A cat will sit on the floor, staring up at you, and you might think, 'See how that cat adores me? After you feed it, it will ignore you until it feels like having its chin scratched."

"Your cat eyes drink my common sense dry and make me want to please you."

So, there was no avoiding it—she wanted to hear, and he would tell her.

July 1967, Santa Lucia

Carlos never went out with the men, but here he was, lured by Rafael to this dance at the church hall—Rafael, who'd now disappeared. Which left Carlos to do what? Tap his foot to the music, sip fruit punch from this little glass cup, and gaze up at the gold streamers hanging from the rafters?

Across the room he saw a woman alone, like he was. Why? She was striking, with a bountiful figure. Watching him? It had to be his imagination. But there she was, still looking. When he went for punch, she appeared beside him and brushed against him. He set his cup down and led her to the dance floor. During fast dances, moving to the rhythm, their eyes fixed on each other. During slow dances, one after another, she pressed close and closer, saying not a word. How had it happened …?

Sometimes dancing seemed like a bullfight—women displaying themselves in the red of a matador's cape, or some other entrancing color, revealing a bit, using smiles and the closeness of bodies to arouse men, not giving too much—horns passing close, ruffling, brushing the clothing, but not goring one another. More and more distracted, men tried to entice them further. Men, like bulls, were doomed to conquest. And María's body so alluring …

He led her out to a courtyard between church and dance hall.

They walked to a dark corner where only a bit of moonlight found them, embraced and swayed, murmuring to each other.

She came from Monterrey in the northern state of Nuevo León, but she was legal, with a green card, and worked as cook and housekeeper at a ranch near the Bookers. He told her about his village in Mexico and his work in California, but said nothing of Isabel. He didn't want those eyes to stop sparkling in the moonlight.

At only around ten o'clock, with his brains residing somewhere below his belt, María pointed to her watch. "Sorry. I have to go. A friend is picking me up."

"No." Carlos felt suddenly desperate—he knew it was crazy, he was a married man—but she pulled away.

"Stay there. Don't try to follow." She headed toward an opening between the buildings.

"The next dance isn't for a month. Please."

She turned back. "Mass at *la iglesia* San Antonio tomorrow. Nine-thirty. Afterward I have a few hours."

Carlos had no more use for church than for a second big toe on each foot, but he arrived early the next day. María entered the vestibule, and he went to her.

"I can't sit with you," she said. "Meet me after mass." So he waited outside.

Later, as they strolled, she said, "I have to be careful, so the wrong people don't see me." They followed the railroad tracks instead of the road, passed through the orange groves and toward the ranches where they both worked. He took her hand and their fingers interlaced. They glanced at each other as they walked, her posture, her luscious body, almost regal. His arousal brought him back to those first days with Isabel, which reminded him to feel guilty.

Later, he would scold himself for not asking questions. But what if she queried him—about his family, for example?

A freight train approached. "Quick, let's hide," he said. She laughed as they ran together and found shelter behind a sycamore. He held her from behind, one arm around her waist and the other across her chest, his body pressed to her back. The train moved past. Its rumbling subsided, but they stayed. He felt his pulse pounding, felt her breathing filling her. She turned to kiss him, brief, but intoxicating.

Later, they sat on rocks, eating the cheese and apples she'd brought and talking, but mostly just looking at each other.

"We can meet like this again next week," she said.

"The mass is nonsense. We could skip it and—"

"The church is my salvation." Her deep brown eyes held him.

"You know they forced it on our people."

"Don't speak against it, not ever." She crossed herself with two fingers raised. "Not if you want to see me."

He walked her home. Isabel didn't come back to his thoughts until he arrived at the bunkhouse.

Now, in the kitchen with Lilia, he knew he was blushing. What had, all those years before, seemed romantic—this instant intoxication with María—now felt foolish.

Lilia piled eggs and potatoes onto two plates, not looking at him. "Like your old girlfriend, I follow the church, but I don't mind your mistaken beliefs."

Carlos put toast on the plates and set them on the table, then grabbed butter from the refrigerator. "So the pope and cardinals have divine guidance?"

"My church is familiar and holy, a place where I ease my

mind. My priest listens and helps me think things through." She brushed the hair away from her face with a hand.

"Isabel used to say, 'Don't ask me to reason it out, or I might stop believing what I know is true.'"

"Your wife was very sensible."

Carlos laughed. "I guess that's one allure of God's creation: Nothing is known, nothing logical. Tell me, what advice did your priest offer about your boyfriend?"

Now Lilia blushed. "We were discussing María. How did this devout woman react when you told her about Isabel?"

"You're a nosy one."

"I am."

Lilia had wheedled so much out of him—things she had no business asking. He felt suddenly annoyed, because—the realization struck him like a blow—her quiet questions exposed what he'd done back then, and it felt shameful. He'd avoided that thought all these years. "You didn't come here to ask me about María or about my dead wife."

Lilia narrowed her eyes, offended.

He took a deep breath. "Sorry. Let's not be serious. There's a lake called Pátzcuaro an hour's drive away, a beautiful place, in a basin of volcanic peaks. Do you have a bathing suit?"

When she nodded, he said, "The lake's too polluted to swim." Her delightful, confused smile made him laugh. "But my friend owns a small hotel with a pool. We'll swim with a view of the lake but not foul our toes."

"Don't you have to pick plums or something?"

"Let the plums rot. I'll see to the sheep, and then we'll stop by your hotel for your suit."

"On the way, you'll tell me all about María."

Carlos gave her a mock frown. "From now on, we share

information. I tell you something, and you answer questions for me."

Carlos retrieved his swimsuit and they headed off in his truck.

CHAPTER SEVENTEEN

April 1994, Berkeley/San Francisco

After his sociology test, Benito slept away the afternoon. When he woke, he looked up at the rally posters he'd taped to his bedroom wall, pictures of Mexicans working the fields, like his father, the oppressed immigrant. He tried to imagine his room was a bunkhouse. One of his fellow workers played guitar. Others sang. Then he was outside, marching with his dad beside César. The dad with no voice when he spoke, no face that Benito remembered.

Questions swirled in his mind, day after day. What had his father been like? Had they killed him? Locked him away somewhere?

And his mother—Benito had always been proud of her appearance. Back in high school, his friends had checked her out when she wasn't looking, gestured with their hands like they were stroking her body, made comments that had pissed him off, but also secretly pleased him. Still, she'd never shown any interest in men. Clearly, her heart had been crushed when she'd lost his father, and she hadn't dared to risk that again.

Years ago, she'd told Benito that his father's *patrón* had used the police to attack him. He'd worked hard in the fields, but he'd supported the "cause," the union that was fighting for a better life for migrants. So, they beat him and drove him off.

Juan had urged Benito to take part in the rallies. His father had been the immigrant, not him, but Benito could understand. Benito could speak of that oppressed man's tragedy.

One afternoon, he took the bus to his mother's apartment. She mixed a pitcher of iced tea. He took glasses from the cabinet, and they sat at the kitchen table.

"I want to apologize if I upset you the other day," he said.

"It's all right, *mijo*." But her eyes were suspicious, no doubt wondering why he'd come again so soon.

"Is everything okay at the hotel?" he asked.

"Same old job," she said. "The housekeepers complain of too much work, and my boss calls them 'lazy sluts.' 'Make them work harder,' he says. 'I pay them plenty.'"

"You should have his job, but they discriminate against you."

"Don't. Blaming others for our shortcomings only keeps us down."

That started her telling the same old stories about her job. He pretended to listen, gazing from the gray walls to the old beige refrigerator and back to her, but his imagination wandered to a different time, when his mother had lived with that good man who'd fought for the workers.

Benito sipped his tea and kept his mother's glass full. Finally he said, "Tell me more about my father. I have to know."

She waved a hand in the air as if shooing a fly. "I told you when you were younger."

"He was a hero for the union?" Benito asked.

"Didn't I say so?" She shook her head, suddenly on the verge of tears.

"He spent his nights organizing workers? Did he lead them in strikes?"

"He did, *mijo*. Luis was a principled man. Field hands were treated like dogs. But you are not. Forget this and build your own successful life."

Benito leaned toward her across the table. "His *patrón* and the police came after him?"

"Yes. Yes. I told you all of this."

"They lied and accused him of what?"

"Stop it, son. I don't want to—" She stood. "Don't think about him, Benito. He died or he left us. Either way …"

He waited, hoping she'd disclose a little more, but she only glowered at him. "See what you've done with all this tea."

When his mom headed to the bathroom, Benito made for her bedroom. He skirted the single bed—neatly made as always—and headed for the bureau. Beneath the underwear in a drawer, he found the papers—just where he'd once seen them as a teenager living in this apartment: her equivalency diploma from Delano High School in 1970 and two pictures, one of his mother and father with their arms around each other outside a mobile home. In the other, his dad stood alone, wearing a string tie and a broad smile.

Benito replaced the diploma but slipped the pictures into his pocket.

When they were back in the kitchen, he said, "Sorry, Mom, I have to go." He hugged her by the front door. "One more thing—would you tell me the name of my father's town in Mexico?"

She blinked, then blinked again. "I don't know, Benito. That was long ago."

"You must know."

"Stop it, *mijo*. I don't remember." But her hesitation, her sharp words, and that expression told him she was lying.

CHAPTER EIGHTEEN

The Spaniards gave beasts of burden to relieve the natives of drudgery... meat to eat which they lacked before. The Spaniards showed them the use of iron and oil lamps to improve their ways of living ... They taught them Latin and other subjects which are worth a lot more than all the silver taken from them ... it was to their benefit to be conquered and, even more, to become Christians.

> **Francisco López de Gómara, Spanish historian** chaplain and secretary to Hernán Cortés

The Broken spears lie in the roads;
We have torn our hair in our grief
The houses are roofless now, and their walls
Are red with blood.
Worms are swarming in the streets and plazas,
And the walks are spattered with gore
The water has turned red, as if it were dyed
And when we drink it,
It has the taste of brine
We have pounded our hands in despair
Against the adobe walls,

For our inheritance, our city, is lost and dead
The shields of our warriors were its defense.
But they could not save it.
We have chewed dry twigs and salt grasses:
We have filled our mouths with dust and bits of adobe.
We have eaten lizards, rats and worms
When we had meat, we ate it almost raw
Aztec poem about the conquest

Winter 1964, Michoacán.
Two-and-a-half years before Carlos met Julie.

Spending months away from home, a man had many lonely hours to consider what was true and what wasn't. Other men in the bunkroom shared family stories, information they'd heard or read. After seven or eight months away, a man returned home changed, perhaps angry.

Bitter realities. That's how Carlos thought of them now. When he was growing up, they'd been concealed realities. Lies.

Padre Miguel, his *fútbol* coach, dispenser of God's righteous truths to the children, to all the people— Lies.

He'd made Carlos an altar boy like it was some privilege, offered him access to the church, to Jesus and Mary, as if it could heal him. Maybe it had relieved some of the pain, like a sugar pill to a sick patient, but what of truth?

The truth was his family. The truth was life in this village. Now that he was back from the North, he vowed to make peace with his homeland and its superstitions, make peace with Padre Miguel, despite the lies, because he loved him. But there could be no peace without honesty. He'd have to hurt the padre's feelings again.

Carlos caught up to Padre Miguel in the little vineyard behind the church.

The priest embraced him. "Carlos! How old now? Nineteen?"

"Yes, Padre." Carlos felt some of the old warmth, and a nervous rumbling in his gut. He looked around to make sure they were alone.

"And your reunion with Isabel and the baby?"

Carlos saw the priest glancing at him—assessing. *Stay calm*, he told himself. *He's as close to a father as you possess.* "It was glorious. Isabel and I love each other so much. And Rita makes my heart beat a sweet serenade."

Padre Miguel cut a branch and tossed it onto a little pile. "It must be painful to abandon that joy every year." He cut another.

"You know why I go. But now the *Norte* government is ending the Bracero Program."

"What will you do?"

"Not join the seminary." Carlos's voice was harsher than he'd intended.

The padre slipped his clippers into his belt and gestured toward the far end of the vineyard. As they walked, he said, "Having a little one is more reason to stay here in Mexico."

"Is it God's plan to impoverish us?"

"Suffering while keeping faith is a blessing."

"I'm going to be a wetback and sneak in."

"A dangerous crossing, son. Against their law."

"Not your law, Padre. Not the law that you say came from God."

The priest paused and glanced back over the vineyard. "God sustains us, Carlos. God gave you a wonderful woman and now this infant to share your life, all of it, not five months at a time. Appreciate your blessings and recognize God's hand in things."

Padre Miguel had been Carlos's hero once. He'd supported Carlos's family over the years, but his advice was useless. "You speak of *God's hand,* which reminds me …" Carlos knew he was raising his voice and tried to take it easy. "The history books you gave us children were full of lies."

"Oh?"

He saw the priest's hurt expression, and he wished he hadn't come. But he had to finish now. "The benevolent church in Mexico converting natives, people welcoming the friars and the church." Carlos walked his hands toward each other in midair, like stick figures. His voice mocked. "Everyone happy. Ha. Ha. Ha."

Past the vineyard now, they came to a large tree. Padre Miguel leaned against it. "Native rulers were tyrants, cannibals who sacrificed thousands to their pagan gods. Christianity brought a gentler path."

"That's your excuse for enslaving and slaughtering?"

"No, but—"

"Why not be honest? They forced the natives to convert."

"Missionaries suffered and sacrificed spreading God's word."

Carlos held the padre's eyes with his. "Not easy to resist, when they were tortured."

Padre Miguel shook his head. He sank to the ground, leaning back against the tree. "Some of the soldiers may have—"

"And missionaries condoned it."

"Who's filled your head with these foul thoughts?"

"Men where I worked told stories passed down in their families—great-great-great-grandfathers who hid in the hills to escape slavery. Conquistadors attacking women and planting seeds in their family bloodstreams. A book, written by a priest, describes it all."

"You have to understand the times."

Blood pounded in Carlos's temples. Why so angry? Because he'd accepted the church's benevolent lies for so long. Because Padre Miguel had offered him salvation and a chance to clean the holy chalice, and Carlos had jumped at it. As the priests who'd enslaved and slaughtered his ancestors had offered that holy cup. "The Spaniards worked people to death in the mines. Conquistadors attacked. People fled to the friars, and they said, 'I'll protect you, if you slave to build my church.'"

The padre looked at his feet as he spoke. "They came for a holy cause, Carlos: introducing souls to Jesus. Juan de Zumárraga, a Franciscan, defended the natives. Vasco de Quiroga gained the people's love and respect as the bishop here in Michoacán." He swallowed hard. "Friars inspired the people and built churches not from compulsion but devotion. They tried to end the harsh treatment."

The padre's distress bored a hole in Carlos's fury. "I'm sure some were good men."

Padre Miguel got to his feet and held out a hand to Carlos. "You see what I'm like. I'm a priest, and I'd never—"

"See the color of our skin, Padre? We're descended from their victims and from the torturers."

Carlos noticed beads of sweat on the priest's forehead, tears welling in his eyes. "Before judging, consider the church's good acts. Educating children. Caring for the poor. Building hospitals."

The padre believed it all, didn't he? All the good done by the church, the sacraments that brought you closer to God. Carlos felt hollow regret pour into his chest. This was his coach and his mentor, a man who'd only wanted Carlos to believe what he thought was right and good.

He held the padre's hand for a second. "I know your heart is true, but the church is supposed to be *always* good, not just sometimes. I believed those books the priests wrote and felt foolish when I realized."

"You were a child. A child doesn't need confusion. A child must believe in virtue and reap the seeds of goodness." Tears ran down Padre Miguel's face, and he turned away. "When you questioned before, I told myself you were like many young men who doubted for a time. You were my special boy. I loved you so." The padre cleared his throat and faced Carlos, holding out his hands. "Now, the way you speak to me ... I can't."

He waved a hand in front of his face. "That's enough. I'm going back." He pointed toward the church. Carlos stepped forward for their usual hug, but the padre shook his head. "Please don't follow me."

That night in bed, Carlos thought of Jesus's compassionate words and of Padre Miguel's past kindness. He vowed to go back the next day and tell the priest he loved him.

CHAPTER NINETEEN

Carlos glanced at Lilia as he drove them to his ranch. "I'm going to answer a question you haven't asked. I don't know about the picture you saw of me at Julie's house, but sometimes Mrs. Booker drew parts of my body she never saw."

Lilia looked skeptical.

"No, really."

June/July 1967

In Mrs. Booker's studio, week-by-week, he received less to wear—a shirt without buttons. No shirt. Tight-fitting pants. At first, his body responded to her looks and her touches. But the humiliation wore at him. He began to dread his weekly visits.

One afternoon, Carlos entered Mrs. Booker's cottage to find a small piece of black cloth on the stool, like a woman's bikini bottom—black, flimsy, barely enough to cover. Anger settled like a stone in his gut. *Humillación*, self-loathing. How would Isabel feel if she saw how her proud husband earned extra money?

But his children deserved good clothes and nourishing food. They deserved their father at home all year. If he made more money this year and next and the one after, one day he'd buy a *ranchito* in Mexico to provide for them.

And Isabel would never find out, thank God.

He showered and put on the scrap of fabric, then wrapped a towel around himself and stepped into the studio.

"Drop the towel," she said.

"You want I show my leg?" He sat on the stool and exposed one.

"Take it off." She came close, drawing her hand back. He tensed for a slap, but she didn't hit him. "If you want the money ..."

He took a deep breath, let the towel fall, and allowed her to pose him leaning on the stool. But he refused to leer or even to smile.

She set him up the way she wanted and touched him, but his body had lost interest.

"Get it up," she said.

"He won't do it." *My flute has more pride than I do.*

"You're useless, not even a man." Mrs. Booker brought out magazines from the long cabinet that ran along one wall. She flipped through the pages, found a photograph and stuck it in front of him. "See, a real *hombre*, with a real pecker. Do you know what that means, *muchacho*?"

He did know. Her daughter had taught him *pecker*.

"Smile at me, like you did before."

All right, for money he could smile.

The next Wednesday, he found the stool bare. As he was supposed to be? Should he do this? For fifty dollars? Or maybe for his safety. He showered, then unhooked the shower curtain and wrapped himself in it.

When he entered the studio, Mrs. Booker looked him over and chuckled. She tugged the curtain, but he held on.

"You want the money? I'll make it a hundred."

He struggled to find the words in English. "You not need

me to make picture." He gestured at the magazines she'd left on the counter.

"Fine. Wear the friggin' curtain."

She brought out a tube like the ones containing toothpaste, squeezed it over a bowl, dipped a paintbrush in. She stepped toward him, her hand darting at his face. He closed his eyes and felt a wet brush on his nose. Amy Booker laughed. "It's all right. You'll be able to wash it off." She parted the top of the shower curtain and dabbed paint on his chest, a blue flower to adorn his right nipple.

Back at the canvas, she said, "Smile."

Instead he looked out the high window at tree leaves fluttering in the wind.

Afterward she showed him the image: A manly body, with a blue head and a blue daisy on his chest.

"One hundred," he said.

She snorted at him.

"Or I not come back."

"Get out."

He retrieved his clean clothes from the porch and washed off the paint. On the stool, he found two fifty-dollar bills.

Every night that week, he vowed not to pose again. But he was under Mrs. Booker's protection. What would happen if he refused her?

Returning the next Wednesday, he found the drawstring pants on his stool.

When Amy Booker entered, a sleek, chocolate-brown dog followed her in, limping on three legs.

"His name is Teddy," she said. "Handsome, isn't he? Lost the leg in an accident."

The dog gave Carlos a sniff and returned to Señora Booker, pressing his head into her thigh. She bent, nuzzled her cheek against the dog's face, stroked him and kissed his forehead. "Lie there," she commanded. The dog settled in a corner. "Good boy."

When she turned back to Carlos, her expression hardened, "Take a look between Teddy's legs and you'll see what a penis is."

She pointed at the stool. "Sit and be quiet. Don't ask for a hundred dollars ever again."

The dog watched his mistress as she drew, and when she finished, he limped behind her out the door.

Carlos pulled the truck to a stop by the sheep pen. "My job became easy. I put on those loose pants and tried to leer at her. She used a bit of me and parts from the macho magazine men, each painting revealing a very excited Carlos, with a very excited …"

"She made you naked with an erection," Lilia offered.

"An impressive one too." Carlos felt himself blush. "When I told Julie, she laughed, until she saw how it shamed me."

"Pictures to keep the *patrón* company at dinner?"

"Yes."

"Dangerous as hell," Lilia said.

"I took risks—I did. I humiliated myself. When I called Isabel that next week, she didn't ask how I earned so much. She said, 'Thank God for the extra money. Anita had a terrible rash. She was shrieking and I couldn't get her to stop scratching. We had to go all the way to Guadalajara for a special doctor.' Isabel cried on the phone, and her gratitude made me forget my shame. It was hard for her, being without me, but the money was so important. It wasn't as simple as giving up and going home."

Lilia reached across and touched his arm. "I'm sorry for what Mrs. Booker did. Did she call off your Wednesday afternoons after that?"

"I thought she would, but no. Julie explained to me later that her mother couldn't let Señor Booker know my interest had vanished."

Lilia gave him a mischievous grin. "You said she kept drawing your flute larger. How big did it get?"

"It's humiliating."

"If you aren't embarrassed by now …"

With one hand on the steering wheel, he raised the other up to the roof. "Big as a cat. She even drew a cat in one of the pictures."

Lilia whistled.

CHAPTER TWENTY

The victim ... slowly began to climb the steps of the pyramid. In this ascent he represented the course of the sun from east to west. ... He reached the summit and stood in the center of the great Sun Stone, which represented noon, the sacrificers approached the captive and opened his chest. Once the heart had been wrenched out, it was offered to the sun and blood sprinkled toward the solar deity. Imitating the descent of the sun in the west, the corpse was toppled down the steps of the pyramid.

Diego Durán, Dominican friar, describing an Aztec sacrifice

Carlos checked the water trough. He brought hay from his shed and tubs of greens from the back of the pickup and laid out a feast for the bleating sheep. Then he jumped back behind the wheel and headed toward Lilia's hotel.

"So now are you willing to talk about María?" she asked.

"I might. But first you'll tell me: Did Julie ever marry?"

"No. She finished college in San Diego and moved back to Santa Lucia to care for her mother."

"She was unhappy in that house," Carlos said. "Only planning to stay until she was twenty-five."

"Her mom was very ill, her father meaner than ever. Some event in Delano had set him off." She looked at him. "That's something you know, Carlos—something Julie mentions but doesn't explain."

Her comment took his breath away. *Delano. The Deputy.* Lilia could never know about that night. "Julie's still pretty, I bet."

"Forty-seven and beautiful. She lives in the downstairs of that big house. Her sister, Ivy, and Ivy's husband live upstairs."

Julie's life had turned out so different from her dreams. She'd had none of those foreign adventures, and now living with her sister. Why? *Norteamericanos* didn't seem to like their families.

He pulled up in front of the hotel. "Shall I help carry your bathing suit?"

"No thanks." She reached for the door handle.

He touched her arm and said, "There's no need to spend money on this hotel. Pack all of your things and stay at my house tonight."

She looked him over, skeptical.

"Last night you said you missed sleeping with a man."

She turned serious. "I was pretty drunk then, and you are quite a forward fellow. You can't think that I would—"

"Innocent sleep, like last night."

"Two people, two bedrooms."

He raised his palms in surrender. "If you prefer."

After a few minutes, Lilia returned to the truck with her suitcase and kissed him on the cheek.

As he drove the pickup, she watched him. "I told you about Julie. I even kissed you. But you haven't finished your story."

"You didn't respond to my most important question. So, I'll tell you what's on *my* mind: our ancestors."

"Who?"

105

"Lilia, you said your family lived near Mexico City before moving north, so your forebears could have been *Azteca*. Like many Mexicans—especially those a bit lighter and taller—with some Spanish blood. In your features, I see an Arabian prince who helped conquer Spain in the 1100s, fell in love, and produced beautiful children with the darkest brown eyes on earth. One of this Arab's descendants, a Spanish soldier conquering Mexico, became your long-lost great-great-great-grandfather … and a few more greats."

Lilia laughed. "All this from my eyes?"

"Eyes, lovely skin, and geography. I know little about those Spanish or Arabs, but your local ancestors were interesting. This land around us belonged to a tribe called Purépecha, who battled your Aztecs like wild dogs. The Aztecs anointed high priests and built temples for the deities, like the sun god Nahuati. And there was a hummingbird warrior god. Yes, a hummingbird! The people had to worship and behave properly, to save the bird and the sun god from their enemies."

He savored Lilia's incredulous frown and had to remind himself to look back at the road.

"You're doubting this, but it was serious. Imagine how cold these hills would become without *la luz del sol*. Humans were sacrificed to support these gods. Your pretty mouth is twisting up, Lilia. You find these beliefs questionable, but this is your heritage. You wonder how the priests knew all of this, but priests command magic. People believe and follow to gain a joyous *eternidad*."

Carlos saw the first sign for Lake Pátzcuaro: sixty kilometers. "Your ancestors took prisoners from other tribes—my great uncles perhaps—slaughtered them, cut out their hearts and offered them up to the immortals."

"How do you know my ancestors weren't among the victims?" Lilia asked.

"Too bad for them. Aztecs lost in the end anyway. Spaniards destroyed their temples. They brought new racial mixes and new beliefs to force on the people. The high priests who guided the Spaniards were anointed by a new and jealous god, whose hacienda was apparently in Rome."

"I get your message." Lilia folded her arms.

"There are many strange beliefs. Some are called religions."

"I see why María wouldn't discuss her faith with you."

"If you came from India, you'd bow before a god with the face of an elephant and make confessions to a six-armed goddess riding a tiger."

"I'm comfortable talking with Jesus and Mother Mary." She stared ahead, annoyed. "When you mock priests—*my* priest—you're being hypocritical. You say they pretend to know what they can't know. But you pretend to know they're wrong."

Of course she was right. "I apologize. None of us knows. But people who feign certainty trouble me."

Time to lighten the mood. "I think you'd make a beautiful Hindu princess. Your skin is almost dark enough, and with a little red dot right there ..." He reached toward her forehead, and she flicked his hand away.

CHAPTER TWENTY-ONE

Lilia rode silently for a while. Then she said, "Here's something good about the United States—scientists."

"Oh?"

"You have such a bad opinion of my country, I need to remind you. You know we landed a man on the moon, right?"

"Of course."

"People from all over the world come to our universities. We have an amazing telescope that orbits the earth. It can see stars billions of miles away." She sat straight in her seat, self-satisfied.

Carlos was beginning to admire Lilia's pride in her country, and the way she challenged him with it. "Yes, very good scientists."

Without a pause, she said, "So you began seeing this María woman, and you fell for her."

Her question startled him, and amused him, too. He took a moment to recover and said, "Every Sunday after mass we followed the railroad tracks and ate lunch in the sycamore grove. I wanted to tell her about my family, but she twisted my heart in complicated knots. She stared into my eyes as we ate, and then we held each other for hours. I felt every inch of her body, caressed every contour of her sides and back, always through her clothing. We kissed cheeks and lips and necks. I wanted so badly to touch more of that lovely skin, but couldn't ask. Julie had drawn me into the American free-love sixties, while María remained a *mujer mexicana tradicional*."

"You were still posing for Mrs. Booker and having sex with Julie?"

"I had dreams about using that money. And Julie was still a comfort to me."

"So, that's *your* word for it," Lilia said. "None of this worried you?"

"It wasn't just the sex with Julie. I was lonely. I was terrified many days in that land, not just that year. All of us lived with questions and fears. What if *la migra* comes for us? What if the foreman attacks for no reason? What happened to men who left the ranch without a word? If I caught the scent of a dead animal, I hurried past, fearing I might find a human corpse.... I could tell Julie all of my fears. My sadness, too."

Lilia raised her voice. "I meant worried about *your* actions?"

"I guess not." But seeing the look on Lilia's face—disappointment?—he was starting to see his past through her eyes, to consider those actions. For the first time beginning to regret what he'd done.

July/August 1967

He'd been seeing María for two weeks when he finally mentioned her to Julie. She gaped at him like someone who'd discovered dog shit on her shoe. "You're seeing a woman who won't put out for you?"

"True."

"You love Isabel and your girls, but you're falling for this *other person*," she said. "You say you'll always go back to them.

You'd better. This will hurt you deeply and hurt this woman. Who is she?"

He shook his head. "I'll only love her a little bit, the way I do you."

"You're making a horrible mistake, Carlos. Promise to think it over."

He promised, but still Julie sent him back to the bunkhouse with not so much as a hug. That evening, as he pictured the disappointment in her eyes, he realized, *She's my only true friend here, and I could lose her.*

The next week, after another session with Amy Booker, Carlos headed toward Julie's hideout, hoping she'd calmed down. He snaked his way among the orange trees, then stopped to look around, listening for the patrol truck on the dirt road. He heard a sound—a breeze blowing branches? A crack. There—a patch of denim-blue among the trees just down the hill. He stood still, heart pounding in his throat.

"I'm following you, Montoya." It was the foreman, Conteveras. He came forward, shaking his fist. "What are you doing up here?"

"Seeking peace."

Carlos thought the man would hit him, but Conteveras just beckoned with a finger. "Sure, Montoya. Come with me."

Julie will worry when I don't come, Carlos thought. But he had no choice.

Conteveras drove him to the celery field. As the vehicle slowed, Carlos spotted Ruiz glaring, and Conteveras said, "Out. Now."

The truck still moving, Carlos opened the door and hopped onto the dirt, hopped again to keep from falling before the truck stopped ahead. He was only a meter from Ruiz, who delivered a stinging slap. "Lazy bastard. Get to work."

As Carlos picked up the short hoe to begin, he saw that his hand was shaking.

At the end of the day, Ruiz ordered, "You get time off to fuck around with Mrs. Booker, but from now on, once you're done with her, get your *culo* back here."

Carlos felt his heart hammering. If they were following him—if they had been following him—how much did they know? How much did Hiram Booker know? He couldn't go to Julie, and had no way to contact her. Would he ever see her again?

The next morning, Carlos and Rafael were cutting up a dead avocado tree when Rafael suddenly straightened, staring. Carlos turned to find Señor Booker close behind him. He whipped off his hat.

Booker's eyes were cold as granite beads, his voice gravel, his Spanish coarse. "Ruiz made my wife angry yesterday," he said. "She insists you have Wednesday afternoons to yourself. We *do* what my wife wants, remember?"

"Yes, señor."

"Ruiz thinks you're lazy. He wants to beat the shit out of you, like he does with other crappy workers. But I protect you, don't I?"

"Yes, señor."

"I'm not happy about this business." The *patrón's* eyes narrowed, making him look almost sad, and Carlos saw that Mrs. Booker's drawings upset him after all.

Booker's expression hardened. "You are crap, Montoya, but I told Ruiz to leave you alone. They won't follow you again." Booker eyed Carlos's sombrero and held out his hand. Carlos passed it to him. Booker spat in it and handed it back. "Put your damned hat on. It's hot out. Get sawing on that tree. And keep your dick in your pants around my wife."

What he asked for was, of course, contradictory, and Carlos

was tempted to say, *I swear she hasn't seen my penis.* The thought almost made him grin, but Booker's glare prevented him.

As the *patrón* strode away, Carlos savored the words, "I protect you."

The question was, would that protection last?

"Jesus," Lilia said. She covered her mouth with a hand.

"There's more. If I tell you, you'll see how blind I was."

"You *didn't* go back to Julie the next Wednesday?"

He shrugged.

"Don't say you did it because you're a man the way God made you, unless God made you very stupid."

CHAPTER TWENTY-TWO

August 1967

Carlos fretted all of the following week. Did he dare go to Julie? And why did he want to so badly? Sex? Having someone who cared about him in this hostile country? Her irreligious thoughts that raised questions he couldn't answer? The next Wednesday, after posing for Mrs. Booker, he reassured himself with her husband's words, "they won't follow you," and set out. After a slow and careful transit, he found Julie at the hiding place. Her pale green shirt was buttoned all the way up, and she didn't rush to hug him. He might have asked if things were okay, but instead he said, "They were watching me."

She surprised him by smiling. "Not anymore."

"You know?"

She touched his cheek and looked into his eyes. "I worried when you didn't come last week. But I found out what happened that night at dinner."

"Ruiz wants to beat me. That's what your father told me."

"Ruiz isn't in charge." Julie looked so confident that it calmed him a bit. "At dinner, my father called you Mom's *macho muchacho* and told her how the foremen had hauled you back to work. Mom was irate, but she kept her cool."

"Your father joked about it?"

"Mother used his ego against him. He wants everyone to know he has the power. 'You're the boss out there, aren't you?' That's what she said. 'If Ruiz came after my beautiful *muchacho*, you must have sent him.' She gave him a big smile and said, 'It's sweet that you're so jealous about me, dear.' That really pissed him off, but he couldn't admit that Ruiz pursued you on his own. He turned really red, and it was so funny. Then he said, 'Ruiz won't bother the fucker anymore.'"

Julie ran her hand through Carlos's hair. "You must have been really scared."

They sat on Julie's hammock, and every creak it made sent a chill up his spine. "Can we trust him? The *pendejo* spit in my hat."

She laughed. "My father's a mean son of a bitch, but he won't let Ruiz go after you."

"This isn't a joke, Julie."

"It's all right. I'll keep watching my parents. He told you to do what Mom wants, right?"

Carlos thought that over. He wanted to see Julie, and maybe, as long as he was careful …

Julie waited for him to settle down. "Lie beside me."

It was a windy day, but down between the palms, the breeze was gentle. It rocked the hammock as they watched the sky. Her closeness comforted him.

He turned toward her and touched her breast.

She pushed his hand away and faced him, serious. "You're still seeing that woman?"

"Yes."

"You thought about what I said?"

He caught himself before saying María's name, tried not to show emotion. "Seeing her is more important than I realized."

"This is an awful mistake. For Isabel. For you, too, Carlos."

He shook his head. "You're angry?"

"No. But let's be normal friends for now."

No more fooling around, then. "I hurt your feelings? I thought we weren't falling in love."

She shook her head. "It's not that. I thought you were such a good man."

"I'm the same man. Never perfect." Yes, he was intoxicated by María. A mistake? Probably. But not Julie's business.

"This is my way to show how much I disapprove. It hurts me as much as you—more." Still looking into his eyes, she said, "Still, I'd like you to keep coming."

Julie, the free spirit, was telling *him* what to do. Maybe he should be angry. But the emptiness in him felt like disappointment. He had to decide: Had he just been coming for sex?

Without saying anything, he rolled onto his back. Clouds drifted overhead.

Whenever he spent time with Julie, he realized a little more how special she was. He learned things from her, stretched his consciousness, considered her unique brand of morality. She sympathized when he told her how hard the work was, how degrading his visits to her mother's studio. No, he decided. Despite the danger, he did not want to give her up. Still … what would "normal friends" be like?

"Tell me about Julie," he said. "How was it being a rich girl growing up on this ranch?"

She laid her head on his shoulder. "We had horses to ride, Ivy and I, and days at the beach, trips to the LA Zoo or shopping. One of the maids would take us, with a ranch hand driving. The maids got to swim with us, visit stores with us. We ate ice cream together."

"Your mother didn't go?"

"Rarely." Julie thought for a moment. "Rosa and the others became my true moms. On quiet days, I hung out in the kitchen or went for groceries with them. They loved me, and I loved them.

"When I began school, I missed my 'Mexican moms,' and I fought with little boys in my class." She laughed. "I gave Toby Smith a black eye in second grade. Mom screamed at me. After that she started really bossing me around. Her neglect had been okay, but discipline pissed me off. And I still believed my father was the strongest, most important man alive. He ran our ranch, which seemed like the whole world."

"That's the way we're supposed to see our dads." Carlos swallowed, imagining how it would feel if his father would be there to hug him when he returned to Mexico this fall.

"You told me how good your father was, Carlos. Which raises the question: if some God is watching over us, why did my father stick around and your dad ..." She squeezed his hand. "This will surprise you.... I used to think our priest was the wisest man alive."

"What turned you upside down, so that you love your mom but hate your father and priest?" he asked.

"My father started coming in from work ranting about lazy Mexicans, but I loved our Mexican maids and cook. He'd shout insults at black people marching for their rights on the TV news. Now, it's the Vietnam War. 'Nuke the gooks,' he shouts. I started to argue with him maybe in fourth grade, and things got really bad between us."

How difficult this would be for a sensitive girl. Julie, perceptive, wiseass and smart—unique.

"I really began listening to Father Henry's sermons," she said. "God commands this and God commands that. In the confessional, I questioned him and refused to admit any of those stupid phony sins."

"Is that the priest you called a 'dickhead?'"

"Yep. Two dickheads—my father worse than my priest, because he shamed Mom every day. Mom turned out to be smarter than I'd thought, and she was on *my* side. When I hit puberty, Father Henry gave me a lecture about masturbation—my father had put him up to it. I was twelve or thirteen. Can you imagine how embarrassing? Years later I learned that the church had made a saint out of the guy who declared that pretty much any fun was sin."

Julie was getting worked up again, making Carlos uncomfortable. "Take a breath and watch the clouds," he said. And Julie surprised him by lying still beside him.

After a while, he said, "My priest is a good man. I used to believe God spoke to the saints. But then I decided that those rules they taught us were made up. I was furious with Padre Miguel at first, but I realized he'd only told me what he believed."

"After your father died?"

Carlos nodded. "I read about other ideas and decided to think for myself but—you'll mock me—I still believe God gives us gifts, like this day, these palm trees and clouds."

She sat up in the hammock, making it squeak. He put his finger to his lips for quiet.

"I'll say it softly," she said. "That's a load of crap. And your priest—"

"Please don't judge Padre Miguel. Maybe this is my *fantasia inocente*, Julie, but *you* are the true gift of this angry country. God brought you to make my time bearable."

She grinned. "I thought I was here to give you sex."

"And now you're not."

Her smile faded. "You have another woman to please you, but I hope you'll still come see me."

He wanted to. They could share ideas and memories, feelings he couldn't disclose to his cousin—the emptiness of missing Isabel, the hurt inflicted by the foremen's casual cruelty. Men didn't talk about these things. "I do like talking with you."

"I point out when you spout your priest's bullshit."

"I understand you better now," he said. "God has disappointed us both, but your father wounded you most of all."

"So, you're a friggin' psychologist?" Julie blurted this in English, but he understood. "Sorry. I don't want to take it out on you."

"You need to make peace with this, Julie. It only hurts *you*, hating your father and your priest and God."

She gave him a quirky smile, lay back beside him, and stroked his chest. "You'll come back next week?"

"If no one kills me first."

That night in the bunkhouse, he worried about the foremen, and Hiram Booker, and finally Julie. *My ideas may not make perfect sense, but I can never give up hope and inspiration the way she has.*

But he *had* given up hope and inspiration, hadn't he, twenty years later, when Isabel died?

CHAPTER TWENTY-THREE

September 1967

Señora Booker usually appeared after his shower, but the following Wednesday, she met him on the studio porch, her eyes intense, lips clenched in a hideous smile. "We'll do something different today." She repeated the words, "different" and "today" in Spanish.

Carrying a box with her drawing pencils, she led him to a clearing where there was a boulder and flowering bushes. A burlap bundle lay on the ground beside a shovel and pick, with an artist's easel set up nearby.

She pointed to the sack. "My Teddy. Would you dig a hole, so we can bury him?" Tears ran down her face.

He cut into the earth as she drew with her pencils. When the hole was deep enough, she showed him the sketch—the bushes and hills and part of the boulder, but she'd left the center clear. "You'll hold my darling, and I'll draw you." He understood "darling" not from the word, but from the misery on her face.

He unwrapped the dog, handsome and lean, with that glossy brown fur and that missing back leg. There was a gash across his throat, the fur stained black. He recoiled at the sight, then lifted the body.

She stroked the dog's head and kissed him between his ears, tears dripping onto his fur. She looked into Carlos's eyes. "He did this. My husband."

Carlos did his best, in English, to ask if the dog had been sick.

"He was seven and very healthy. My perfect friend." She pointed at the stump of his missing leg and said something, too fast for him to comprehend. He shook his head, and she positioned him by the boulder with Teddy across his lap, the dog's head cradled against his elbow. "Look at him," she said. "Like he's your son who's just died."

She drew with a plain pencil and then colored ones as he focused on the dog, trying not to picture Señor Booker slaying it.

When she finished, she said, "Bring him here."

As she caressed Teddy's face he admired the picture—the fine brown pencil strokes in the dog's coat, the furrows in Carlos's cheeks, and thick black eyebrows that made him seem to mourn the dead animal.

She nodded at the hole in the ground and walked away. He wrapped the dog, laid him in the grave, and shoveled dirt on top.

Afterward, he went to Julie. As they hugged, he told her.

"That son of a bitch." She began to cry and pace. "He killed Teddy for what? He was innocent. He was one fine dog." She stopped and patted Carlos's cheek. "I have to go to Mother." And then Julie turned and ran toward the house.

A week later, Julie told him, "He cut the dog's throat in the laundry room and left the carcass and blood for the 'help' to clean up. I screamed at the prick and all he said was, 'I've put up with that pathetic thing too long—limping like an old lady.' Mother set her drawing by the dining table that night and called it the *Pietá for Teddy*. That pissed my father off, him being so uptight about Jesus. He ripped it up and stalked out without eating." Julie gave a grim smile. "Mom's better at the game. His victories come through idiotic force."

"Tell me you ran away then," Lilia said, looking incredulous.

He shook his head. "Julie's mother still assured my safety."

"If he'd shot it or drowned it, that would have been despicable," Lilia said. "But he left that blood for the maid to clean up. She was Mexican, wasn't she?"

He nodded.

They'd reached the lake with the lovely black hills beyond. Lilia gazed out the window from time to time, but mostly focused on him. "You understood that Hiram Booker wasn't angry at the dog?"

"The *patrón* told me to do what his wife wanted. She told me to pose that way."

Lilia gave a derisive snort. "Any man who'd kill a dog would take you down in a second."

"Easy to see now, but I was making better money than ever. A hundred dollars again that day."

"And fooling around with Julie. Men will do anything for sex."

"I told you, Julie ended that."

"As you moved on to María."

Maybe Lilia couldn't see. Yes, there had been sex, also so much more. "Looking back, I see that I was crazy foolish. But I wasn't risking my life for María or for Julie. I was in California for a good reason: to make money for my family. I modeled for Mrs. Booker so I could triple my income. If I fled, I'd lose my pay for the rest of the season. And if I just stopped modeling, without Mrs. Booker's protection, I might have been beaten or worse. So,

EDWARD D. WEBSTER

I took risks. I made mistakes. I was human, yes? The way God made me."

"Sorry," Lilia said. "I didn't mean to upset you."

They drove in silence. The lake was obscured behind a stand of trees, and then he recognized a familiar fruit stand. "The hotel's just around this bend. It's beautiful, and you'll meet my friend Freddie."

Carlos had always admired the two-story hacienda-style hotel with its white beams and wide porches on two levels. Freddie came out to greet them. In his sixties, with trenches chiseled across his forehead and from chin to nose, he looked them over, then hugged Carlos and winked at Lilia. "Stay here tonight. A fine room for you and the lady, fifty pesos."

Lilia's smile vanished, and Carlos wondered what was bothering her. "When I called, I explained, Freddie. We just came for a swim in your pool."

"No, no. Stay the night. Have a nice dinner at one of our restaurants. Tomorrow you'll show your sweetheart around the lake." Freddie looked from Carlos to Lilia and back, no doubt trying to figure out what was annoying her and worrying him.

Carlos moved close to Lilia and whispered, "We *could* stay here and drive back tomorrow."

"In one room?" she murmured. "You see what he thinks."

Freddie *had* been pretty obvious about it. "Please don't be angry," Carlos said.

Freddie was watching them closely now. "Two rooms, same price. One room or two, no difference. Pay me nothing, just bring your leftovers from dinner."

Lilia was settling down. She looked the hotel over. "It *is* a nice place."

She nodded, and Carlos said, "We'll take both rooms. I'll pay full price."

"Nonsense. Eat at Josefina's and bring me a chile relleno and some arroz con pollo."

Carlos tried to hand him two hundred pesos, but Freddie waved it away. "None of that. Buy me two chiles."

He and Lilia were given two adjoining rooms with a door between. He changed into his bathing suit. Lilia knocked, then entered.

He didn't want to embarrass her, but with her in that one-piece swimsuit—dark blue with crimped fabric around the waist and white lilies running from shoulder to hip—how could he not skim his eyes down and up and back again?

A minute later, down at the pool, she flew from the diving board, a graceful blue streak, and came up shrieking. "It's really cold!" Her laughter was musical joy.

He dove in and swam with her. She found a small beach ball by the pool and said, "Jump off the board, and I'll try to hit you with this."

So he did. When she threw the ball, he caught it, and when he came up in the water, she said, "You get a point for catching it. Now I jump, and you throw."

"How many points to win?"

She twisted her mouth, considering. "Twenty."

"And my prize?"

"A hug."

"And if you win, Lilia?"

"I want …I want a hug, too" She paused on the diving board and asked, "Do you think I'm too bossy?"

"Why?"

"Always making rules."

"You're a woman."

She grinned and jumped, and he bounced the ball off her knee.

Soon they were laughing and jumping in the pool and hugging wet bodies, sometimes after only a few points had been scored. She seemed completely happy for once. Her laughter and her body and her bright smile thrilled him.

But as they headed for their rooms, she seemed more serious. "I'm going to walk by the lake."

"Shall I come with you?"

She shook her head.

Back in his room, thinking about their play at the pool, he wondered what made women so irresistible—appearance, yes, but also a feminine sweetness, a natural gaiety that no man could match, laughter as delightful as fine music. When a woman smiled at him—open, sweet, spontaneous—what man could resist?

Around five that evening, he answered a knock on the door between their rooms. She stepped in, wearing a short white dress. "I'm starved."

They had Josefina's dining room to themselves, looking out a huge window at the lake and mountains. "Have a good walk?" he asked.

"I did."

"Beer?"

"Wine, but don't think you'll make me as silly as last night."

"Of course not. They have excellent white wines in this region." He ordered a beer and a small bottle of wine. The waiter left, and he said, "At last, you'll tell me Julie's request?"

"You could tell me about—"

He shook his head. "It's time."

Lilia studied him. She took a breath and said, "She wants you to visit her in California."

It didn't surprise Carlos, not completely. "Don't you understand how much I ... Lilia, I'm scared to go there."

Carlos waited while the waiter poured wine into Lilia's glass and left. "I haven't crossed that border in twenty-six years. It's dangerous."

"Julie knows a congressman. She'll get papers."

"It's not just the crossing. *Policía*—"

Lilia raised her hand. "Julie's lawyer checked. There are no warrants against you." She gave him a dubious look. "Of course, nothing you've told me explains why there could be."

He chose his words carefully. "There was a small crime that I didn't commit. But in your country, a powerful Anglo can accuse you anyway, and ..." He felt a knot of anger in his chest, a twist of fear. That one false accusation, for a minor crime that never happened, had threatened his life.

What about the major crime that had?

He took a swig of beer and thumped the glass on the table. "I'm having trouble comprehending. Julie could come here."

"She can't."

"Or meet me in northern Mexico."

She shook her head. "There's a good reason. That's all I can say."

"I'm supposed to let my fruit rot in the orchard and face the *Norte* authorities without understanding why?"

"Don't be angry." Lilia stroked the back of his hand under the table. "Julie will get you a visa to come to the United States for ten days in June or July, whenever it's good for you, and I'll return to get you." She paused. "If you don't agree, I'll have no excuse to see you again."

He tried to think rationally. If the *Norte* police knew what had happened that night in Delano, if they suspected him, they would have hunted him down before this. Lilia said there was no warrant.... If the only way to see Lilia again was to go to California... "I'll think about it."

Later, they stood in the doorway between their two rooms. "Whose bed shall we share tonight?" he asked.

She didn't answer.

"You're only here for a short time, and we both miss closeness."

"I shouldn't have told you that. I drank too much." She stood on her toes, held him close and kissed him then, a good long kiss. When she backed away, he saw lust in her eyes, lust that lingered, then dissolved to regret. "Good night," she said, and retreated to her room.

In the night, visions tortured him—a *Norteamericano* jail cell, a policeman, his mouth right against Carlos's ear, screaming indecipherable words, a baton raised high, pain slicing elbow to shoulder and into his skull, arm bound in a blood-soaked cloth.

He woke sweating and about to scream, but he stopped in time. Lilia was in the next room.

CHAPTER TWENTY-FOUR

A fter lunch at a lakeside restaurant, Carlos pointed the pickup north. "Have you decided to stay at my house tonight?"

She leaned against the truck door, mocking him with a smile. "I've told you what Julie wants, but you have more to say."

September 1967

Despite the murder of Teddy the dog, ranch life didn't change much. Ruiz scowled, but did not strike. Hiram Booker rode out on his black stallion, watching Carlos and the others with the expression of a stalking hyena.

Carlos was no longer fooling around with Julie, but María's meager allowances made up for it. Her eyes told him she shared his wild desire. Her virginal reluctance stoked his flame and fed his guilt.

One Sunday after mass, he and María followed the train tracks to their sycamore grove. She wore one of her bare-shoulder dresses—pale green with yellow roses, her beauty making it so difficult for him to say what he had to. He laid a blanket on the ground by a tree, then sat and gestured for María to join him.

But she stood, holding the bag of food she'd brought. "I see it in your face, *querido*. Is there a problem?"

He took a breath and blurted it out. "I return to Mexico in a few weeks."

María's mouth fell open. "You can't, Carlos. I'd miss you too much."

"I have responsibilities."

"Go for a week and come back," she said.

He couldn't look at her. "I'll spend the winter, as always, with my family."

"No. No, dear."

"I'll miss you, too." He looked at her, serious. "You have to understand."

She studied him for a moment and then dropped to her knees. "How can you even ..."

He imagined staying and getting closer to María. But his home was in Mexico, his true love Isabel, his girls. He forced himself to be strong.

"Two weeks then return to me," she said, beginning to cry.

He shook his head. "I'm sorry."

She watched him, her lovely mouth distorted in a grimace. "You break my heart." Then, all of sudden, she pounded her chest, wailing and gulping air.

"They depend on me. They ..."

He was about to speak of Isabel and the girls, but María grabbed his arm. "Don't. Don't speak about *them*."

Could she have guessed about Isabel? If so, why hadn't she cast him off like a rotten mango? "My—"

"No. I don't want to hear." She unwrapped his burrito and held it out to him. "Eat, *querido*, and with each bite, think how good it is here with me."

He wanted to cry, for himself as much as for her pain. "I'm sorry."

María kept observing him, her expression anguished and then perturbed as he held her gaze. "It's very hard for me, too," he said.

Moments passed. Fury flared in her eyes. She jumped up, ripped the burrito open and flung it at him. "Son of a dog."

He stood, flipping beans and rice off his shirt. "María."

She slapped him hard and turned her back, leaning against a sycamore tree. He thought she'd stalk away, but instead, as he approached, she reached for his hands and wrapped him around her. She slipped one of his hands beneath her bra. He'd never touched her breast before—so firm and full, such an intimate offering for this devout woman. As he hugged her from behind, he felt her body jerk with sobbing, and he cried, too.

"I'll treat you better," she said. "We can touch and hug and kiss. You'll see. Don't go back there."

Lilia watched him as he drove. "That whore wanted to destroy your family. She was so theatrical, and you fell for it."

How could he explain desires that stole a man's sense? How even to understand himself?

"I'm mad at María, and Julie, too," Lilia said. "If she hadn't talked you into sex, you might have followed your better instincts. How long did you see this María before deciding to confess about Isabel?"

"A couple of months, I'm ashamed to say. I would have told her that day if she'd let me."

Lilia crossed her arms in front of her. "I wouldn't have liked you back then."

"I agree."

"Maybe not now, either."

CHAPTER TWENTY-FIVE

April 1994, Berkeley

B enito copied the old pictures of his parents and returned them to his mother's drawer.

He was certain she'd lied about not knowing his father's hometown in Mexico. Why? Whatever her reasons, it was clear she wouldn't help him find his father.

At least he had his dad's picture now and a few sketchy details. His father, Luis, had been a leader in the union. He'd been in trouble with the law. Benito had been born in Delano, and his mom had a diploma from there. There'd be union rosters, police records, maybe prison files. *No, stay away from police!*

Benito took a bus to the state capital and was shown to the dusty cellar of the main library. There, sitting at a long table with four viewing screens, he scrolled through rolls of microfilm, finding stories in the *Sacramento Bee* about César Chávez—the strikes, battles with teamsters, his march to Sacramento, a meeting with Robert Kennedy. One of the union leaders had been named Luis, but not Ortega. Could his mother have changed her last name after his father left? She wouldn't tell him if she had.

More articles and a couple of grainy images. The Luis in the union looked older, more hefty than his father seemed in the picture. Another article, better picture—still not his father.

For two days in the library, staying until closing, Benito found no mention of a Luis Ortega with the union, and no images of union men that he could match to his father's picture.

Back in Berkeley, he phoned the United Farm Workers offices in Delano, Keene, Oxnard, and Salinas, asking to speak to longtime union members about Luis Ortega. If not Ortega, any Luis who had trouble with the law back in the sixties, who may have died or fled the country.

"We had many named Luis, but only one who organized."

"We all got into trouble with the law … what kind of skunk would quit over a little jail time?"

"Maybe he organized for another union. The teamsters were active then. They used to bust our heads with bats. Big growers loved the teamsters."

No way his father would have worked against César.

After days of frustrating failure, Benito answered a knock on his door and found Juan pacing the hall. "Benito, how are you coming with the Bakersfield rally?"

"That's a month away."

Juan put on a fake smile and spread his hands. "*Amigo*, remember, you agreed to arrange a venue, contact newspapers and radio stations? And don't forget that fine speech you're preparing."

Benito called in sick at 7-Eleven the next day and got to work on his speech, but questions about his father nagged him. This political organizing, his schooling—everything in his life—now seemed like one huge bundle of obstacles keeping him from his search. Not to mention his mother, who held back all the answers.

She answered the door in a stained blue robe, a wide-eyed look of surprise on her face. "Son, I wasn't expecting you." She looked him over, wary. "Is something wrong? Come have tea in the kitchen."

"I'm not staying," he said, stepping inside and looking her square in the eye. "I want to know about *him*. My father."

She stepped back. "I've told you everything, I—"

"I'm going to look for him."

"No, son. He's probably dead."

"What town did he come from? You know, but you wouldn't tell me."

She sighed. "I worried you'd start this. Just accept that he's gone."

He needed to be calm, but she was pissing him off. "Even if he died, I want to know about him."

"This can only make you sad." She moved toward the kitchen. "Have a beer. Come. Tell me about school."

He stood firm. "I don't want to drink. I want to know. Stop the bullshit, Mom."

More of her tears, but now a hostile glare. "If he's not dead, he should be." Her hands flew up to her eyes, like she was trying to cram the tears back in. "Don't bother with him. He left us."

Her words stunned him. "Mom, what are you talking about? If you know he's alive—"

She held up a hand. "Sorry, son. Forgive me. I … I don't know anything."

She was furious at his father. He'd never imagined. Did she really think he was alive? He already knew that she lied—maybe about everything—and she wouldn't budge. He had to go to Mexico and find the truth. "What town was he from? It's a simple question."

"Don't do this, *mijo*. You'll break my heart." Now she was pleading, another of her tactics.

"Was his last name Ortega?"

She looked into his eyes, pathetic, tears streaming. "You're Benito Ortega. You don't need any more. Please trust me, Benito."

"You told me they injured him. Maybe he got better, and he's been trying to find us." Her eyes turned cold as he said, "You should want me to find him."

"*Stop!*" She stood rigid, angry. "You'll make me lose control, and you don't like it when I do that."

Actually, he hated it. But maybe if he pushed her, he'd learn something useful. "If you won't help me—"

"He doesn't deserve the same name as you. You can't take his side against me."

"You mean he's alive?"

"I didn't say that."

"He's a hero, mom. You always told me."

"He left us. How much of a hero is that?" She turned and fled into her room.

He followed and tried the knob—locked. "Just answer my question."

"Get the hell out."

Confused, doubting everything, Benito left, shaking. He stalked all the way to the BART station. *Did I piss her off so bad that she turned on my father? No. She's covered her rage all these years.*

Without understanding why, every missing fact and misdirection fueled his yearning to know.

CHAPTER TWENTY-SIX

Lilia hadn't spoken for half an hour. Was she angry or just pensive? As they approached his village, Carlos cleared his throat. "Want to go to a restaurant for dinner?"

She paused and then said, "I'd rather just be with you."

He was surprised, but pleased. "Wonderful!"

She leaned against the passenger door, facing him. "I'm mixed up about you, Carlos, but I don't want to be out where people will watch us."

He stopped to buy beer, a roasted chicken, bread, and grilled vegetables. As he turned the truck into his street, Lilia bolted upright and pointed to her red rental, still parked in his street. "*What's that on my car?*"

One windshield wiper was sticking up with something furry under it. He pulled the truck forward and jumped out, raised the wiper, and poked the thing. "Dead possum."

"Is this one of those Mexican curses?"

"No. My daughters aren't into that."

"You said Rita wouldn't make a scene," Lilia said.

"She must be pretty upset." He walked around the little red car. "Doesn't look like she damaged it."

"How nuts is she?" Despite her words, Lilia seemed to be enjoying this.

He thought a moment. "We have to show her she can't bully us, right?"

"Right." Lilia looked uncertain.

"May I have your keys?"

"Maybe you're nuts, too." She handed them over.

He drove around the corner to Rita's beige stucco house and parked the car out front.

Back at his place, he opened two beers and settled with Lilia on his front step. "Rita's watching from her upstairs window. Don't look. Just raise your bottle and clink it with mine."

"This runs in your family?" she asked.

"Probably."

After a while they moved inside, to the kitchen. Carlos carved and Lilia divided the chicken and vegetables between two plates. There was a rap at the window over the kitchen counter and Rita's voice, just loud enough to hear. "*Papá*, come here."

He opened the window and looked out. Rita's hair was a mess, her lips drawn in an angry line.

"We're trying to have a peaceful meal, *hija*." Carlos couldn't help but grin as he glanced at Lilia and winked.

"Move the car, *Papá*. It embarrasses us."

"The dead animal?"

"It's gone."

"Where did you get the possum?"

"Pepe found it in the arroyo."

"Oh." He shut the window.

"Wait, *Papá*." Her voice was muffled. "*Papá!*"

He stood back by the refrigerator, where she couldn't see him. He knew he shouldn't enjoy his daughter's discomfort so much, but maybe she deserved it.

When Rita stopped tapping on the window, he peeked out and saw her trudging home.

But when he turned toward Lilia, she looked annoyed. "I'm not hungry," she said. "I'm going to take a shower, and…don't ask."

He was waiting on the living room sofa a half hour later, trying to decide what he'd done to anger her. She came to the doorway in those pale blue pajamas, damp black hair trailing down one shoulder. He stood and stepped toward her.

Her expression confused him. Angry? Uncertain? Regretful? "You say you have no expectations for us, but you do," she said. "When you were taunting your daughter, you let her imagine we'd have sex, and back at Freddie's hotel, there was a reason he insinuated what he did…. I'll be in the guest room tonight—door closed."

A lump formed in his throat. He was tempted to apologize, but why? He thought back to that time when she went to hug him but pushed him back instead. Other times when she sent him those seductive looks, then backed away.

"Wait," he said. "Did I really do anything wrong? Maybe Freddie noticed that I seemed happier than usual and made an assumption. I *was* happy—to be with you. I hope you've enjoyed this time with me too."

She watched him with her arms crossed in front of her— calming down?

"With Rita just now… I don't know. Maybe I was smiling because it gives me pleasure to frustrate her. Maybe—"

She let her arms drop to her side. "It felt like more than that."

"Lilia." He took another step toward her and reached for her arm, but stopped short when her look didn't soften. "If I get ideas about you, it's not an insult. It's that you're *so* lovely. When you look at me with those amazing eyes, I can't help it."

Carlos thought he detected the hint of a grin on Lilia's lips.

"You're not being fair. I'm not going to apologize for finding you attractive."

"Maybe not," she said. "Still I have to think about all of this. Don't bother getting up early to see me off."

As she disappeared down the hall, he was tempted to have a shot of tequila. But that would dull his thoughts when he needed to think clearly. Later, alone in bed, he worried that his tales of Julie and María had set Lilia against him. He'd been so foolish back then. Resenting Padre Miguel for preaching falsehoods, trying to decipher for himself God's intentions, he'd let selfish desires seduce him. He knew that now. But how foolish he was still. With Rita just now, and with Freddie too, had he acted like he expected sex from this lovely woman? He'd been trying to mask his deep desire and not scare her away.

CHAPTER TWENTY-SEVEN

April 1994, Santa Lucia

Lilia's voice came from the speakerphone. "You said to call after I'd spent some time with Carlos."

"And?" Julie asked.

"I like him ... but I shouldn't."

"You spent the weekend together?"

"Three days. I had Monday off," Lilia said.

"Are you sleeping with him?"

"Do you mean sleeping or *sleeping*?"

"Sleeping with a small *s*."

"Well ..."

"That must be a 'yes,'" Julie said. "So you like him a lot."

"Maybe. But I didn't sleep with him or SLEEP with him last night."

Julie focused on Carlos's picture on her bedroom wall, his bare chest and sexy smile. "Why not?"

"It's too fast for me, Julie. And what he's told me about 1967, you and this woman, María—he wasn't a good man. Then I thought he acted like he expected sex, and I got mad."

"He *was* good, Lilia. He missed his family so much, and he sacrificed to support them. He loved his wife in a sweet, abiding way, deeper than what he could have felt for María. I was there.

I saw it. He cried with me about missing her." Julie waited a moment, then said, "So you had an argument?"

"A little one. I calmed down before I went to bed, but I left early in the morning for work, so we didn't get to talk any more."

"At least you kissed him good night?"

"No."

"You like him, Lilia. Don't make yourself too hard to get. When you see him tonight give him a good hug."

"I'm working the rest of the week and won't see him until Saturday."

Julie couldn't believe it. "Why not tonight?"

"Because." Lilia sounded reluctant.

"Screw it, Lilia. If you like him, have dinner with him."

"Julie, in a few days I go home to California. He stays in Mexico."

Carlos—in the picture and in Julie's memory—so strong and virile. "My advice is to sleep with him with a capital S. It will make you forget every bad thing that's happened."

"I'm going to change the subject now, Julie. I told him what you want him to do."

"And?"

"He's making me wait until Saturday."

"When you sleep with him."

Lilia laughed. "I'm taking vitamins to strengthen my resistance."

After Lilia hung up, Julie's thoughts rambled. Memories of carefree afternoons with Carlos lately had been followed by horrible dreams. The crappy deputy had invaded her sleep. Now, fully awake, fierce anger welled in her; that guy was seen as a hero, even now, all these years later. He'd been about to murder Julie's lover in that cotton field outside Delano, and everyone had paid a price for it.

CHAPTER TWENTY-EIGHT

After a long four days without Lilia, Saturday arrived. Carlos cut wildflowers in the field near his orchard and filled vases in the kitchen, living room, and guest bedroom.

He cleaned house and waited, glancing at the clock, worrying that Lilia would still be angry with him.

She'd said she would arrive midafternoon. Four o'clock. Five. He went to the market and purchased roasted pork, tortillas, and refried beans, but when he returned, there was still no little red car.

The food grew cold on the counter.

Finally, he heard her at his front door and rushed to it. He opened the door and hesitated, waiting to see if she'd recovered from her resentment the other night. She wrapped her arms around him, and relief flooded him.

"Sorry I'm late," she said. "After we finished work, the teachers insisted I meet their families. We walked from house to house in their village, with all the children following." She shrugged. "I loved it. They invited me for dinner, but I broke away to be with you." She stroked his cheek. "I *really* wanted to get here sooner."

It was a tender touch that thrilled him. "So you're not angry with me anymore?"

"Only a little." She kissed him then—not passionate, but a

good kiss that lasted several seconds. "I'm sorry about that too. I was too hard on you. I've thought a lot about this, and I don't want to be that way."

He brushed her hair away from her face. "It's all right," he said.

"Can we forget all about it?" she said. "I hope so."

He sighed. "That sounds great. I'll go heat our dinner."

"Not for me." She puffed out her cheeks and patted her tummy. "They made me eat at every house."

And just like that; everything was all right.

She sipped lemonade as he ate, leaning her elbows on the table, chin propped on her hands. "I've had a long day." But the gleam in her eye made him hopeful. "I planned to be strong and sleep alone."

"You know I'm trustworthy."

She sliced a hand level in the air. "You wouldn't dare piss me off."

"Right. Your karate."

She showed up in his bedroom a few minutes later wearing the blue pajamas. He set two beers on the night table and made a mound of pillows against the headboard.

He rested against them, and Lilia settled back against his side, her head nestled between his cheek and the pillow, long hair tickling his neck. He slipped an arm around her waist.

She tugged it off and laid it across her chest, his hand on her shoulder. "My stomach is off limits."

He sipped a beer and passed her the bottle. "You're a surprising woman."

She drank and gave it back. "You're not the only one with secrets."

They finished the first beer and then the second.

"If you lie on your back, we could snuggle," she said.

They shifted, and he kissed the side of her head. "I like this," she said. "I like this a lot." She kissed his chin and murmured, "No more than this."

"It's God who designed men without a switch that says, 'off.' Delay your trip a day. That's all I ask."

"It's not half of what you ask." She lifted her head to look at him, "If you were ever so lucky, we'd use a condom."

"You're not on the pill?"

"It's the nineties. We have AIDS to think about."

"I've made love to no one but Isabel since 1968."

"I'm not a virgin either, Carlos."

He was half surprised, after the way she'd darted from lustful to reluctant. Did virgins exist anymore? The world had changed, and it had happened in the sixties, with the birth control pill, free love, and drugs, happened for him with Julie's ideas and her easy lustfulness.

"When you're back in California, will you talk to your priest about me?" he asked her.

"He'll remind me that God wants people to sanctify relationships before…"

He shook his head. "I don't understand the logic."

"Faith isn't logic, Carlos. It's faith. You'll never figure it out or prove it." She rolled onto her back.

Carlos got up to turn off the light and returned to lie next to her. They held hands, fingers intertwined.

He watched the moonlight from the window play across her thighs—the miracle of Lilia. Life was God's miracle, beautiful or not, desirable or not. Even a rat or lizard was miraculous. Carlos had ignored this kind of miracle since Isabel's sickness. Now it felt like a discovery.

In the night, he awoke to find Lilia gone. He waited, but she didn't return.

CHAPTER TWENTY-NINE

The next morning, with the guest room door closed and no sign of Lilia, Carlos went to the bakery. When he returned with a bag of pastries, he found her spooning fresh grounds into the coffee pot. She wore her white dress, the sexy one that ended well above the knee.

She leaned against the counter, smiling at him. He kissed her forehead.

"Julie was a *firecracker*." Lilia said. "That's an American expression that means 'wild and fun.'"

He nodded.

"I'm not like that, Carlos."

He took plates and coffee cups from the cabinet. "That's why you retreated to the guest room last night?"

"It was a lot for me."

"It was very nice."

"Too nice, Carlos. Too tempting."

He brushed a strand of hair away from her face. "We did nothing to regret or worry over."

Lilia didn't respond, and he said, "Julie could be like that, too—one minute a firecracker and then intense. She felt things very deeply. I wondered how someone, born to a rich family and money for life, could disdain God. But later, when she sobbed about the latest news—seven hundred North Americans killed that month in war, seven thousand of the enemy—I understood. Julie didn't see enemies or even strangers, only people. She had a conscience wider than her rich-girl's world, and she rejected God because she expected Him to be good."

Lilia stroked his arm. "That was an awful time in my country, Carlos, and it wounded her. It's not like that anymore." She studied him. "Now—you can't delay Julie's answer any longer."

He took a deep breath. "You tell me that Julie can't come here, and she wants to see me badly. You've checked and there are no warrants?"

She nodded.

"You seem like a most honest woman. I can only believe you."

He wanted Lilia to return. Wanted her back in his bed, her body close. Wanted to savor her sweet company and lovely smile. "I'll go."

She beamed. "Wonderful."

"I haven't told you yet why I'm so grateful to Julie."

"Go ahead."

"You have to leave for the airport, and it's a lengthy story. Call the airline and delay your trip."

"Not a chance. Come to the airport with me and tell me on the way."

Carlos retrieved the little red car from Rita's house, and then Lilia drove as he told her the story, keeping a few of the most embarrassing details to himself.

Late September 1967

One Wednesday, after finishing his shower at the art studio, Carlos entered the art room to find Amy Booker. Her left eye was a swollen purple mound. "Pretty, isn't it?"

His breath caught in his throat. He reached for her face. She grabbed his wrist hard, but then her look softened, and she let go. "All right. Touch me this once."

He brushed her cheek with his fingertips. "Your husband?"

She denied it with a shake of her head, but he knew. He'd known other men—workers at the camps, guys back in Mexico—who beat their wives. Some did it in secret. Others boasted, as if it were a man's right, even his duty. Could this be another need that God placed inside men, making them stronger in their bodies but weaker in other ways, more aggressive, so many bullies among them?

He pictured Isabel and couldn't imagine doing such a thing. If he couldn't, there were many like him. So it was not one of God's irresistible appetites.

"I'm winning, Carlos. *Ganando*." She tried to smile. "He's showing weakness."

"Danger for you."

"No. He cares about me." As she spoke, Señora Booker looked away.

He searched for the words in English. "And what he do to me, when so angry?"

"He won't. If he harmed you, they'd all know why."

Señora Booker led him to the easel and handed him a pencil. He took it, bewildered, as she moved to the stool. "Draw me, Carlos. Outline my body." She shadowed herself with both hands, indicating her waist and hips. "Make me naked. You have seen a nude woman?"

145

"Please, no."

She blew out an annoyed puff of air. "Start drawing."

He stood, blushing and foolish.

She marched over, took the pencil and made a curving line on the paper. "That's one side of the hair. Fit my face in here." She outlined a shoulder and upper arm, the curve of her hips and upper thighs. She placed the pencil back in his hand. "Use these lines to start."

She leaned against the stool and unbuttoned her white blouse all the way down. She wore no bra. He hadn't noticed before, hadn't looked past her wounded face.

He gaped at her. "Bad idea. You must see."

She pulled two hundred-dollar bills from her pants pocket and let them flutter to the floor. "You will do this, and I'll hide it from him." She pointed to her face and body. "Draw my eye the way it is and show my open blouse." She spread it farther, exposing a purple bruise below one breast. More gestures. "Show my nipple, show this bruise, and this." She pointed to a small black mole near the bruise. "I'll give you another five hundred before you go home."

Her misery silenced him, but he was drawing the most dangerous portrait—a man's disgrace.

She knew it, too. He saw it in her anguished eyes that darted to the door and back. "Don't worry. You'll be safe."

He sketched, revealing the top half of her body, her open blouse, the one breast exposed with the outline of that bruise. He did his best to trace her lips, the shape of the purple area, and curve of her swollen eyelid. His eyes wanted to cry at the sight of her. Finally, he set the pencil down. "Bad picture." He gestured to the drawing.

She came over and helped him add shadows, darkened the

eyebrows, added curly pubic hair where the thighs came together. She handed him pencils in purple and darker purple, pale pink, and the blue of a bright, clear sky. "Color in my bruise and my eyes—one blue, the other closed, like the door to hell. You see where to use the pink." She gestured to her face and body.

His heartbeat pounded fast and hard. He set the pencils down. "You can no let him find this. He do horrible something."

"I'll lock it away and wait until he's dying to bring it out."

But how could she stay with the man that long—until he was dying?

There was a sound outside, and Mrs. Booker jumped. "Oh," she said. "Rosa's bringing your clean clothes."

"Can't show this to him," Carlos said. "Never. Never."

She reached for the picture. "I'll do what I want."

He snatched it off the easel. She glared and held out her hand.

He ripped the picture in half, then ripped it again.

She clenched her fists, about to strike.

He tore again—now in eight pieces. His heart beat like a bulldozer engine pulling out a stump.

She spun and headed to the door, buttoning herself up as she stomped out.

Minutes later, up in their secret place, Julie gaped at him as he told her what had happened. "Where's the picture now?"

"I flushed it down the toilet."

Julie shook a fist in the air, crying. "Goddamn it." She paced, keeping her eyes on him. "Goddamn *him*. You have to get out, Carlos. I hate this, but you have to."

He thought of the fear in Amy Booker's eyes, her agitation. But it was Julie's next words that convinced him. "He hasn't beaten her in years, but when he does, no one's safe." She shook her head. "Get food from the bunkhouse kitchen. Bring it here and

147

wait. I'll help you, but if he's in a fury, he'll come after everyone. He'll toss her closets and burn her clothes, and then he'll choose someone he dislikes and beat them half to death." *Someone he dislikes.*

Julie kissed him long and deep, tears dripping from her lips to his. "Get the food. Then come back here to hide. Be careful." He reached to touch her cheek and saw that his hand was shaking. She ran from him then, toward the ranch house.

Stealthily, Carlos followed the long row of eucalyptus to the ranch. Near the bunkhouse, he saw Ruiz, Conteveras, and another man, carrying clubs. They circled the building, and then Conteveras and the stranger trudged off into the orange grove.

Hunting, and he was the quarry.

Terrified, Carlos retreated along the windbreak and up the arroyo, past Julie's secret spot.

At dusk, he heard a truck inching along the road and men talking. He hid deep under the foliage. The men moved on, but he stayed hidden, waiting for his heart to stop hammering.

Later, under the cover of darkness, Carlos crept into the fields and ate picked-over celery stalks. He drank irrigation water, came back and slept on the ground in the arroyo, just above their secret place. How foolish he'd been to pretend he was safe. Hiram Booker had told him to pose for his wife—to do what she asked. But any husband would be furious at those pictures…. He'd valued money over safety, over his family's well-being, and now he was desperate to return to them.

He lay awake, whispering to the moon, unable to sleep from fear and cold, worry for Julie and her mother, and dread about leaving María without a chance to reconcile after he'd disappointed her so.

The next morning, he heard rustling and hid behind the

palm trees. A woman's voice: "Carlos, it's Ellen. I'm alone." He peeked out and recognized Julie's friend. She'd brought Ellen to meet Carlos once. Now he wondered if Julie had been preparing for this moment.

She led him through neighboring orange groves to her car and drove him to a motel in the city of Oxnard. He slept there most of the day, until Julie arrived that evening with food.

She wore a long-sleeved shirt, and she winced when he touched her arm. He looked into her eyes as she rolled up her shirtsleeves. Plum-colored marks marred both arms, spots where fingers had dug into her.

She gave him a wry smile. "I yelled at the bastard for hurting Mom."

His fists clenched and fury burned in him. "The son of a whore."

"Don't get all macho," she said. "You can't protect me, only yourself." She took a wad of money from her purse. "A thousand dollars. Mom gave it to me. She's worried about you."

He stared at the money, more than he'd sent home that whole season, and wondered how Amy Booker knew to give it to Julie and why she would even care.

They held each other, and he murmured, "I have to tell María."

"No, dear one." Julie stroked the side of his head. "Don't you know that ranchers conspire against their workers? María's overseer would beat you for fun, then hand you to my father."

He thought of the foremen with their clubs and imagined what Señor Booker might do when he untethered the rage he must have corralled all summer. And he thought of his little family in Mexico, who needed him.

He wrote a note for María, promising to find her next spring, and handed it to Julie. "You have to get this to her."

149

EDWARD D. WEBSTER

She shook her head. "I don't trust this *woman*. I don't like this."

"Please."

"All right, Ellen can take it. But, Carlos, forget this woman. She wants to ruin everything."

They lay together until morning, Julie crying in his arms. "Lovely, darling, Carlos," she murmured over and over.

Then it came to him that he'd never see Julie again, this true, kind, caring friend. And Carlos cried too.

Lilia turned right, following a sign for the Guadalajara airport. "You were really lucky to get out alive."

"There's more to tell. Stay, and I'll buy you some delicious wine."

Her smile was both wistful and sexy. "Sorry. Hey, I need a phone number where I can get a message to you."

"Use Rita's. She'll love to chat."

Lilia laughed.

Carlos wrote the number. "With more time, I could tell you how María came after me here in Mexico."

"She chased you?" Lilia half-shouted. "You're a good seducer, Carlos, but I'm going. Two months from now, in California, you'll have days to tell me."

In the parking lot, she gave him a brief, disappointing hug and a long, soulful look. She cupped the side of his face, turned, and marched into the airport.

As he rode the bus toward home, Carlos brooded. He'd been carried away with desire for Lilia, and he'd promised to go see Julie. But could he truly bring himself to visit that horrible place?

Back home, he entered the guest bedroom, thinking of stories he wanted to tell Lilia, wishing he could hold her for another moment.

On the bureau he noticed an envelope. Inside was a thousand dollars—and a note:

Carlos

> *It's 3 AM. I'm in my room feeling lonely after leaving you just now, but also confused about why I wanted so badly to share your bed, why I fled and why I've shared such personal information.*
>
> *Here, so far from home, I wanted to feel bold and free, as if what I do doesn't matter, but it does.*
>
> *I still plan to come and get you in two months, as long as I'm feeling brave.*
>
> *Oh, yes. Julie sent this money for you.*

Lilia

The uncertainty in her note reminded him of the way she'd fled from his bed the night before, and her half-hearted hug at the airport. *As long as I'm feeling brave!* What did that mean?

CHAPTER THIRTY

Isabel, October 1967, Michoacán

My children are my solace when Carlos is away. The baby, Anita, is healthy again. She's been walking for months, and now runs in her wiggle-wobble way, tumbles to the floor or crashes into my legs as I work in the kitchen. She cries little, as long as I give her what she wants—my milk much of the time, applesauce, a clean diaper and my body against her as she sleeps.

Rita, the dutiful helper, sweeps with a toy broom; scrubs the vegetables with a little brush; "helps" me change the baby—her favorite doll, Anita. She scolds me—at the store if I forget her favorite cereal, walking home, about letting the baby carriage bounce on rough pavement, in the bathroom if I don't wash Anita according to Rita's suggestions.

These girls demand everything, but also give everything. They fill my heart.

My heart fills twice. Carlos telephoned—he's back in Mexico, arriving on this afternoon's bus. I want to see him. I long to see him. I need to see him.

But why three weeks early? And the call before this one—I heard worry in his voice. So, I ask myself, how is it that he's able to send more money than ever before? Why not tell me the details of such good fortune? If he faced danger, he'd never worry me with it, so when he reassures me, I fret still more.

But now he's coming! He'll be home and safe.

His touch makes me tremble. His embrace warms me. Whatever I wanted to ask, my worries run out of my head. Rita shrieks with joy to see him. He tickles and teases her. "Why the serious face?" he asks, tapping her nose with a finger. She tries not to laugh, tries to confront him for being away so long, for making *mamá* worry. But he just tickles her more.

He picks Anita up. "Your eyes are as brown as coffee beans," he says. She doesn't understand, but they gaze at each other and grin like monkeys as Rita watches with a sour face.

That night, Rita sleeps in her bed in the living room, past the hanging quilt that separates us. My mother sleeps in her own room beyond the kitchen. She deserves this privacy—it's her house.

I lie between them. Anita, asleep against my chest, takes long breaths. I move away a little. Carlos, behind me, his arms around, caresses me, his hard body against my back. I raise myself up and he adjusts my nightgown. His fingers send tingling delights—as a modest woman I cannot explain—all through me. He holds me so tightly; I feel how he cherishes me. Heaven.

After a few days, I ask if he's visited Padre Miguel. "Not yet," he says.

They argue, but Carlos loves the padre as much as I do. "Don't you want to see him?" I ask.

"I do," he says, but I hear hesitation.

I wish he would go. I wish he would find a way to believe again, even a little, to lighten his burdens.

One afternoon, we sneak away to love each other at my sister's house. I kiss him everywhere, and he kisses me. We shout for joy and ecstasy and love.

"The devotion I see in your eyes is the most beautiful thing in the world." That's what he says to me.

Before we leave, he shows me a thousand *Norteamericano* dollars, but averts his eyes when I ask where it came from. His only explanation: "They finally appreciate my work." I give him my look from the devil—the one I use with the children when they're sneaky. "Trust me," he says. "I've done nothing wrong."

I do trust him, but I see that he's sometimes sad and thoughtful. My heart can't release the doubt and worry. I would ask him not to go north again—it's risky—but to him, this is part of being a man, supporting his family.

He has a dream. He's buying an orchard. In a few years, when the trees grow full and the fruit comes heavy, he won't have to go north anymore. I long for that.

"Be careful, *querido*," I say. "It's dangerous there."

CHAPTER THIRTY-ONE

November 1967

Parishioners had reported seeing Carlos Montoya around town. Miguel waited, but Carlos didn't come by the church. Then one day, Miguel spotted him carrying a bag from the grocery store. The young man must have seen him, but he kept walking. So, he was not only lost to Jesus, but also to Miguel.

A few days later, Carlos came to his cottage. Miguel led him in, worrying after their last encounters. Would they argue? Would Carlos berate him again?

"I apologize, Padre. I've been home for weeks but …" Carlos looked away. "I'm thinking you wouldn't approve of me. I mean. I'm not a believer. You know that, but …"

"What is it, son?"

Carlos sat in one of the wooden chairs by the table. "I don't know how to say this."

"Take a breath and have some apple juice."

"No, thank you."

Miguel poured himself a glass and joined Carlos. "About your work on the other side?"

Carlos shook his head. "This year, something different happened. It's—it's what I didn't want to tell you. I don't go to confession. I'm not guided by those rules, so …"

Miguel had seen this sort of shamefaced blush before. "You're seeing a woman."

Carlos flushed.

"You're not my first parishioner who's strayed." Still, the realization disheartened him—thinking back to his first days in town, drying Carlos's cheeks during the baptism.

Later, when Miguel played *fútbol* with the little ones, he'd tell Carlos he had a "good foot." A keen mind, too and a loving heart, destined to something special, even as his father died in an accident and Carlos questioned his faith. But what had seemed special seemed it no more.

"Is it straying?" Carlos asked. "From God, I mean?"

"It's clear."

"You know I don't believe."

"God—no matter what you think of Him—sanctified your marriage."

"I don't know if He demands anything of us. You're a good man, Padre, generous, but nothing you've said has any authority."

"You used to love Jesus and revere Mother Mary above all. Perhaps—"

"I've abandoned those myths."

"You can be skeptical of her divinity and still think of her as a good woman. Visit her statue in the church. Seek her advice."

"I don't think so, Padre." Carlos eyed Miguel's glass. Miguel pushed it across the table, and Carlos drank it down.

The problem, of course, was that Carlos was a "sincere disbeliever." He'd learned many things from books, but somehow knew little of importance. "Even ignoring miracles, the Bible holds many truths."

"Possible truths. I have only what the world preaches, the world of plants and wind, the sun, the senses in my body." Carlos touched his chest, but Miguel knew he was referring to feelings lower in his anatomy.

"You could read Saint Augustin," Miguel suggested.

Carlos surprised him by smiling. "Hiding behind a saint's robes again?"

"Believe or not, these were wise men. Augustin's revelation was that God created love for procreation, not selfish pleasure. He forsook lust—which he had fully experienced—not ignorant of his sacrifice at all."

"Haven't you wondered why God would give such a boon and deny its pleasure? Have you always refused your nature, Padre?"

An audacious question. Miguel took in a breath, wondering how to respond in a way that was both truthful and inspiring. "My son, men are part animal and part God. We have a beast's needs, but also conscience and soul."

"You, as a priest, have a greater share of God? Then why not answer me?" Carlos scrutinized him for a moment and then shook his head. "Sorry. It's none of my business." Carlos stood and stepped to the window above the sink. "I do. I have a relationship up there. I've been avoiding your judgment."

"My judgment is unimportant. Think of Isabel."

Turning back toward him, Carlos said, "I'll be a better husband than any other in this village, even those who succumb to your ecclesiastic guidance."

"Believe me, son, this *will* affect your marriage. And you'll hurt this other woman. Do you care about that?"

"I value your opinion, Padre. I do, and I'll consider it. Now maybe we can talk about something else."

Miguel poured juice for both of them. They talked for another hour—about farm work, marriages in town, births and deaths. Miguel hugged Carlos for a full minute before letting him depart.

He believed there was good in Carlos's heart. His weakness was the burden of too much freedom, because Carlos would not accept the church's certainty.

Miguel saw Carlos only once more that winter, the day he stopped by to bid Miguel *hasta la vista* before going north, but he had hope now that their relationship might heal.

CHAPTER THIRTY-TWO

May 1994, Santa Lucia

Julie closed her eyes as Lilia mopped her forehead with a damp washcloth, then dabbed at her tears. "I want so bad to go with you to Mexico, Lilia."

"I know."

"You're my special friend."

"I know that, too," Lilia said. "I told Carlos you're a firecracker. He likes those American expressions."

Julie recognized misgiving in her friend's eyes. "You meant something worse than 'firecracker.'"

She glanced at the glass of water on the table. Lilia brought it to her. "What you did with him was wrong. You know that."

Julie sipped through the straw. "You pulling some kind of Catholic shit here?"

"He was married."

"And I made him happy for a few hours."

"I've been thinking about this since Mexico," Lilia said, and Julie heard reluctance in her voice. "I'm supposed to head back in a few weeks, but …"

"You're not quitting on me," Julie said. "You can't."

"Someone else could go."

Julie felt a wave of panic ripple through her. "No!"

"You told me he was a good man."

"I get it, you're judging Carlos and me, but—"

"How good could he be if …"

"Even if you think it was wrong, which makes no sense, that was over twenty-five years ago. Carlos was scared and alone."

"You're my friend, Julie. You were disillusioned back then, young and wild, influenced by other students and not intending harm—I guess," she said. "But I don't really know Carlos."

"You like him a lot, don't you?"

Lilia gave a subtle nod.

"You can't judge another person, sweetie. Can't even judge yourself. If you're struggling to believe he's a good man, trust me—he's the best." She saw Lilia trying to suppress a smirk. "Oh! You want to mess around with Carlos, but you're stressed out over some moral BS?"

"When I slept in his bed, it felt so good. I wanted more, but I got scared…. If I go back, I'll …" Her voice trailed off.

"If you don't go, Carlos won't come to see me, will he?" Julie hadn't meant to sound so resentful.

Lilia opened her mouth to speak, paused, and said, "I have to do what's best for me. If I fool around with him, it might not be just fooling."

"He isn't married anymore," Julie said. "I give you my blessing. I'd cross myself, but it's a little awkward."

Lilia chuckled. "I'll let you know if I decide not to go."

But Julie was pretty sure Lilia had made up her mind. If only Julie could do the same. Like a cancer rotting her spirit, that night in Delano haunted her. It was beginning to feel like there was only one way to excise the tumor.

CHAPTER THIRTY-THREE

May/June 1994, Michoacán

Carlos had been drinking again—not like the drinking he'd done with Lilia, light-hearted and joyful. Lonely drinking. I-don't-want-to-be-mad-at-God drinking. The drinking of a *miserable*. Disgusted with himself, he knew he had to cut back. It took a few weeks, but he finally returned to his old routine: Sunday nights at the cantina, and sometimes at lunches with Anita (but never Rita).

Carlos received a note from Julie in late May saying his visa application was progressing, and she hoped to send for him soon. At the end, Julie added, "Lilia says hello." Not "Lilia will be happy to see you." Or even "Lilia will come to get you." He took Lilia's note out of his dresser and reread it. "I still plan to come and get you in two months, as long as I'm feeling brave." He took a long walk in the opposite direction from the cantina, thinking about how unpredictable Lilia could be with him.

Another month passed, and every day his agitation grew. Had the visa been denied? Had Lilia backed out? Would she write him if she had?

Then, one Monday, Rita appeared at Carlos's door with a sour face. "I brought tomatoes, but you don't deserve them."

"Really, *hija*?"

"Anita's coming. We'll talk when she arrives."

"How are the children?"

She held her flat stare on him. "Anita will be here soon."

In the kitchen, he poured three glasses of lemonade. Rita sat but didn't drink. A scowl etched her forehead and set the creases beside her mouth.

The front door opened and closed. Anita breezed into the kitchen. "Hi, *Papá*. I brought more lemonade." She set two jugs on the counter. "Can't have you dying of thirst."

Anita was blessed with the soft *cafe con leche* skin and the curly hair of Isabel's mixed-race forbears, the trim middle of young womanhood, and, best of all, Isabel's sparkle.

They kissed cheeks, and all three sat.

Carlos looked to Rita. "So what's upset you today, daughter?" He glanced at Anita, who winked.

Rita picked up her glass but didn't drink. "I had a phone call from *that woman*. Lilia. She's arriving tomorrow. I guess I'm your messenger maid now, serving that *puta* of the North."

His pulse sped up. "Wonderful."

"I didn't ask before," Rita said. "I've tried to be respectful, but we're the village joke. So, you'd better tell us now. Is it serious? Is she sleeping with you?"

"*Papá*," Anita said. "Did you fool around with that pretty woman?"

"Yes and no."

Anita touched his hand. "I was hoping for *yes* and *yes*."

Rita banged her glass down, sloshing lemonade onto the table. "Thanks, sister, for your support."

"*Mama's* gone. Why begrudge *Papá* a life?"

"I guess the old women don't laugh behind your back at the market. Maybe you don't care, with no children who get teased at school."

Anita shook her head. "God, Rita, if he has a little fun with a pretty lady, it only makes things … spicy."

"What does she see in you?" Rita demanded.

Anita laughed. "He's handsome as hell. My girlfriends are jealous of this new *chiquita*."

He raised a hand. "Girls, you're making me blush."

"I blush as well," Rita said. "My children blush. My soul turns red when I confess to the priest. If she stays in your house again, I'll blush and cry, too."

"Perhaps your cheeks will go crimson when she takes me north for a few days." He tried to keep smiling even as the thought unsettled him.

Rita jumped up, her chair scraping the tile floor. "What?"

"You're going to sneak across?" Anita asked.

"She's bringing a visa. I'll be visiting the ranch where I lived in 1967."

"You returned from there with that … arm." Rita pointed. "And you want to go *visit*?"

"Now you're worrying me," Anita said. "They hate us in California. It's all over the news, this proposition."

"That bothers me, too," he conceded. "But I won't wander around up there. I'll stay on the ranch, and it wasn't there that I was injured."

"The *patrón* hated you."

"He's conveniently dead. I'm going to see his daughter, who was very kind to me."

"And you're going with this *puta*, Lilia, is that right? You're going to sleep with her here in your house and shame us. I know you will."

Anita beamed at him. "You're coming back to life, *Papá*."

When they departed, Carlos hopped in his truck and visited

163

markets in the closest three towns for bouquets of roses, savory chocolates, and genuine French champagne.

Rain was pouring down by the time a green station wagon arrived outside. He grabbed a towel, thinking to shield her, but when he opened the front door, Lilia came rushing to him, a blur of pink cotton and shiny black hair.

He'd known it would delight him to see her, but the depth of his joy took his breath away. She came inside, and he closed the door. "Sorry about the weather," he said. "These storms come up in summer."

She wrapped her arms around him, and they hugged, kissing one another's cheeks and ears and foreheads.

"I was hoping you hadn't stopped liking me," he said.

"I've been deciding." She kissed him on the lips. "Liking you might be good for me."

"I bought bubbly wine for you. It's in the refrigerator."

"A celebration," she said.

He stood back to look at her. "You seem different. Your skin's darker."

She turned her body side to side. "You like it? I'm exercising and spending time in the sun."

It was more than her skin tone, though. She seemed freer in the way she looked at him, almost … jubilant. "You were thinner."

"You said I was perfect then."

"You're even more pleasingly perfect. You must understand from our conversations—there are many ways for a woman to be perfect, all subtly different and stirringly wonderful."

"How can a woman believe a fellow so full of compliments?" Her smile was open, unreserved.

"If you could see into my heart, you'd know that I like this new Lilia very much."

"I gained a couple of pounds. They seemed to settle in the right places." She stretched in an exciting way.

"Very nice," he said. "Will you stay here tonight?"

She gave a slight nod.

"I'll get your suitcase before you change your mind."

He retrieved the suitcase and led her to the kitchen, popped open a bottle of champagne, and filled two stemmed glasses.

She clicked glasses with him. "I've been thinking about this since I left."

"About me?"

She nodded, smiling into his eyes. "Julie's encouraging me."

"Oh?" He waited.

She looked down for a moment. "I have something to tell you—but not yet. Ask me after a couple of drinks."

They moved to the living room. Lilia snuggled against him on the sofa.

She pressed her forehead against his cheek. "How are your fruit trees and those outrageous sheep? You'll be able to leave them for ten days, won't you?"

"My fruit trees prosper with this rain. My grandsons can tend the animals. But—"

"You *are* coming with me?" Her voice held a note of alarm.

"I said I would, but I worry."

"If you're scared of *la policía*, I promise—they aren't looking for you. Julie wouldn't consider this if they were."

"Californians are in a frenzy. On the news ..."

"You won't be protesting. No one will bother you."

"Going to the ranch where I was treated like a dog and from which I fled for my life." He shook his head. "There was María, too. You don't know everything about that."

"But you'll tell me."

Certainly he would. He almost looked forward to it. "We'll confide in one another and become more intimate."

"Good," she said. "I don't want to hide myself from you anymore." The words touched him in his chest, where his heart beat.

Carlos poured the rest of the bottle into their glasses. "This is very good. I wonder how you taste after drinking it."

He sat next to her again, she shifted onto his lap, sitting sideways, and took a sip of her champagne. Then she kissed him, pushing wine from her mouth to his. It surprised and delighted him.

"There's something I want to ask," she said. "You told me you'd been with no one but Isabel for the last twenty-six years?"

"That's true."

"And she was faithful to you?"

"I'm sure."

"Have you had any blood transfusions, any private diseases?"

He was getting her meaning and liking it very much. "No diseases, no transfusions … no AIDS."

She reached down and produced papers from her bag. "I had tests done, and I'm clean."

He pushed them aside. "You're taking the pill?" It shocked him a little, how this woman, who looked like a Mexican señorita, could speak so boldly. But, of course, she grew up in Julie's country. *What must the women there be like now, so many years past the crazy sixties?* "You said you have something to tell me."

"I'll show you my secret *and* tell it, when the wine vanquishes my inhibitions." She finished her glass of wine. "You have more champagne?"

He retrieved the other bottle, popped the cork, and sat beside her. They kissed and drank and kissed some more.

Lilia took a deep breath. "Okay." She stood, unfastened her shorts and dropped them to the floor. His eyes ran up her supple thighs to the *V* in her black undies. She pulled up her pink blouse and glanced down at herself.

On her stomach he saw little crooked scars—stretch marks. "You have a child?"

"Almost did."

He waited.

"There's this, too." She pushed the top of her underpants down a bit, revealing a ten-centimeter scar. "When I was here with you two months ago, this was red, like your plums. My tummy was … bloated. I couldn't let you see, and I wasn't ready for you to know or to …" She swallowed and gestured to the wine. "I'd like some more, please."

Her intimate disclosure moved him, and he looked away for a moment as he poured her glass.

"I lost the baby a month before she was due. Lost my family, too."

He saw tears trickling down her cheeks. He leaned forward and skimmed his fingers over the little lines on her stomach. "This doesn't make you less than beautiful." He knelt on the floor and kissed her belly left and right and then the scar. He rose and wrapped his arms around her, thinking about saying something reckless about loving her. "Tell me."

She sobbed, pressing herself against him. "This is what I had to show you. It's enough for now. Right?"

"Of course, dear."

She gave him a forced smile. "All the time I was away from you, I thought about what I'd been tempted to do, what didn't feel right, what could become right once I was ready. I'll tell you everything soon, I swear. Right now I need to wash my face."

Several minutes later, she returned wearing a black lacy nightgown. He took in her slender, graceful legs, the body of the gown that showed patches of skin between black flowery filaments, intriguing but illusive. He skimmed a hand up from her tummy, along her side, and ended by stroking her cheek. Looking into her eager eyes.

"More fun than talking about upsetting secrets." She kissed him and led him to bed.

Afterward, he lay on his side, looking her over, her gown bunched above her waist.

She laughed. "An hour ago, I was terrified about confessing. Now I can't imagine why."

Carlos was about to respond when he heard a banging on the front door. He threw on a robe as more thumps sounded. "All right, all right."

At the front door, Rita faced him, hands on her hips, a look of defiance and scorn on her face. "At least her car isn't prostitute-red this time, but we all know what you're doing. You flaunt your sins and disgrace us. It's time for you and your bitch to face me."

Carlos usually overlooked Rita's outbursts, but the word *bitch* annoyed him. "No."

She gawked.

"If Anita would like to meet my friend, she's welcome, but you are not."

"Not welcome in my father's house?"

"Not until you're civil." He gently closed the door.

An hour later, Anita arrived, bearing a custard tart covered in strawberries.

CHAPTER THIRTY-FOUR

June 1994, Bakersfield, California

Benito's spring classes ended, but he skipped summer registration. Putting college off until the fall wasn't such a big deal.

He sat on the platform in the Bakersfield College auditorium. Light streamed in from windows set high in white, paneled walls. In a hall built for hundreds, only sixty or seventy people were scattered in the seats. The crowd cheered as Juan spoke from the podium. "The governor and his soulless cronies scare people with fake stories of immigrants' crimes and lies about the cost of services to our people. They sneer from the television screen, their white faces, their expensive suits and bright ties, prominent men who lie easily. People see our brown faces, dirty hands, simple clothing in photographs, not on television. Our people have no TV cameras and no voice. Many will vote from ignorance and prejudice. And if Proposition 187 passes in California, where next?"

Beside Benito, a girl named Olivia nudged his elbow. She'd come down from Berkeley with a friend named Juanita to support the cause. They'd split a cheap hotel room last night with Benito and Juan—guys in one bed, girls in the other. Juan had made a pitch to switch partners, but Juanita had stood firm. Too bad; Benito knew from experience what a good bedmate Olivia could be.

She laid a hand on Benito's thigh, which would have felt hot, but he was trying to concentrate on his notes, jotted on a series of three-by-five cards. He'd sketched out the speech a month ago. It was a good speech, good for the cause … but knowing so little about his father, he had to wonder—how much truth was in it?

"You'll do great," Olivia murmured.

And now Juan finished. He waved Benito forward and adjusted the microphone for him. "Be cool, *amigo*," he said as Benito took the podium.

"Can you all hear me?" he asked. People nodded, and a few waved. "My name's Benito, and I'm here to tell my story." He swallowed and took a breath. "It's your story too, whether you're Chicano, Black, Asian—even Native American. They rant about Mexican gangs as if they fear us, but we are the ones in danger. In danger because of racists, threatened because they lie about us." There were a few cheers from the audience, and he tried to smile.

"California has always been hazardous for foreigners. The Chinese came to build the white man's railroads, and they were beaten and deported. Filipinos toiled in the fields beside our Mexican brothers, and they were threatened if they stood up for decent salaries, beaten if they struck their employers. Blacks were hanged just for speaking to white women.

"It has always been dangerous because *they* are violent—the rich Anglos, their souls full of hate for anyone who looks different. They believe that they are better, that we should stay in our place, stay out of their business. Proposition 187 is racist and hateful, and we must defeat it."

The crowd shouted approval, giving Benito time to glance at his notes. "How do I know about the white man's hate? Because I feel it in the way they look at me, in the way they talk about us as 'parasites.' All of them—California's governor and his kind."

He took a breath, steadying himself. "This conviction resides in the marrow of my bones. I inherited it. My father picked grapes in Delano and celery up the San Joaquin. When they treated him like dirt and paid him like a slave, and when they didn't respect the women who worked beside him, he joined the union. My father became a friend and advisor to the great man, César Chávez."

Benito knew that he'd gotten a little carried away with the crowd's energy. But he'd said it now, and what was the harm? "Father marched with César to the state capital, walked the walk of righteousness, strode the trail of justice, stood with César when he fasted and let himself waste away to make them listen." The crowd cheered again. Benito wished he had a drink of water to prepare for the most difficult part.

"César died last year. He's gone. And I never met my father." He paused as the crowd went quiet. "Never met him, because, after he joined the union, Dad was assaulted by the police. Beaten and maybe killed." Benito felt tears welling. He steadied himself against the podium, trying to take the tremor out of his voice, wanting to finish, but there were more notes on his card.

"My father was never seen again. My mother gave me life months later. She raised me alone, worked for slave wages to feed a baby son, had to go on not knowing what happened to her husband, and I not knowing my father's fate. We had to live that way because of racism and hatred. We must defeat Proposition 187. We must raise ourselves up to build our people's dignity, to build our children's hope and self-respect. All people must be treated as equals. We cannot let them see us as less than, cannot accept less than, cannot accept a law that penalizes children because their parents came here to make a living."

Everyone was cheering. Juan stood at the side of the stage, clapping.

"Leave and spread the word. We hundred men and women will contact hundreds more. We can defeat this evil plan. God bless our cause."

After the rally, Benito's heart wouldn't slow down. As Juan drove the old Nissan, he opened the window, gulping air. They were on a bluff with barren hills to the right, oilfields, by the look of them, with plumes of steam rising here and there. They headed for a restaurant called Zingos, where they planned to meet the girls for lunch.

Juan glanced at him as he drove. "Olivia brought her car down, right?"

Benito nodded.

"Pretty girl. And you like her?"

"Sure."

"You impressed her today. She could drive you back, and I could take Juanita with me, singing as I drive, *Juan and Juanita, at the casita.*"

Benito laughed for Juan's sake, but he had other thoughts. His father had lived in Delano, only thirty miles away. He'd never been closer to his dad, closer to the truth. "You go back with them, Juan. Enjoy both girls. I want to borrow your car."

Two hours later, Benito drove alone, north on Route 99.

CHAPTER THIRTY-FIVE

Carlos and Lilia lay naked under the covers that night, a sliver of moonlight peeping in from between the curtains.

"That standoff with Rita was tense," Lilia said.

"Mexican women can be jealous for their fathers."

"She doesn't want to see you hurt." Lilia stroked his cheek. "With Julie, you couldn't get hurt because you didn't love her." She paused. "Did we make love before, or sex?"

"If I said love, would it scare you?"

"I'm scared no matter what, and I have another question: Would your loving daughters tend your sheep for more than ten days?"

"Are you kidnapping me? I like this."

"We could fly to California, but Mexico has a beautiful coastline. It's a four-day drive."

His pulse kicked up at the idea. "Driving together sounds wonderful. The first year I was a *bracero*, waiting for admission to the North, I visited Guaymas, a lovely town by the sea. It could take more than four days."

She gave him a glorious smile. "An extra night in Guaymas?"

"If my daughters won't feed them, the sheep can starve. A seven-day drive wouldn't be out of the question."

"An adventure," she said.

"Romantic journey." Carlos banished the word *honeymoon* from his thoughts.

They lay holding hands. "Still awake?" he asked.

"Mmm-hmm."

"I've been thinking."

"Another religious revelation?"

"How did you guess?"

She kissed his hand.

"You know, Lilia, I mentioned God giving us presents, like our drive for love and lovemaking, but everything's an enigma, a trick wrapped in pretty paper. No man would freely give up that desire. But when Isabel was dying, I abandoned any thought of it—the delight dried up, gone, not missed or wanted." He looked at her in the darkness. "You've brought it back. Not just the sex. My heart is opening up to life."

What gratitude he'd felt for God had dried up, too. Too soon to say if that would return.

"I'm glad."

The next morning, in the kitchen, Lilia handed him a sealed envelope. "Julie asked me to give you this. I don't know what's in it."

The note was typed in Spanish:

Dear Señor Montoya;

I am Julie Booker's attorney. Ms. Booker asked my advice because of the sensitive nature of events that you and she experienced on a particular night near Delano, CA, 1968.

Ms. Booker wants you to inform Lilia Gomez about those events. However, upon my advice, she asks that you confine your description to generalities. Please do not discuss any use of lethal weapons, which may or may not have occurred.

We trust that you will use discretion in this matter.

Cordially,
Malcolm Honeywell
Attorney at Law

Jesus. With or without a letter, Carlos wasn't about to talk about that night. He folded the paper and shoved it into his pants pocket.

"Interesting?" Lilia asked.

"Some business." He knew that made no sense, but Lilia didn't challenge him.

Outside, Carlos noticed the rented station wagon resting too close to the ground. "We'll have a slight delay."

The garage sent a repairman to patch the four punctured tires. As they watched him work, he knew what Lilia was thinking. "I know," he said. "I put up with a lot from Rita, but what can I do?"

Carlos took the wheel, and they headed north.

Lilia sat silent for a while, looking thoughtful. Then she softly stroked his thigh. "You said María came to Mexico to find you?"

March 1968, Michoacán

He was repairing a bicycle chain in the shop where he worked sometimes. Rafael's urgent voice startled him. "Carlos."

He saw his cousin framed in the doorway, looking serious for a change. "María's here," Rafael said. "María from Santa Lucia. She came to my home, asking for you."

Carlos felt his stomach fall out of him, his heart about to follow. He said, "Liar," but he saw the truth in Rafael's gaze.

"I took her to wait at the abandoned filling station. You're in trouble, cousin."

Carlos ran to the station at the edge of town. He found María around back, near the open doorways that used to lead to the toilets. She stepped toward him, arms outstretched, but he pushed her away. "What are you doing here?"

"Don't be angry."

He backed her against the wall, harder than he'd intended. "You keep our relationship secret in California. You don't even accompany me down the main street. But now you'd expose us to my family?"

Tears ran down her cheeks, and she reached for his face. "I love you, Carlos. Don't you care for me?"

The words made him release her. He took a step back. "I have a wife and daughters."

She nodded. "Rafael told me soon after I met you."

Crazy! She'd known the whole time? He remembered their shared confidences, María declaring that a woman must save herself for marriage, their chaste intimacy under the sycamore trees. She'd tried to keep him in California with her, the whole time knowing about his wife? His family? It made no sense. But one thing was clear: María must love him, or she wouldn't have come.

"I'm here to protect you," she said. "Sheriffs came to my ranch saying you'd stolen Mr. Booker's money, demanding we help them find you. A thousand dollars, they said! I know it isn't true, but they have papers for your arrest. You can't go back."

He'd known he couldn't return to Santa Lucia with Hiram Booker in pursuit. But now police all over California might be hunting him. He could hardly breathe. "Mrs. Booker gave me that money. I never stole." He shook his head. "You have to go back."

"No! I might never see you again."

"You will."

"You left me five months ago. You vanished. I've been alone."

"I wrote to you. I explained what happened. Ellen was supposed to give you my note."

She jerked her head. "I'll stay here. I will go where you go."

"Go home. You have a green card. You can cross without trouble. I have to break in like a thief."

"Don't ask this. I've cried every night." And she was crying now.

If Isabel learned of her his life would be ruined. "Leave," he said. "If you hurt my family you'll never see me again."

She knelt on the dirt by the filling station, crying, wounding him with her pain.

Tears, anger, pleading … he insisted she leave, she threatened. In the end, he compromised. In one week—two weeks earlier than he'd planned to leave Mexico—they'd meet in Zamora and take the bus together to the border, but only if she left tonight.

Rafael drove María to Zamora and found her a room.

All week, Carlos chastised himself: *My God, what I have done! Estúpido! What I have risked!* And questioned: *What choices do I have now?*

It's safer to stay in Mexico, he told himself. *Give her up.* His heart ached to think of it, but he'd do it, if he had to. But then María, crazed with love and jealous rage, would return and reveal all to Isabel, wouldn't she?

Going north was the right thing to do. His family deserved their own home, some meat at dinnertime, dresses and a good education for the girls, for the boys to come, if God felt generous.

A husband and father had to provide, not pretend they could make a living from seedling trees that wouldn't produce for years, and a bit of work repairing other people's bicycles.

He'd need false papers. He swallowed his fears and disdain and approached a loan-maker who demanded exorbitant interest. A forger produced Mexican identity papers in the name Luis Ortega. How had that name been chosen? Maybe a fellow named Luis had died.

He made up an excuse to tell a tearful Isabel. "I'll get started early and maybe find a better job."

And then he took the final step. As he did every year, he purchased a fresh pair of work shoes and walked the streets of his village, so the earth could seep into the soles. His shoes would agree with his feet and his feet would obey his heart. They'd take him home when it was time.

He spent a tender afternoon with Isabel and a farewell dinner with his little family, and then headed out to meet María.

CHAPTER THIRTY-SIX

March 1968

Carlos and María took the bus to Nogales. With help from an acquaintance, he found a good crossing place and trekked with María through the desert, carrying water bottles and a single bag of their belongings.

After a while they came to a canal, and he knew they'd crossed into Arizona. The water was running fast. He stripped off his shirt and trousers.

"You have to take off your clothes," he said. "They'll weigh you down."

She hesitated, then removed two layers of clothing and her slip.

His eyes skimmed the perfect legs, her white underpants, narrow waist and firm stomach, breasts bulging out of her bra. Her expression excited him, too—she was calm as she looked him over, not reluctant or shy.

He bundled their clothes and threw them across. They climbed into the canal and pushed off together, the current not as bad as he'd feared. He boosted her out on the other side and filled the water bottles. They held each other and kissed, his fingers touching skin that had been forbidden. But they had to move on.

Crossing ranchland with tall cactus, cattle grazing the sparse brush, he saw her weeping. "Are you all right?"

"I want to be with you."

"That's what I want."

"I tried not to."

He wrapped his arms around her.

She pushed away. "Would you swear your love to me?"

He did love her, loved with a crippling, irrational passion—loved everything except the way she confused him. "Of course."

Near dusk, they found a one-window shed with a water trough and a well. "I can sleep outside," he said. "Or in the far corner. You take the blankets."

"No. We'll share them for warmth."

They took turns cleaning up at the well and ate the last tortillas they'd brought, sitting together on a boulder. An almost-full moon rose over the hills.

María gestured to the sky. "The north star guides us to our new home."

He wrapped an arm around her.

"Our ancestors worshipped the sun, moon, and stars," she said. "You told me that, Carlos."

"And you said, 'Stick to Jesus.'" He kissed her temple.

"We can't be together without marriage."

The word filled him with a sense of panic. "But I—"

She touched his lips for silence. "I've agonized about this, darling, prayed, with my heart aching. You were married in Mexico in the church?"

He nodded.

"We can't marry there." She cupped his cheeks in her hands and searched his eyes.

"No matter. I'd never leave Isabel."

María grimaced. "Don't speak of her. We'll couple the ancient way. I pray that our Lord will understand."

"I—"

"You will vow to love me, and I will relinquish to you, the universe as our witness."

What? There were wild Mexicans at home, chanting to volcano gods and demons, but who would have suspected her? He took a deep breath, trying to make sense of it. Of course he longed to be with her tonight and every night until he went home in the fall. But what craziness was she planning?

María stood, pulled her dress over her head, and removed her bra. Moonlight revealed the largest, roundest breasts he'd ever seen.

His confusion vanished. Carlos shucked off his clothes as she finished with hers. Standing straight, naked, facing the moon, she said, "We come to you, as you made us, goddess of the moon."

Dios mio. His blood pounded and his hands trembled.

She faced him and took his hands. "Do you swear to the moon that you love me?"

"Do you?" she repeated.

"I swear that I love María."

To the moon she said, "I swear that I love Carlos. I seek your blessing to live with him." She turned to Carlos.

"I wish to live with María," he said.

She whispered, "Ask for her blessing."

Her body glowed silver in the moonlight, with dark exciting shadows. What was a little feigned piety to the moon or any spirit? "Señora moon, I ask your blessing to spend my nights with her." As he said the words, his gut turned over.

María addressed the sky again. "I pledge that I will always love Carlos and will always be with him."

EDWARD D. WEBSTER

He couldn't help thinking of his true wedding, to Isabel. But he loved María, too. "I swear to be with María when I am in the North."

She pouted for a moment, and then said, "I commit to marriage with this man all the days of my life."

Marriage ... no. This wasn't marriage. Would never be. "I can't." He released her hands. "I'm married to Isabel."

She watched as he shook his head. She touched his chest, and he said, "No."

Her eyes grew angry, like that day when he'd told her he was going back to Mexico. "I followed you a thousand miles ... *Maldito sea*!" She turned and marched into the shed, slamming the door behind her. The door reopened, and she threw a blanket at him.

But sometime later, as he lay on the hard ground, she opened the door. "Have you changed your mind?"

He shivered. "It's not fair for you to ask."

"Come out of the cold." She beckoned. "I don't forgive you." But they made exquisite love there on the blankets.

He watched her sleep as moonlight streamed through the window, opposing feelings battling inside him. He missed Isabel and her comfortable love, and felt shocked and guilty at how easily he'd fallen for another. Yet part of him was thrilled that this pure woman, María, loved him enough to go against God and church and to jeopardize her salvation.

Carlos drove on, descending from citrus groves to sugarcane fields, volcanic mountains rising to the east, telling Lilia most, but not all of the story.

Lilia shifted in her seat. "You're being a little vague.... María wasn't exactly wearing a white gown and veil?"

"Right. We were naked."

"I see." Lilia gave him a derisive smile. "You lived together after that, but not in Santa Lucia, right?"

"Another of my cousins, Carmen, worked with the grape growers, two hundred kilometers away, in Delano. We went there."

"This woman was going to be trouble," Lilia said,

"Heaven and hell in the body of a goddess."

"Nuts, too. And you felt guilty."

"True."

They stopped at a taco stand for lunch, eating in silence. Lilia's mood had shifted, and Carlos didn't know why.

He took the wheel again. Lilia sat with her back wedged against seat and door, silent—brooding? He waited.

"I lied to you," she said. "I told you my boyfriend deserted me. He was my husband, not a boyfriend. He said cruel things but never told me why he was leaving. Maybe he couldn't handle becoming a father. Maybe I disgusted him."

"That's absurd."

"He said, 'Now that you're pregnant, your breasts are passable, but your stomach's like a friggin' watermelon.' He called me names—'stupid Mex,' 'lazy bitch,' other swear words. Ramón deserted me, and I carried her for eight months. Then my baby and I developed a blood infection, and she was turned the wrong way. They discovered too late."

"I'm sorry." Carlos reached for her hand, but she avoided him.

Tears ran down her cheeks. She turned away from him. "Don't look at me."

He pulled off the road. "My eyes won't allow that."

"I have marks on my stomach, a scar across my abdomen, a sad heart, blemishes you can't imagine, and I...." She looked down at herself.

He took her hand and kissed it. "Lost your baby."

She shook her head. "The worst is that after Ramón left, and before I lost her, I thought about giving her up for adoption."

Carlos wanted to comfort her but had no words. The idea of giving up a child, when babies were so precious…. He thought about confiding his heartbreak when he and Isabel had lost an infant son to the fever, but Lilia was miserable enough.

"I know, I've shocked you," she said. "I shock myself."

"Couldn't your family help with the baby?"

"My mother died when I was ten. Later on, my father had more children with another woman, and she ran off. I stayed to raise my new sister and brother."

"And your father?"

"Drunk more than not. He screamed when I married Ramón, calling my new husband a bum. He threw things in a drunken rage when Ramón left, calling me a disgrace. Maybe he was right. I'm worthless. I can't go there anymore."

He wanted to tell her she wasn't worthless, that she was lovely … but he was still shocked by her idea of giving her child up for adoption. Did that make her selfish? She wasn't planning to abandon the infant, wasn't considering abortion…. Hadn't Carlos been selfish with Julie? And María? Who had he considered then, besides himself?

"If my father knew about the adoption agency, he'd have killed me. But you think I'm terrible, too. I see it in your eyes."

"I can't comprehend it, I admit, but your situation was difficult."

He held her hand until she calmed, and then pulled back onto the road.

After a while, she said, "Julie took me in after that. I live in her mother's old studio."

Lilia took the wheel. To lighten the mood, Carlos spoke of his daughters' schooling, his grandchildren, the practical problems of raising sheep. She asked questions, giving him hope that she felt better.

Then another thought came, and he had to voice it. "The way you wrapped yourself around me last night—I did that with Julie sometimes. She'd say, 'Pretend you're with Isabel.' So, as I held her, I'd imagine I was home with my marvelous wife, and Julie would channel Isabel's love back to me."

Lilia glanced at him, silent.

"When Isabel died, I rested my head on her chest, pretending she was still close, but she'd gone. Her body had been stripped of its flesh by illness, but it had never been empty before. I was empty, too, and I've stayed that way."

He might tell this lovely young woman that she was filling him up again, pouring life into his desolate body the way she'd jetted champagne into his mouth, but he didn't feel like speaking. This was all so new, and life could drain out again when he returned home to Mexico.

Silence again, and he realized he'd made it worse speaking of Isabel's death.

That night they stayed at a small hotel, in a bed larger than he'd ever seen—a *Norteamericano*, the proprietor called it. They ate take-out Chinese food and donned pajamas. Under the covers, Lilia turned on her side, her head on Carlos's chest, legs tucked in so her knees touched his thigh, crying, confirmed by the moisture on his pajamas. He stroked her hair, feeling lonely again. He missed Isabel whenever he had a moment to think and feel. And remembering their tiny, lost son added to the weight.

CHAPTER THIRTY-SEVEN

Michoacán, 1992

Twenty-one years ago, we lost our infant son, Roberto, to the fever. Carlos and I were crushed with grief, but I had to stand up for him, and he for me. Together we had to help our girls through. I saw Carlos, the way he longed to escape into the bottle, and I could not allow it. I stood him before Rita and Anita, both of them sobbing and looking to us for answers. The girls were eight and six then, impressionable. "Not one glass of beer," I said. "You cannot let them see you that way."

"Pray to our savior," I said. "Go see Padre Miguel."

"God is my enemy," he said. "The padre has nothing to offer." Without God, without faith in our padre, I feared for him, but I stood firm. Then Carlos—God bless him—had an idea.

He borrowed a tent and a camp stove from a neighbor, and he hauled them up that mountain, over there. We kept the girls out of school, and we brought provisions to his campsite—no alcohol in that isolated place. For a week, Carlos cooked breakfast and I cooked dinner. After breakfast each morning Carlos would walk into the forest. Sometimes, I heard his distant screaming, too far away to understand the words. Cursing God, I was sure. He returned a few hours later, his voice a raw whisper.

The four of us would hold each other and talk about Roberto.

And Carlos didn't object when I told the girls that our dear baby was in God's hands. Maybe he halfway believed it. After that week we managed to go back to our lives. Carlos and I somehow found strength because the girls needed us strong.

But this next loss Carlos must face without me.

I'm just forty-five, but the cancer eats me from bone to skin.

I try to ignore the pain, to pretend for him. "Prepare," I say. "I won't be here forever." A few months, I guess, which is more than I can imagine, more pain than I might be able to bear.

He says, "God will save you." They would be amusing—these beliefs of his, as he sometimes imagines this and sometimes that— if we weren't facing my brutal end.

After the sorrows Carlos has endured in this life—his father and sister so long ago and later Roberto—you'd think he'd be realistic. Still, impractical or not, he's my *amor verdadero*.

I don't worry for Rita, with her family to care for. She'll boss Carlos, tell him to clean the house and rake the yard, demand he go to church.

Anita will comfort him, she promises me, with jugs of lemonade and lunches together. She already begins. She gives him a kitten. "Please *Papá*, you'll be saving its life," she tells him.

Anita accepts, as Carlos pretends not to, that I'm dying. The kitten will remind him that life renews itself. It helps a bit—Carlos laughs sometimes when it scampers and leaps.

The girls will be all right, so mostly I pray for him. He's a good man who deserves heaven, but will Jesus forgive all his questioning?

What temptations might he have embraced on the other side? I wonder about that year when he sent extra money, and the next when he returned with a shattered arm and a new desire for alcohol. Later: More money, unexpected. Why? What did he do?

Instead of questioning, I thanked God for him and prayed to the Virgin he'd never leave again. And now, blessed Virgin, dear Jesus, please don't let Carlos make any final confessions that could only hurt us both.

Two months later

The kitten came into our lives for a purpose, but not what Anita intended. The little creature grew sick and died five weeks after entering our house.

Carlos held that dead kitten in his hands, furious and sad. He wanted to shout at God, I know, but he stayed silent for me. He wanted to drink a case of beer, but he refrained.

Now I know God's purpose for the kitten. Carlos finally believes I will perish.

CHAPTER THIRTY-EIGHT

"Guaymas tonight," Lilia said as she headed the station wagon north the next morning. "We'll have a party there." They passed a string of high-rise hotels. The Gulf of California, sparkling in the morning sun, appeared off to the left and then vanished behind dry hills.

She seemed happy again and very much aware of him as she sat straight, focused on the road, the fabric of her pink tee shirt riding her chest in a smooth curve, thighs seductive in tan shorts, delicate fingers on the wheel. He loved the look of her chin and jaw line, exquisite, vulnerable yet strong.

What was it that made one woman attractive, another plain? Why could one with small, perfect breasts drive one man mad and another not? Fine details, subtle symmetries that invited a luscious embrace; was it this way for every man—a connection passed down in his genes that sent excitement coursing over a delightful smile, the taper of a waist, curve of the buttocks, the grace of a slim wrist?

Lilia glanced at him. "Julie said she went to Delano to meet you. If my body isn't distracting you too much, you can tell me how she found you there."

April 1968, Delano

María had paid for a room in the barrio, with a bathroom shared by five families—humiliating for her to support him, but Carlos had no money. Work was scarce, but one night at a cantina, he shared a pitcher of beer with his cousin Carmen and four others. Mexican music blared from speakers by the bar as men played pool in the back. A tall Anglo approached their table. He was a few years older than Carlos—twenty-six or twenty-seven—with brown hair combed back to show a wide forehead. He shouted over the music. "My name's Travis McKenzie. I'm the fellow who knows where to find you work."

They followed him outside. "Strikes in the vineyards mean opportunity, men," McKenzie said.

One man walked away mumbling, "Strike-breaking scabs." But the rest agreed to meet the next morning.

Just after dawn, Carlos and Carmen rode in the back of McKenzie's white van, crammed in with a dozen others. Carlos couldn't see outside, but he heard men and women, yelling "*Huelga! Huelga! Huelga!*" Something banged the side of the truck, scaring him. More banging. The van lurched and bounced on.

In the bright sunlight of the vineyard, a dark-skinned Anglo foreman wearing a black cap showed them how to clip some of the grapes from the vines so the rest could thrive. Each man tried it with the foreman watching, and then he set them to work.

That Saturday night, Carlos brought María to the cantina, where McKenzie paid his wages. McKenzie bought pitchers of beer for the men and told jokes about the rich ranchers.

But this money came from strikebreaking, bringing Julie's words back—strikers fought for dignity; *patrones* abused Mexican workers. The pesticides, the low wages, lack of sanitation. It was all true, but when a man had a family and dreams to build, he had no space for guilt.

María found a housekeeping job, and McKenzie offered to rent them a small mobile home in the cotton fields. He loaned them an old maroon Chevrolet so they could round up workers each morning. María drove—she had a California license—gathering men from trailers and shacks on the way to town. The men jumped out and entered McKenzie's van to hurtle past the picket lines.

"You see, Carlos," María said. "The Lord favors us with this new home and car."

After a week, however, she began to complain. "It's too quiet here with only cotton plants for company. The car smells like *mierda.*"

Over just a few weeks, life degenerated from lovely picnics up the canyon and passionate lovemaking, to María's "suggestions" that he stay after the fall harvest and work the lemon groves, to her demands and declarations. One day, sweetly: "If you stay in the North all year, you could become a foreman and make real money. We could have babies." Another day: "We've taken vows to each other. I won't let you run away again." On the next payday: "Give me half," she said. "I'll save it for us."

He kept his voice even. "You know where I'm sending this."

"Don't you dare." Her eyes flashed fury. "I paid our rent those first days. I clean your home. I give you ..." She glanced down at her body. "Everything, that's what."

"I have children. I have a wife. You know this."

She threw a kitchen towel at him. Then a plate—it smashed against the refrigerator. "Shut your stupid mouth."

"She's Isabel. My girls are Rita and Anita. You have my love for six months. Be happy with that."

María covered her ears. "Get out."

He hitched a ride to the Western Union office and sent the money home. He called Isabel from the telephone there.

Trudging toward their mobile home, he muttered, "I should leave María. I have to." But then he thought of snuggling with her, eating sandwiches by the lake, those days in the sycamore grove, remembered her naked body in the moonlight.

He rebuked himself for his absurd weakness and God for creating her exquisite flesh, (sometimes) sweet voice, and moonlit eyes that bedeviled him.

"Blaming the woman?" Lilia asked. "There are countries where they'd stone her to death for tempting you. But we know who was wrong."

Despite her words, Lilia didn't seem upset with him anymore.

CHAPTER THIRTY-NINE

Barren rock mountains plunging to a crystal blue bay.
They found a small, modern hotel on a hill above the city of Guaymas, a bright room with a view of the sea.

Lilia hung their shirts in the closet. "I apologize for yesterday. You must think I'm a moody witch." She spoke English and repeated in Spanish, helping him practice. Carlos had understood all except "moody."

He closed his suitcase and set it in a corner. "We were both filled with sad thoughts."

She pressed herself against him, looking into his eyes. "But now, in this paradise, we'll just have fun."

They rode horses on the beach one day and swam most of another. On the third afternoon, they bought marinated shrimp, corn-and-bean salad, bread, a slice of chocolate cake, and a bottle of wine. With the sun low over the hills, they rented a skiff at the marina and motored out past some islands.

She stroked his thigh as he steered the vessel past the lower peninsula, jagged mountains towering to the west, clouds turning creamy above. They found a deserted cove and swam in the sea. Sitting on their towels, they drank wine, fed each other shrimp and salad. They made love and lay on their backs gazing at the darkening orange sky before motoring back in the moonlight.

At the hotel on the fourth morning, he woke to find Lilia coming in with two paper cups. She grinned. "I brought us coffee."

He sat up in bed and sipped as she climbed in beside him.

"I'm curious," he said. "When you were in Mexico in April you seemed…"

"You're wondering about our lovemaking these last few days and the way I kept backing off before. Sex is great. I just wasn't ready then."

"And now?"

"I'm following Julie's advice."

He scrutinized her.

"She said, 'Don't worry about everything. Let Carlos please you.'"

"And your priest?"

"We Americans don't accept all of Rome's rules. It would be absurd not to use birth control. Father Anselm would skip that and talk about waiting for marriage. I did marriage before sex once—I was the only girl in America—and look what happened. The church is becoming more tolerant, and the people more …"

"More sexy," he said.

She set her coffee on the table and lay down, gazing up at him. "We've made no promises. It's just fun and closeness, right?"

Her words made his stomach go hollow, but he said, "Like me and Julie."

"No one gets hurt." She studied his face for a minute and said, "We haven't talked about María for three days. Ready to tell me more?"

CHAPTER FORTY

April/May 1968, Delano

Guilt on top of guilt. Working to the end of a row of vines, he'd see picketers holding signs. *Strike, Fair Wages, Join Us*—women, some striking men, volunteers or unemployed people hired by the union. They taunted the workers or threatened, appealed to their sense of justice, told them to work slowly, hack up the vines to sabotage the crop. He slowed down in sympathy, but during harvest, they'd pay by the crate. Then he'd become a fast, crazy, harvesting machine.

Strikers pelted the workers with stones one day. The next day, a union man shouted an apology over a megaphone as they worked. The ranch owners sent crop dusters to spray the strikers. Carlos heard their coughing even from a distance.

At home with María, he poured out his guilt. "They're our people, and I betray them."

"Don't think about it that way, darling," she said. "You're lucky to have work and such a good employer as Travis." Then she put on her furious eyes and shouted, "But you squander this money on your ungrateful family in Mexico." Later in bed, caressing him—"She could never love you the way I do."

Summer coming—hot and dusty in the vineyard. Young, pale faces appeared on the picket lines sprinkled among the brown—college students sneaking away from their classes.

Hot in their mobile home, too. He brought home pots for her plants, and she smashed them. "Why make our home beautiful? You'll just abandon it." She sobbed and moaned, but a half hour later, she coaxed him to make love before berating him again.

Evenings at the cantina: Mexican music, voices, laughter. Even the crippled old man on the porch appealing for pennies reminded Carlos of home and family. After work on Saturdays, Travis would drink beer with Carlos at the long, polished bar, then leave for a few hours, returning later to drive the men home.

Carlos started to like this man and began to confide, one night saying, "The police here, they hate us Mexicans." Travis gave him a look, and he added, "They have papers out on me."

Travis said, "We've all done some things."

"I wasn't guilty."

"I believe you, pardner."

Carlos felt comfortable because Travis didn't ask questions. "My true name is Carlos."

"Good to know you, Carlos."

Tempted to tell Travis more—foolish thought—he finished his beer and stepped outside for some cool air.

At work one day, he reached the end of a row of vines and heard a woman's voice calling in English, "Carlos! Come join us." He spotted a blonde Anglo with her picket sign and turned away, hoping she was calling another man. "Carlos, I see you." His heartbeat hammered as he slipped between the vines. "I'm Ivy Booker," she shouted. "Julie's sister."

He rushed away, her voice fading.

That Saturday night at the cantina, Ivy Booker came to the table where he sat with five other workers. "Hello, Carlos."

He flinched but didn't look up. *Go away.*

The others laughed. One poked him in the side.

"I'm Luis," he said finally.

"Okay. Luis, come outside with me." She spoke English, but her meaning was clear.

He shook his head, and another man pushed his chair back to stand. "I'll go, pretty lady."

Carmen said, "What's wrong with you, cousin? Take a walk with her."

So Carlos followed her out. Standing in the street, her face red from the neon sign, he saw some resemblance to Julie, but mostly to their beautiful mother.

"You speak Spanish?" Carlos asked.

"Sorry, I don't."

"You can no call me 'Carlos.'"

"I'm sorry," she said. "I understood, when you said you were Luis. It's because of the trouble my father caused? *Problema de mi padre?*"

He looked away for a moment, watching a passing pickup. "You get wrong man."

"I won't cause you trouble."

He looked her over, wanting to believe her. "How you know me?"

"From my mother's drawings. *Mi madre.*" Ivy pretended to draw in the air. "She's a very good artist. Julie's worried for you."

He shook his head.

"I'll tell her you're safe."

"Thank you."

"How can she reach you?" Ivy asked. "Do you come here often?"

How good it would be to see Julie. "Saturdays."

Ivy touched his arm. "You should join the strike. *La Huelga.* You workers need a doctor when you're injured and money when you get old."

Most of her words he understood, from all his time with Julie the year before. "And money today and tomorrow," he said.

The red light shimmered in her blond hair and glinted in her eyes. "I met the man, César Chávez, out on the picket line. He speaks simply, but his words touch me."

"The union, they hate wetbacks," he said. "My wife, my children cannot eat dreams."

She kissed his cheek and walked away. Back inside, his comrades teased him, and he tried to ignore the fear that Ivy Booker had ignited.

The next Saturday night, Carlos and his fellows were drinking and listening to the jukebox at the cantina when Julie entered. He jumped up and rushed to her, suddenly alert and frightened.

"*Estás bien?*" she asked. "Did you have trouble crossing the border?"

He hugged her as his friends whistled. "We should leave."

She held his hands and looked into his eyes. "It's all right. No one knows I'm here."

"But—"

"I was careful."

He walked her to the far corner of the cantina. Julie offered him her wide, lovely smile, and he thought, *She loves me. I should love her more.*

She sat beside him at a table. "Where are you living?"

"Outside of town … with María."

Julie grimaced. "No, Carlos, not her. I told you—"

The cantina's door slammed open, and Carlos jumped. Hiram Booker charged in, looked around and saw him, pointed.

Behind Booker was a sheriff's deputy in a brown uniform, the badge gleaming on his chest. Carlos looked for an escape. There was a back door past the men's room. He pushed back his chair, bumping the wall and stumbling. The deputy came fast, shoving the table aside, and grabbed him. Booker came around, and the two dragged him toward the exit. He thought Julie was yelling, but he only heard the blood pounding in his ears.

"Don't make trouble," Booker snarled.

The deputy shouted something to the people in the bar. He twisted Carlos's arm and shoved him outside. Booker opened a car door.

"Get in the car, you fucking thief." The deputy banged Carlos's face on the car roof and stomped his foot.

Carlos heard a crack. He landed in the back seat, his foot throbbing, the deputy beside him and Booker driving. Booker spoke in a mix of English and Spanish. "I heard *mis hijas* talking about you on the *teléfono*. I've had you followed … I know where you live. I know your *puta*, too."

Booker drove toward Carlos's home, turned into the dirt road. *Oh, God.*

"María used to put out for me," Booker shouted.

"You're a liar," Carlos blurted. He wanted to say, *she's a good woman*, but the deputy jammed the baton into his thigh, and he screamed.

A white van was parked beside the Chevrolet outside his home. Travis McKenzie's van, but why?

The deputy prodded him, and he stumbled out. Booker held a gun on Carlos as the policeman heaved a rock through the bedroom window, and they laughed. A face appeared—Travis McKenzie, bare chested.

"Who the fuck are you?" Booker yelled.

Carlos saw Travis pull on his shirt. "I own this place."

Scared and shocked and crazy confused, Carlos gaped.

"You see, she's screwing him, too," Booker snarled.

Travis showed up at the front door with a pistol. "You're going to pay for my window. Then you're getting the hell out of here."

The deputy stepped forward, lit up by the headlights. "Don't fuck with me. I'm the law."

Travis grinned for a second, but when he looked the policeman over, his expression soured. He lowered his gun. María came up behind him in the doorway.

"We want to talk to that bitch," Booker shouted. "*Get out here, slut!*"

María stayed back.

"Get her, McDougall."

The deputy, McDougall, climbed the front steps. Travis stepped aside. McDougall pulled her onto the porch. "Take a look," Booker shouted at Carlos. "Tell me she's not a whore."

Carlos stepped toward María and felt two lightning bolts of pain, one from his broken foot, the other from Booker's gun slamming the side of his head. Booker tripped him to his knees. He stared at María and the two men beneath the porch light, trying to understand what Booker was saying. "María fucked me every Saturday night. I paid for two abortions for the careless bitch. Now she's fucking that guy in your crappy trailer home."

Abortions! *Madre de Dios*! Carlos saw María sobbing. He would denounce Booker's lies, but the *patrón* still held that gun.

Booker shouted, "Admit it, you whore."

"I love you, Carlos," she bawled.

McDougall twisted her arm.

Booker shouted again, "Tell him."

"Travis helped us, Carlos. He gave us this place to live."

Travis McKenzie put a hand on the deputy's shoulder and spoke to him. McDougall let María go, and she escaped inside.

Booker jerked Carlos up and slapped him. "You understand, you piece of shit? I let you amuse yourself with my wife, and you two did God knows what. I listen in on Julie's phone, and she's scheming with her sister to meet you. Jesus—my wife and daughter and now my old slut."

Booker smashed his fist into Carlos's face. A flash of pain and dizziness. "Load him up, McDougall."

McDougall shoved him in. They flew along the dirt road into the cotton fields as Carlos tried to muster strength to somehow escape when they stopped the car.

CHAPTER FORTY-ONE

That night in 1968 was seared into his memory—Booker and McDougall taking him on that terrifying ride, then pounding his face as he knelt in the dirt clearing by the cotton plants; the deputy accusing him of being a thief and Carlos declaring his innocence; protecting his head with his arm and the bolt of pain when the deputy's baton smashed it; the shots that rang out in the night. Yet parts of it were a sickening blur. Julie had explained later, but he couldn't possibly tell Lilia that part.

"It happened so fast, Lilia. They beat me nearly unconscious. Julie found us somehow and saved me. I gained my senses later in her car." True enough.

A cold chill ran through Carlos, the memories returning that nausea. Now he was heading with Lilia to that land of the corrupt deputy, where an accusation could be a death warrant.

Lilia sat up in bed, looking down at him, incredulous. "Carlos! Tell me how Julie saved you. You have to know."

He thought of the lawyer's letter and shook his head.

"Carlos!"

"It's Julie's story to tell."

"She said to tell me everything."

Not everything about Delano. "I'm sorry. The more I remember, the more I dread going north."

She gaped. "You promised."

"I'll meet Julie at the border. Nogales or Tijuana."

"I told you. She can't."

"You told me, but you didn't say why."

"She'd be angry if I said more."

"Maybe your secrecy irritates me."

She jumped off the bed and stared at him. "We drove this far so you could share a few meals and get laid?"

Her words hurt. "I want to go, but these are horrible memories. Surely you see."

Lilia looked toward the window, where there was a fine view of the sea, but Carlos doubted she noticed it. "She's very sick. Julie is very sick, but she doesn't want you to come out of pity. Either you'll honor your word or not. And if you don't ..."

She didn't need to finish. What had she said a few minutes before? *It's just fun and closeness, right?* If he didn't go north, Lilia would leave him behind ... and Julie had done so much for him. She'd promised there were no warrants out. "All right."

"Thank you." Still not looking pleased, Lilia took her suitcase from the closet and began pulling underwear out of a bureau drawer. Without turning around, she said, "You know, María might have loved you."

He bolted upright in bed. "Ridiculous."

She turned to him, hesitated, and said, "If she had sex with them to get what she needed and made love with you from her heart ... Some women don't know another way."

"I don't like this."

"That's all I'll say, but think about it. If María gave sex to Booker, he might have arranged for favors from her *patrón*. Travis provided a home and a car for you both. She didn't do it with them for love."

His throat ached with long-buried fury. "You said that was all."

CHAPTER FORTY-TWO

June 1994, Delano

It was a Saturday night. Workers crowded Delano taverns. Benito drank a beer in each of six bars, approaching older men with the pictures he had of his father. Finally, in the sixth bar, he settled beside a dark-skinned Mexican on a barstool and laid the picture in front of him. The man said, "That looks like Luis."

A spark of excitement.

The man scratched his head, eying the second photo. "And his wife, her name was ..."

"María." Benito offered.

"I think—maybe. Yes."

Benito waved the waitress over and bought the man a beer. "Do you know where he came from in Mexico?"

The man stared toward the liquor bottles on a shelf behind the bar. He shook his head. "Don't remember Luis saying. Didn't talk much about himself."

"Could I trace him through the union?"

"No. No. There was a contractor, though—Travis, maybe? He might know."

The beers arrived. The fellow lifted his mug and took a gulp.

"Is this contractor still in town? Do you know his last name?"

The man nudged his chin with a knuckle. "Mc-something,

McCann … McKenzie—that's it. Drives a white pickup. Hires workers out by Lumber Mart sometimes."

Benito spent the next two mornings with the idle workers outside the lumber store until finally a man arrived in a white pickup truck. The fellow was probably fifty and wore a big Texas hat that crowded the ceiling of his truck. He rolled down his window and looked the men over.

"You Travis McKenzie?" Benito called.

"Yeah, why?"

"Hey, maybe you can help me. I'm looking for someone."

The other men glared at him, but Benito stepped forward.

"I don't need trouble," McKenzie said, holding up a hand. "If you're a cop or a narc—"

"Nothing like that." He handed a picture through the open window. "I'm trying to find my father. His name was Luis."

McKenzie looked at the picture, his expression inscrutable. "Was?"

"He may be dead. I don't know."

He handed the photo back. "Yeah, Luis. A good worker. But …" The man paused. Trying to remember—or deciding how much to say?

"Anything you can tell me would help," Benito said.

"Your dad worked for me one spring. He and I had a few brews together." Travis squinted at Benito. "Hey, you ain't told me your name."

"I'm Benito." He handed in the other picture. "Here he is with my mom."

"María's your mother?" McKenzie shook his head, smirking. "Yeah. She was a fine-looking gal." Travis shifted in his seat, taking his eyes off Benito. "Your dad may have had another name.… Might have told me once."

Benito held his breath, waiting.

"Not Luis, but …" Travis shook his head. "I don't know. It was so long ago."

"What else do you remember?"

"He was running from something. A deputy came to the bar one night and hauled him off."

The night he disappeared…

McKenzie glanced from the picture to Benito and back. "How's your mom doing?"

"Fine."

"Still beautiful, I bet."

"He never told you where he came from? In Mexico?"

"He kept pretty quiet about things." Travis slapped the steering wheel of his pickup and grinned. "I'll tell you who knows. He had a cousin. I guess you Mexes all have lots of …"

Benito suppressed his anger. "I'm an only child."

"Sorry." McKenzie's smirk said otherwise. "This cousin, Carmen, worked with us and then took a job at a cotton mill down near the Grapevine. If he's still around, he'll know."

CHAPTER FORTY-THREE

Before leaving Guaymas, Carlos drove Lilia to a shoe store.

She gave him a suspicious look. "Buying footwear?"

"For you."

"I don't need—"

"Remember I told you about buying shoes before going north?"

She pursed her lips. "You walk around town letting the shoes get their bearings. But I—"

Leading her to the store, he said, "Your people came from Mexican soil, but those shoes didn't." He nodded toward her sandals and then opened the door for her. "After I return home, you should come see me. If you get shoes here, they'll take you back to Guaymas, and from here you'll find your way. Besides, we Mexicans make fine leather goods."

She chose a pair of blue walking shoes, and Carlos paid.

Back in the car, Lilia drove, headed toward the border as Carlos felt his fear rising.

She glanced at him. "You're worried, but I want to tell you why you shouldn't be."

Carlos waved his hand toward her, about to say he didn't want to talk, but she went on. "Proposition 187 is a setback, but we're making progress. Our people are becoming citizens and voting.

Latinos are elected to city governments and to our Congress. Black men are mayors of cities large and small. They campaign and challenge the system without fear."

He didn't respond.

"It's not a scary place. I don't want you to be afraid."

"Can we speak of something else?"

Lilia waited a few moments. "Okay. You left me up in the air. What happened after that night in Delano?"

He and Lilia were bound for that treacherous land, and she was asking the worst question possible. He shook his head and turned to look out the side window.

But he couldn't escape his thoughts.

May 1968, Delano

In the car, speeding away from the cotton field, Carlos leaned forward in his seat, holding his head in his hands, feeling like he would vomit.

When they reached the edge of town, Julie pulled over and asked someone on the street, "Where can we find a doctor?"

Carlos didn't look up, but he heard a man's voice. "Union headquarters. Beyond the highway."

She drove into a compound—shacks and a larger adobe. Light shone through the windows of a trailer. He opened the car door to step out, but when his foot touched the ground, a bolt of pain shot up his leg. Julie supported him on one side, as they hobbled to the trailer. An older Mexican woman in a white smock opened the door. The flood of light sent another wave of nausea through him. She gave a stoic smile and shook her head. "The teamsters and foremen sure like to bust you men up."

He lay on a cot in a space like the living room he shared with María while the woman wrapped tape around his arm, three of his fingers, and his right foot. He eased himself up, feeling faint. She dabbed his forehead with stinging disinfectant and flashed a light into his eyes. "You have a concussion. Stay here tonight."

Julie and the nurse helped him cross to a square block building—in one room a single bed and a wooden chair. Julie carefully slid into bed beside him. She pressed her face against his shoulder and laid an arm across his chest. He felt her sweet presence close by and hoped that she was sleeping at least part of the night.

In the morning, the nurse looked him over. "César spent many nights on this bed while he was fasting. The great president— Kennedy—his brother came here. He gave César bread to keep him from starving himself. That's how much our leader sacrifices for us. Lousy strikebreakers stab him in the back."

A pang of guilt. "I haven't met him," Carlos said.

She put a bottle of pills in his hand. "For the pain. Take two now and two in four hours. Don't be macho. Just take them."

A man entered, a hollow-cheeked *Mexica*, walking bent, like an old man.

"César." The nurse bowed her head as she said his name.

The man gave Carlos a long look. "You aren't in the union."

"No."

"Wetback?"

Carlos wasn't offended. Mexicans called each other all sorts of names that would piss a fellow off if they came from an Anglo. "Yes."

"You're a strikebreaker, but they beat you anyway. We'll feed you. Then you leave."

"Thank you."

"This compound we call 'Forty Acres,'" Chávez said. "Someday this will be something—respectable offices instead of trailers, tiled roofs like fine buildings in Mexico."

The union leader went to another room and returned with bread and jam. Julie and Carlos ate, and then Chávez told him, "Go back to your country where no one beats you."

As Julie pulled out of the compound, he said, "Take me home."

She gaped at him. "Tell me you aren't going back to María."

He just shook his head, knowing he had to go but not understanding why.

They parked outside the mobile home. He saw María peek at him through the broken window and pull the shade closed. She didn't come out. He waited—feeling the ache in his foot and his side, hearing the buzzing in his head, questions, answers he hated coming more and more clear—before gesturing toward the highway. "Not my home anymore."

Julie drove north on Highway 99. "We'll go to Berkeley. My sister will find us a doctor and someplace to stay."

Carlos took three pain pills and slouched in the seat, trying for a comfortable position as Julie spoke of recent events: the young people's protests in American cities; riots in France and Poland, even Mexico City; Russian tanks rolling into one of their puppet states to put down a revolt. In Vietnam, there had been a great attack. The American president was desperate not only to end the war, but also his reign in Washington.

The great man, King, who stood for peace and freedom, was slain. Protesters marched in great cities of the North and stoned the police. Buildings burned. Farmworkers struck in the fields and picketed grocery stores. César Chávez led the workers in a great march from Delano to Sacramento.

Carlos knew much of this from the men in the vineyards or the television at the cantina, but he didn't interrupt Julie, didn't want to speak or move. He had toiled in those fields, crossed those picket lines, but he'd been on the rich man's side of justice.

Julie glanced at him as she drove. "Still believe in God giving those gifts?"

"Isabel is a gift," he said. "You are, too. The rest are tricks and fantasies that make a man foolish."

"I'm just a woman," she said. "Not a gift or a trick."

May/June 1968, Berkeley

They rented a one-room apartment and found a clinic to mend his wounds. Ivy, who was twenty-five and had received her family trust, paid for everything.

Two of his ribs were cracked but would heal. Doctors twisted his fingers back into position and re-splinted them. It hurt like hell. They sliced into his foot to fix the bones. The foot and his arm received plaster casts. Julie wrote antiwar slogans on them with colored pens.

At night, he missed María, grieved for María, desperately wanted her ... and despised her. Her lies and feigned chastity had made a fool of him. He declared himself a fool as his doubts turned against him. Had María lied, or had he assumed she was a virgin, waiting for marriage? He saw her hiding behind Travis McKenzie in the doorway, closing him out. *Close her out, too,* he thought. *Think of Isabel and home. Isabel, true and loving. Leave the danger behind. Return to her.*

Julie took Carlos, his foot still in a cast, to a student cantina on the night of the great California primary election. "A chance for you to learn about American politics," she said. A television set behind the bar showed two men talking into microphones, pictures of one crowded meeting room and then another, streamers, balloons, and people holding signs.

The bar was full of rowdy students, many wearing badges to support their favorite. On one side of the cantina, badges said "Kennedy." Across the way, "McCarthy."

"Kennedy is César's friend," Julie said. "He'll help the farmworkers." So Carlos and Julie stood on that side, drinking beer. Numbers appeared on the TV; McCarthy several points ahead. His people cheered, raising beer mugs in the air.

Julie looked disappointed. "McCarthy's all right. He'll end the war, too."

Music played from speakers over the bar, some of those songs Julie had taught him: "If God is on Our Side, He'll Stop the Next War." He thought of telling these students that God didn't stop wars; He only gave simple gifts. But the gift of María had turned to *mierda*. He hated the idea, but Julie's non-God was making more sense.

More results showed on the TV. Everyone watched the announcer, who was speaking too fast for Carlos.

"Kennedy's gaining," Julie said.

"We're going to win," someone on their side shouted.

"No, *we* are." A McCarthy supporter.

Carlos leaned his crutch against the wall. He and Julie turned their backs on the television and swayed to the music, jammed in between the others, all dancing now in the smoke-choked room. She murmured the songs' words in his ear—one from the famous Beatles: "All you need is love," and another, "Ain't no mountain high enough to keep me from you." Many mountains lay between his home in Mexico and Julie's angry California, but he believed the song for a moment. They'd always be together in some way. *Maybe I do love her*, he thought.

Near midnight, another announcement—the numbers were almost even, 44 to 43. Kennedy's people cheered. "Kennedy's going to make it," Julie told him. "Look, he's going to speak." On the screen, a man who looked very young to be president moved through a crowded hallway, smiling wide, shaking hands, signing papers people held out to him.

"But the numbers ..." Carlos protested.

"Votes from Los Angeles are coming in now. They love him there."

César's friend Kennedy was at the podium with his pretty wife. Carlos tried to listen to his speech, but it was difficult to understand. Julie pulled him against her side as she watched, the people around them cheering.

Kennedy finished and left the stage. Advertisements showed on TV. But the broadcast did not return to the election. Instead, the screen flashed back to the newsroom. "This is a special report," the announcer said.

"Quiet," the bartender yelled.

The announcer looked nervous. "We are trying to confirm our information. There seems to have been a series of explosions at the Kennedy celebration. We have reports now of shots fired ... that Senator Kennedy may have been shot."

Students covered their mouths, staring at the screen. A shout: "What the fuck?"

"Quiet," a girl yelled. "Listen."

Silence in the bar.

The announcer kept repeating, "We're trying to verify."

A minute later: "We have confirmation now. Senator Kennedy was shot, blood on the floor where he's lying."

"God damn it," someone screamed.

"Shut up!"

After a few more minutes. "We have reports of Senator Kennedy bleeding from his head and abdomen. He's being transported—"

A guy jumped up on the bar, ripped off his shirt and threw it into the crowd, screaming. "This is too fucking much!" He grabbed a beer bottle and smashed the television—a burst of light, a loud pop, glass shards showering people near the bar, yelps and screams. Two guys threw mugs at him, knocking him off the bar and shattering the mirror. Julie retrieved Carlos's crutch and they escaped before the police could come.

Back at their apartment, Julie slept little. She turned the news on and off all night, pacing. Early next morning, the word came: This second Kennedy had been assassinated like his brother. Julie sobbed in Carlos's arms. "They've killed them all. President Kennedy who cared for us, Martin Luther King who opposed hatred with love, and now Bobby, who would have made peace and helped the workers. Now no one can believe in God, you'll see."

Carlos, still clinging to some of his naive notions, thought, *A person could believe, but it's difficult to imagine that He is just or compassionate.*

So he made no reply to Julie on that terrible day in North America.

CHAPTER FORTY-FOUR

At the US-Mexico border, Carlos and Lilia waited in a line of cars as two bored Mexican border guards watched from chairs beside a building.

Crossing a line on the pavement, they inched toward the US *migras'* guard booths. Lilia pulled out of the line and parked by a green block structure. "We have to go in so they can validate your pass. Okay?"

Carlos shivered. "Thirty years ago, in the Bracero Program, I came legally. They herded us into a building, like where they feed cattle. Men inspected our faces and our hands and sprayed us for bugs. The one who sprayed us wore a mask, but we stood helpless. Toxic powder marinated our closed eyes and tickled the insides of our ears."

"I'm sorry," she said. "They won't do that today."

Inside, they stood at a counter before one of the men in brown uniforms. He glanced from Carlos to his fellow officers with a sneer. "Are you his daughter?" he asked Lilia. "Does either one of you speak English?"

Lilia smiled. "I was born in the good old USA. And this document authorizes my friend to visit for ten days."

The man snorted and took the paper into a back room. Carlos noticed a map of Arizona on the back wall, red pins clustered along the border. Nearby, behind the counter, two women typed at their desks, the clatter of their machines rattling in his head. A fly landed on his ear and he shooed it away.

The man returned and stamped the date on the paper, entered another date, and signed it. "You'd better leave when it's time." He jabbed a fat finger toward the date he'd written. Carlos felt those resentful eyes follow them out the door.

Back in the car, he said, "I was going to grin to show him my perfect teeth."

"No you weren't. You were scared *shitless*—you know that English word?"

"I'm trying to make it a joke because I hate being here."

She sighed. "I know."

Long silences. Lilia drove north to Tucson and then west past huge saguaro cacti, glancing at Carlos and back to the road. She appeared troubled, as Carlos felt. Finally she said, "Growing up, my father got drunk and beat me. I married Ramón, and he took over." She glanced at him. "Is it okay if I mention this?"

"Of course."

"Ramon didn't need to drink to get violent. He only had to lose something or make a mistake. If something infuriated him, it was my fault. Maybe I deserved it."

"You didn't."

"Both of them—father and husband—said I was worthless. After he left me, Ramon came back a couple of times. 'Ugly bitch,' he called me, but he still wanted to come inside my body…. He hit me when I refused. I moved to Julie's ranch, and she sent workers to Ramón's apartment. Maybe they attacked him. I don't know, but he didn't come back."

"You're beautiful," Carlos said. "I hope they kicked his *cojones* up to his ears."

"I hated the fact that I'd lain with that monster, married him, wanted a life with him."

Lilia kept glancing ahead at the road and then at Carlos. "You didn't ever hit her, did you?"

"Pardon me?"

"Isabel, you didn't hit her?"

Carlos felt her question like a blow to the stomach. "I'd rather have killed myself."

"I know without asking, but it keeps popping into my head."

Carlos closed his eyes, feeling the pain of Lilia's past. "Cowards beat the sweet-tempered and the weak."

Riding through the vast desert, he knew she was waiting for more of his story. But this was hard, this land, its people—hard. Finally, he dozed off.

Carlos was startled by Lilia's hand touching his arm. She pointed through the windshield. "Los Angeles."

1967-1968

He'd passed LA several times back then, usually in the back of a van, but one time he rode in a sedan and saw this view. He remembered music in English playing on the radio that time, the driver singing.

Julie had given him music, too. Some Wednesday afternoons, especially those last few weeks when she'd denied him sex, she'd brought a portable radio to their rendezvous. Retreating further up the arroyo—away from nosy ears—they played music low. She explained the youths of San Francisco, called "hippies" and "flower children," using crazy drugs, making free love, calling the police "pigs," and burning their government cards on courthouse steps.

He'd heard of the Beatles in Mexico, but Julie taught him about other groups—speaking English as well as Spanish, with Carlos understanding more. Innocent songs like "I Want to Hold Your Hand," fell away to music about drugs, hallucinations, and rebellion. There were rhythms from Africa, and old songs from American blacks, nothing like Mexican music and nothing North American parents wanted their children to hear. Some songs were very serious—two men and a woman named María singing about nuclear bombs, the danger of breathing the air of our planet— poems to man's folly.

Julie had cried when she'd first played that song for him, pressing her face into his shoulder. "In third grade, my teacher made us jump under our school desks. The Russians wanted to nuke us, and if they did, the windows would shatter. Glass would cut us to pieces, so we had to cover up."

He and Julie were close that way, Carlos thought. He might cry about missing his family one day, and Julie could weep over injustices another.

Another song from a man named "Woody," about Mexican laborers who died in a California plane crash. No one in the North cared, as if they weren't human, as if Carlos wasn't human. Music and sex, and later no sex but still music.

"It's an hour to Santa Lucia." Lilia's voice brought him back. "I need to mention something."

She was driving on a three-lane highway through the suburbs—palms, eucalyptus, blocks of houses and then clusters of stores. "You should prepare for Julie and her illness."

"What is it?"

"Just don't act like it's a *big deal*—you know that American expression?"

He nodded. "Did she want me to come because she's …" He was about to say, "dying," but she cut him off.

"She won't want your pity. She may not tell you much, or she might tell you everything. It's up to her."

"I see." But whether dying or not, why would his presence be so important?

"Don't let on that I warned you, or she'll hate me."

CHAPTER FORTY-FIVE

Approaching the Booker ranch, Carlos looked up to those hillsides beyond the avocados. Was it still there, that bed of sand circled by palm trees?

The big white house seemed much as it had in 1967, but other buildings were missing. "The bunkhouse and dining hall," he said. "Am I looking in the wrong place?"

"Torn down years ago," Lilia said.

"Where do the workers live?"

"They come by truck from Oxnard or Piru. Things changed after Julie and Ivy took over."

"Where will I stay?"

"I hope with me."

He took a slow breath at the foot of the porch stairs, remembering Hiram Booker's hostility as he'd tramped down them that first day. Then Lilia led him inside to a sitting room—brown leather armchairs around a low table, tall windows facing the garden. Soft music played. The afternoon sun streamed in, shining on a figure in a wheelchair. The chair rotated, and he saw her.

The wide mouth and something about the smile made it her, but her hair was short and gray. Her head sat at an angle, a strap under her arms, securing her to the chair.

He took three quick steps forward and knelt to look her level in the eyes. "What happened? Lilia didn't ..."

"She wanted to tell you," Julie said. "But I forbade it."

Carlos felt Lilia's hand on his shoulder.

"This must be a shock." Julie said. "Are you all right, Carlos?"

"Yes, I'm just ..." He looked her over, through eyes blurry with tears. "What can I do?"

"You've come. That's all. I'd like you to myself, if Lilia agrees."

Lilia patted her cheek and left.

The wheelchair turned, and Carlos realized Julie controlled it with a lever by her right hand.

He followed her to a bedroom. The bed had side rails like those in Isabel's hospital rooms. On the wall in the corner—he stared—was one of her mother's drawings, of a young lascivious Carlos in white drawstring pants but no shirt.

"One of Mother's best."

He stood over her, feeling sick about her condition, embarrassed by the picture, out of place, and wanting to escape. "What happened? An accident?"

"No. I have *esclerosis*—multiple sclerosis in English—and emphysema in my lungs."

"My God. I've heard of them. Will you recover?" He winced and said, "Sorry."

"It's all right," she said. "Remember our talks about God? I'd get furious, and you calmed me down. When I became ill, I called Him the Big Pisser." She snorted. "Finally I realized that all my life I'd believed in Him. Why else despise Him so?"

"I can't consider that now," he said. "I'm thinking of questions but can't ask."

"Wondering when this will kill me? No one knows. If it was only the one disease, I might live far too long." She blew out a puff of air. "It started with a tingling in my arms or just my fingers. If you'd come a few months ago, I could have wrapped an arm around your neck."

He bent and kissed her cheek, feeling queasy.

She paused, and he waited. "Out cutting roses in the garden one day, I fell and couldn't get up. I lay still and pretended I was in our secret place with that blue sky, palm trees, and my handsome Latin lover." She gave him a fond smile. "Then I panicked and screamed for help."

"And now?"

"Lots of numbness, tingling, like a river of needles prickling from my shoulder into my neck. At least those little jolts tell me I'm alive. Here, I'll show off." She raised her right forearm, her hand several centimeters above the arm of her wheelchair, and pointed toward a desk. "There's a chair. Sit with me."

Carlos set it close, and Julie said, "It's that God you believed in, Carlos, playing ugly tricks. If not God, it's crappy luck and some germ or genetic defect, which is what I believe."

"I thought you said you believe in Him now."

"No. I used to—probably as much as you did. I tried to piss God off by denouncing him. I'd bought into the Christian concept; God was supposed to be good and to care for us. You see? That's crap the preachers made up. My almighty father, who stood in for 'God the Father' in our house, was a shithead." She paused to take a breath. "You know what? It's all right for people to believe if it comforts them."

There was a tap at the door and a middle-aged Mexican woman entered. She wore a yellow apron and filled the water glass from a pitcher she carried, stuck in a straw, and handed it to Carlos. She watched as he held it to Julie's lips.

Julie sipped and then said, "This is my wonderful helper, Felicia."

Carlos held out his hand to greet her, but the woman was already busy pulling the curtains closed. "Too bright in the afternoon."

"Thank you, Felicia," Julie said. Then she asked Carlos, "Do you know about Buddhism? They don't believe in a God who cares."

"I read about it long ago, when I borrowed those books from Padre Miguel."

Julie chuckled. "Oh yeah, good old Father Miguel, who lent you the books that exposed the phony church." Julie nodded toward the bed. "Lying here, thinking about those conversations, I decided I had to see you. And where are you today? Have your beliefs changed?"

He thought for a moment. "When Isabel was dying, anger wrung me out like a wet towel. I had no good thoughts for God, so I stopped talking to Him."

"You used to say He gave out gifts."

"I admit, God bewilders me. Sometimes I hate Him. Sometimes I try to believe. All I have left is a hope of seeing Isabel again."

Carlos glanced at Felicia, still lingering by the door. She slipped out.

"What if there's just some impersonal universe?" Julie asked. "Each of us floating like a molecule of water in a stream. Whether we're diverted into a farmer's field or we travel all the way to the ocean, the stream doesn't care. There's nothing for us to like or hate or worship, just nature running its course. If I have MS and this pain, I'm a drop that ended in a puddle of yucky green algae."

He felt a tear run down his cheek.

She closed her eyes for a few moments. "I'll never be in this body or this place again, but I can take in the sun's rays and feel my breath come and go. Those are gifts, Carlos."

He couldn't see it that way right now, but her words brought back long-ago feelings, sparks of spiritual imagination and insight, thoughts that had evaporated from Carlos's mind, like Julie's water droplets. He took her hand—startled by its limp heaviness, brought it to his lips, and kissed it.

"I guess I didn't follow the rules." She gave him a crooked smile. "I promised I'd never fall in love."

He squinted at her. "You don't mean …"

"You were married, and I couldn't say how I felt. I thought girls were stupid when they fell for the first guy who called them beautiful and tickled their clitoris."

It wasn't too much of a surprise, was it? Maybe he'd wanted her to fall. "I did that?"

"Oh, yeah."

"I apologize."

"Don't," she said. "I have great memories and this picture to cherish. I've missed you, Carlos. I sent my trusted friend to bring you."

"Why have Lilia spend all that time with me?"

"She'd lost her baby and her husband and her faith in people. She needed to see what a good man can be."

He touched her cheek. "Did you really know me?"

"We talked for hours back then. We shared. I knew how cruelly they treated you on our ranch, but you didn't give up. You came to earn for your family. You missed your girls and Isabel so much, and you wore that Saint Christopher medal for her, even though you thought saints were phony."

"She believed it would keep me safe." He reached inside his shirt and touched it.

"When Lilia returned from Mexico in April, she was happier. She took care of herself again. You were working that magic on her, even though she fought it."

"She's lovely."

Julie closed her eyes again. "Stay with me while I rest?"

He sat for a silent hour listening to her breathing, thinking. How would it feel to abandon resentments and float in Julie's stream? Carlos sensed a tide empty and then fill his spirit, rise, ebb and rise again… what was it? Affection for Julie? Pity? Regret?

So different than the way he'd felt when they first came together, so young and full of life.

May 1967

The second time he'd gone to Julie's hideaway they lay on towels on the sand, shirtless, staring at each other.

"Want to know what I plan to do with my inheritance?" she asked.

He ran his eyes over her. "We could talk later.…"

"I don't know. Are you really okay with sex?" She didn't wait for him to answer but grinned and said, "This is going to really piss my father off. I'll spend that family money taking freighters to tropical ports, savoring incense in African markets, trekking the Himalayas, seeking wisdom in temples and shrines—though I know it's crap."

He laughed, partly at Julie's jubilant laughter and partly at the thought; *Padre Miguel would hate what I'm doing now.*

She kissed his cheek. "I'll have sex with beautiful men in India, Ghana, and Tahiti—men like you, Carlos. I'll write an erotic novel about a woman spending days by the sea with a Latin lover, nights on the acropolis with a virile Greek. And I'll send a copy to my father." She kissed his eyelids and ears and chest as she spoke of drinking vodka with Cossacks and smoking hashish in China.

He was touching her, too, enjoying her lovely blue eyes and her perfect body. "Since last week, I've thought about this," he said. "I can't believe the priests, so I have to look to the way God made us. People are born and die. Plants rise from their seeds. Last week you gave me your North American expression, but I changed it: '*If God made it feel good, He wants you to do it.*'" He'd been rehearsing and said the words in English.

She laughed. "The religion of Carlos." She was still examining his expression.

He looked deep into her eyes and nodded as his fingers traced a strand of her hair from the side of her head to her breast.

"Okay. I believe you." She reached into her bag, brought out a packet and ripped it open.

A condom. The workers made fun of gringos who used them. "No, we should do it natural."

Julie frowned. "I'm never going to fall in love, and I'll never have a baby. If you like me at all—if you liked any woman you were with—you would do this."

What could he do but accept?

She relapsed to sheer joy as they had glorious sex. Later, they decided: People spoke of "making love," or "having sex." But making love was for people in love. For them it would be "making sex," or "fooling around," which they said in both languages. No matter its name, they would not fall in love. And somehow he had no doubt—he wouldn't. Julie made him promise that next time, he'd close his eyes and picture Isabel.

He opened his eyes now to see Julie, her mouth open, head lolling to the side, dreams stolen, just a sliver of life remaining.

There was a knock on the door. He wiped his tears away as Julie woke with a start.

Lilia entered. "Time to wheel in to dinner. I'll clean you up a little." She gave Carlos a sympathetic glance and went to help Julie.

CHAPTER FORTY-SIX

Carlos found Julie's sister, Ivy, waiting in the dining room, wearing a sparkling silver blouse and black slacks. She was fifty now, blond and still attractive despite some extra weight on her waist and hips. She ran her eyes over Carlos and hugged him close. The scent of her perfume reminded him of those days back in Berkeley and the way Ivy's flirtations had seemed more like invitations.

Her husband, Ronald, two inches shorter and balding, wore a gray sweater and tie. "He works in the stock market," Ivy explained. Ronald looked very pleased with himself, and uncomfortable shaking Carlos's hand.

Julie wheeled to one end of the long table set with a golden tablecloth, a vase of red roses, and cream-colored dishes. Ronald sat at the other. Carlos and Lilia took places to either side of Julie. Ivy slid in close beside Carlos.

Ronald poured from a bottle of white wine he took from a standing ice bucket. He swirled some in his glass, sniffed and tasted, and then poured for everyone.

Felicia brought tureens of potatoes and beans and a bowl of diced chicken in a red sauce.

"Our food's cut up small these days," Julie said in Spanish. "So everyone gets to enjoy what I can eat."

Ronald grimaced. "Speak English. We *are* in America."

"He's rude," Ivy said. "But English would help me, too, and you know some English, don't you, Carlos?" She patted his wrist.

They waited as Ronald lowered his head and asked Jesus to bless the food. Lilia quietly repeated, "Amen."

Lilia took turns feeding herself and serving Julie, a tender act that touched Carlos.

As she served Julie a bite, Lilia said, "Carlos was telling me about your time in Berkeley back in '68."

Ronald looked to Lilia. "You may not know this, being younger: Two leaders were slain within three months, Martin Luther King and Bobby Kennedy."

"Right," Lilia said. "I was a kid, but I remember."

Ronald caught Felicia's eye and pointed to the empty wine bottle. "But you couldn't comprehend—the disrespect for our flag, the disgrace of our country falling to anarchy. Blacks in the ghettos and students at the universities were disappointed, and they pitched a fit."

Julie raised her hand a bit off the table, which drew everyone's attention. "Screw 'disappointed.' We were righteously pissed. Do you remember how heartbroken and furious we were, Carlos?"

Carlos was working to remember words, hoping his pronunciation wouldn't be too bad. "'The establishment,' what you call it."

"Right," Julie said.

Ronald looked at him as if a new, more-intelligent guest had taken the Mexican's place.

Felicia arrived with another bottle of wine. Ivy leaned closer to Carlos so the maid could fill her glass. "There was no beating the establishment, no ending the war, no limit to racism."

"It all came to a head in Chicago," Julie said.

Under the table, Ivy slid her hand onto Carlos's thigh. "Rich people wanted the war, some for profit, some because they feared the 'Commies.' Are you following us, Carlos?"

All of this was making him queasy. "I remember, so yes." *But no*, he thought. *I don't want you touching me. And I don't want to think about Chicago.* He pushed Ivy's hand away.

Julie turned her head partway toward Lilia. "Carlos carried protest signs with me at rallies in Berkeley."

"'Peace,' 'End War,' 'Free Love,'" Carlos said. "Everyone smoke 'Mary J.'"

"Marijuana." Ivy grinned. "There were 'Dow Shalt Not Kill,' signs and anti LBJ signs—Johnson, he was the president. We hated the piss out of him."

"'Hey, hey, LBJ, how many kids did you kill today?'" Julie added.

"Eugene McCarthy," Ivy said. "He was the peace candidate. Then Bobby Kennedy jumped in. McCarthy had ideals, maybe Kennedy, too."

"McCarthy was a dreamer," Ronald growled. "Kennedy an opportunist. Humphrey was clueless. There was never any hope of ending that war."

"We were young radicals off to disrupt the Democratic Convention in Chicago," Julie said. "I asked Carlos to go with me before heading home to Mexico. Did he tell you about this?" she asked Lilia.

Lilia gave Carlos a wide-eyed gawk. "No."

He felt so anxious now, not about Lilia's reaction, but about the memories.

"Going there was a horrible mistake," Julie said. "I was to blame. I coaxed you to come."

CARLOS CROSSES THE LINE

August 1968, Chicago

Julie and Carlos traveled there by train and stayed in a hotel the first night. The next morning they walked through a park that ran from the lake up a gentle hill, strewn with tents and sleeping bags, toward the skyscrapers.. So many kids with long hair, smoking weed, having sex under blankets, some without blankets. Tattoos and long, dirty hair. Kids cheered as students took turns burning their federal cards.

A bearded guy held out a lit cigarette. "Hey man, take a toke." He gestured to a plate. "Or one of these fine brownies."

"I love this *vibe!*" Julie declared. "We've got to join them."

They gave up their hotel room that day, bought blankets, and slept that night on the grass, listening to guitar music, couples making love, and long-winded discussions of the war and the "pigs." Julie took a joyous breath. "I smell rebellion in the air."

The adventure fell apart the next afternoon when police and soldiers formed a cordon along three sides of the park. They wore khaki uniforms with helmets and belligerent fury on their faces. Carlos stood with his back against a tree, panic rising. Julie took his hand and they fled down to the lake. When they were far enough away, she said, "You're remembering the deputy?"

He nodded.

"It's not your country that's screwed up," she said. "It's mine. I have to face them, but you don't."

They walked the streets, holding hands, passing scores of young protesters heading for the park. "You guys know where we can get a room?" Julie asked over and over.

Finally, three students from Michigan invited them to share their room on the fifth floor in a downtown hotel. Julie left Carlos there the next afternoon as she headed across town to protest at the convention. "I'll be late," she said. "Stay here and be safe."

But she didn't come back and didn't come back. Eleven o'clock … midnight, Carlos alone in the room. He opened a window and surveyed the quiet street, wondering and worrying; did police only beat Mexicans or would they club a pretty white woman, one who might get angry and tell them to fuck off?

Finally he took the elevator down and stepped out into the street. It was quiet; no sign of Julie. Turning back to the entrance, he found a hotel porter blocking the way. The fellow wore a dark red tunic and cap. "Quiet tonight, ain't it?"

"Yes." Carlos said.

"You stayin' at the hotel?"

"I am." From behind him, Carlos heard the clumping sound of footfalls coming from the side street. His heart beat faster.

"Where you from?" the porter asked.

Carlos looked at the man's face. He was young, maybe twenty, with the condescending scowl of a newly appointed ranch foreman.

The foot beats were louder now, echoing off the buildings. Carlos nodded to the entrance. "I go in."

"Hold on. I gotta check on you." The guy held him back with an upraised palm.

Panic half choking him now, Carlos made for the revolving door, but the porter grabbed his shirt and yanked him back. "You don't belong here, do you?"

Carlos glanced around to see a squad of police turn the corner, shields up and clubs ready. He turned back, hoping for sympathy in the porter's eyes, but the man, still clutching his shirt, glanced at the police and shoved Carlos across the sidewalk into the street.

"I left Carlos at a hotel and joined the protest," Julie said. "Hundreds of us outside the convention center, facing the troops. Phil Ochs sang, 'I Ain't Marchin' Anymore.' We chanted about the rigged convention and fighting the pigs. Cops and soldiers attacked and suffocated us with tear gas."

Ronald gave a satisfied nod. "Law and order. Blacks were burning down cities, students seizing universities. Someone had to draw the line."

Carlos bristled at the term "law and order," one of the slogans politicos used to justify maiming the weak.

"Ronald's namesake was governor of California back then," Ivy said. "Ronnie Reagan smashed lots of heads on the campuses. Mayor Daley in Chicago did, too. So, the blacks had reason."

Ronald grabbed Ivy's wrist. "Not to destroy or kill, not to disrupt our educations."

There was Ronald, parroting the politicos, churning Carlos's resentment.

Ivy shook off his hand and gulped from her wine glass. "Was your precious schooling interrupted, dear? Oh, yeah—they cancelled graduation."

Ronald made a fist, about to slam it on the table, but he held back. "Our country needed order. Okay, Vietnam was a mistake, but you don't advance your cause with riots."

Julie raised her hand off the arm of the chair, capturing their attention. "Black people couldn't take a piss in a clean toilet or eat at a lousy Woolworths counter. They wanted an education for their kids."

"Things were improving," Ronald said. "LBJ passed legislation to take care of it."

"All the money went to that ghastly war," Julie said. "Young men either unemployed or dying overseas."

A derisive sneer spread across Ronald's face. "Excuses. That's all they had. Burning the ghettos hurt their own people. That futile tantrum must have taught you that."

"It taught me not to trust pricks and stockbrokers," Julie said.

"Ouch." Ronald rubbed his cheek as if he'd been slapped.

"Remind me why you married him," Julie said to Ivy. "Oh yeah, you told me. He's cute in jockey shorts."

"Rich, too," Ivy said.

Carlos held up his scarred arm. "This is your 'law and order.' Cops beat innocent man from hate."

Ronald scoffed. "What did you expect? You were illegal."

Carlos rose slowly, somewhere between humiliation and violence. He glared at Ronald for a moment, itching to strike him. Then he turned and fled to the living room. He stood by the window staring out into the grove, still clenching his fists. Insults had come his way before, but he'd never hit a man since becoming a man himself. Did that make him a coward? If so, he forgave himself. Not striking a rich fellow in this land meant survival.

August 1968

The police crammed Carlos into the back of a crowded panel truck and took him to jail. As he stumbled down a ramp getting out, a policeman yanked his arm—the arm that was still mending from the deputy's beating—and he yelped.

"Can't take it?" The cop's face was just centimeters from his. "Where'd they pick you up?"

"Hotel."

"A foreigner, eh? Come with me."

The cop grabbed his arm again—grinning as Carlos winced—

and dragged him inside, to a windowless room with green walls. He backed him into a corner and pressed his baton into Carlos's stomach. "Show me your papers."

Carlos squirmed to reach into his pocket as the stick bore into him. He handed over the identity papers.

"Yeah, Mexico," the cop said. "That's a screwed-up shithole. Chicago's a nice city, you Mexican fuck. But you Communist shitheads come to destroy it." The cop jabbed the baton hard into Carlos's belly and he crumpled to the floor, wheezing and desperate, feeling that panic from the night in Delano. There were no cotton plants to hide behind here, no Julie to save him. The policeman menaced him with the baton. "You want to ruin America, don't you, Communist Mexican fuckjob?"

Carlos backed into a corner, raising an arm to protect himself. The cop whacked him with the baton. Agony, fear, like that horrible night. Carlo yelped in pain. "Had enough?" the cop demanded, brandishing the baton.

"No. Please, no!" Carlos cried. He raised the other arm, the one already broken in Delano.

"No, not enough?" The policeman struck. The snap of breaking bone. A lightning bolt ran down his arm.

Carlos heard a faint sound behind him and saw Julie roll in. Tears ran down her cheeks. "I'm so sorry. I never got to apologize before."

"I chose to go with you."

"I was frantic when you disappeared that night. The police wouldn't help. I hired a lawyer who found out you'd been deported. When I got back to California, I sent someone to Mexico to see if you were okay."

He shook his head.

"I loved you, Carlos," she said. "I've checked on you from time to time, but I never let you know."

Why he'd accompanied Julie to Chicago rather than returning home from Berkeley right then, he could no longer remember. Maybe he'd wanted to heal more completely from the deputy's beating before Isabel saw him. But it was one of his fateful mistakes, like falling for María but never for Julie—Julie, who loved him openly and truly. Who could explain any of it?

CHAPTER FORTY-SEVEN

September 1968, Michoacán

The grocery clerk fetches me. I run to the store for the telephone call. It's Carlos on the line. "I'm coming home, *mi amor.*" I want to cry for joy.

Customers loiter by the fruit display. Their eyes pop sideways from their heads to see what they pretend not to see, hear what they pretend not to hear.

I feel relieved and, at the same time, those worries—he's coming home early again—and crazier fears, too. Days ago, a rough man came to the house demanding money. He said that my Carlos owed him for making false papers. I paid this *sanguijuela* with money Carlos sent.

I didn't ask about it when Carlos called this morning. He'll explain when he's home.

As I wait in front of the city hall, he exits the bus with no belongings, his arm wrapped in white cloth. He supports it with his other hand. I run to him.

"*Querido*, what happened?" I hug him and kiss his cheeks.

"An accident," he murmurs. But his eyes say it is more. Then, minutes later, he confesses. "My *patrón* accused me of a crime."

"Is that why you came home early last year?" I asked.

He doesn't answer.

"And the reason you arranged false identification?"

"Yes."

I don't want to ask, but the fear won't be silent. "Did you … commit a crime?"

He wraps his left arm around me, and I see that it hurts him to let the right arm swing free.

"I was innocent, but the police beat me."

He takes long, even breaths as we walk.

At my mother's house, Carlos picks Anita up with his left arm and hugs her, that painful arm in white linen resting across her back. She kisses his neck, and I see the mixture of joy, sorrow, and love in his eyes. All of it hurts me so, but I can hope; maybe this means he won't go north again.

Rita runs in after school and shouts with joy. She stops, hands on her hips as she sees his bandaged arm. "Mama told you to be careful, but you got hurt."

I wonder how Rita will make out in this life. Will motherhood coax more compassion from her? Will she make a man happy or drive him to drink?

And now, lying in bed, I wonder again: What could he have done last year for the thousand dollars to buy his orchard? What had he tried and failed this time? I must honor my husband and not question too much.

Three months later

Carlos began drinking after he returned from the other side. With that broken arm and the medications, he was in pain, of course, but it became too much. Slurring his words, staggering in front of the children. Living with my mother as we do, it shamed and shocked me to see Rita and Anita afraid that way. When I told Carlos to look at what he was doing to us, he smirked like a foolish man. So, I shouted at him to leave until he was ready to be a father and husband. He opened his eyes for the first time and saw the girls cowering from him. He surprised me then. Out of control as he had seemed two minutes before, he walked out. He spent some nights in his truck, some at his orchard, until he gained control.

Carlos lost his way for a little while, that's all. Things had happened to him up there, something very bad that he'll never tell me. He's overcome it ...

All right—the truth— He's not quite the same. He might wander away from the house for an hour now and then, spend more time away at his little ranch. But when he's home, he's our cheerful husband and father, who takes care of us in every way.

That's all I intend to say.

Summer 1971

Carlos received a package from California today. I know this because Rita accompanied him to the store where the mail arrives. She rushed in with the news.

"I received some mail," he says later, and I wait. "Money. Lots of money."

In my mind, I'm thinking about the thousand dollars he brought home four years ago, and the police who beat him the next year. I can't help but wonder: Would he have told me about this money if Rita hadn't been there to see? "I don't understand."

"From the ranch where I worked in Santa Lucia." He swallows, nervous, trying to decide what to say. "The *patrón* there was stingy with us, but his family knew what he did to me. They want to make amends."

My silent questions, like uncooked tortilla dough, are lumps in my stomach. *Be grateful*, I tell myself, *and hope no more danger comes from it.*

He smiles at me. "Now we'll build a proper home and buy a truck that runs."

I smile too. Our life is good. The girls are healthy. Carlos seldom drinks more than one beer—except on special days when we get away from the kids for our own little party. Mostly I smile because, since his wounding, Carlos stays here in Mexico. With this new money, he'll never leave again.

CHAPTER FORTY-EIGHT

While Lilia and Felicia readied Julie for bed, Carlos sat alone on the living room sofa, trying to shut out memories of Chicago, and shut out the guilt for what he'd done back then. Isabel hadn't known of Julie or María, thank God, but he'd scared her by purchasing false identity papers, horrified her with his mangled arm and the operations to repair the damage, and threatened their family with that bout of drinking. When Julie turned twenty-five and sent money from her inheritance, it shocked Isabel all over again. He'd been afraid, too, day after day, year after year, that *Norte* police would come to their door, accuse him for what had happened outside Delano that night, and take him.

He deserved his wounded arm for what he'd done to Isabel's heart and soul—and for risking her health, having sex without protection.

When Lilia returned to Carlos in the living room she shook her head. "Julie's too tired to see you now." He followed her outside, and she stopped on the porch. Without looking at him, she said, "I asked her what happened with you and the deputy in that cotton field, and you know what she told me?"

Lilia looked up into Carlos's eyes. "She said, 'I shot that shithead deputy.' I thought Julie was joking, but then I saw she wasn't. She began coughing then—too much coughing. I gave her water. It's been an exciting day, and she was tired. So I told her to rest, and she promised to tell me everything tomorrow. Or you could do it now."

"Sorry. It's her story to tell or not."

CHAPTER FORTY-NINE

After Felicia fed her breakfast, Julie wheeled out to the living room where Carlos and Lilia waited on the sofa.

Lilia greeted her with an inquisitive smile. "You had more to say about Delano."

"Good morning to you, too," Julie said. "We can't talk here."

Carlos opened the French doors, and Julie led them across the porch and down the ramp to the garden. They followed a dirt track between the avocado trees to the road at the back of the property. She rotated the wheelchair to face Lilia. "Just up that hill is the rock where Carlos and I first embraced."

"I know," Lilia said.

"And our love nest among the palms."

"About the deputy?"

Julie glanced at Carlos, who looked worried. "His name was McDougall."

May 1968, Delano

Julie skidded into the clearing in the cotton fields and saw her father's car with headlights shining on The Bastard and the deputy. Carlos knelt between them. The deputy menaced with his baton, and Julie saw blood on Carlos's face. Hot fury ran through her as she jumped from the car, its engine still running.

The Bastard came toward her. "Now, honey, you can't be here."

"Out of my way, prick."

"Go on, now. Go home, doggone it. It's none of your business."

Behind her father, the deputy stood watching them, and she saw Carlos crawling toward the cotton plants. She had to keep their attention so he could hide back there. "You can't just beat him to death. I won't let you."

"He stole something, and we're teaching him how to act," her father said. He glanced over his shoulder at the deputy. "Watch out, McDougall. He's getting away."

The deputy charged after Carlos.

As The Bastard looked back toward her, Julie slipped past and ran for the cop, who grabbed Carlos by the belt and started dragging him. Carlos wriggled and almost broke free. McDougall raised his baton high over his head. Still running, pumped up with adrenaline, Julie saw the gun holstered at his waist.

She slammed her shoulder into the deputy. He grunted, and his elbow came down on her back as she fumbled to unsnap the holster. She grabbed the gun and rolled away, rolled again, came up on her knees. The Bastard had trained her with firearms. She knew there'd be a safety. She leveled the pistol at McDougall, found the lever, and switched it off. The deputy froze.

Julie spotted her father coming from the right, and she turned the gun on him.

"Now, you wouldn't shoot us would you, honey?" The Bastard took another step, his hand out. "Just give it to me."

She shot a round into the dirt near his foot. "You're going to release him, *now.*"

The prick screamed something at her, but she ignored it. Another shout—Carlos warning her. She turned and saw the deputy charging. She pulled the trigger. McDougall fell close to her. She backed away, still on her knees, still aiming the gun at him. A black stain streamed down his trousers. He started to stand, grabbing his leg like he was trying to hold himself together, but crumpled to the ground. The lights from the car turned his leg all red.

"Mother of God." Lilia covered her mouth. "You hit the artery."

"I threw the clip of bullets and the gun at my father, and got Carlos the hell out of there. I was freaked out that night and later, after we fled to Berkeley, expecting detectives, but none came. When I dared call my mom, she said that a friend of my father's, Deputy Sheriff McDougall, had gone missing. I worried for months—for years. But now I don't give a shit—and they haven't found McDougall."

Lilia looked from Carlos to Julie and back again, speechless.

"He must have bled to death in that cotton field," Julie said. "My fingerprints were all over the gun, and my father covered it up. Buried it with the body or … I don't know. I couldn't believe he'd protect me that way, but later I realized, it wasn't for me. It was about his precious reputation."

Lilia shook her head. "Wow."

"Every year, the newspapers write about Deputy McDougall." Julie felt her fury rising. "The son of a bitch is still out there in the pictures they run on TV. They call him 'an American hero,' and say it's a 'haunting mystery.'"

"*Gracias a Dios*, it's a mystery," Carlos said.

"It pisses me off. I want them to know McDougall for the pile of crap he was. Instead they claim he was investigating Mexican gangs that night. Killed doing his duty."

"As usual," Carlos said. "Everything blamed on us."

"That asshole wanted to kill our Carlos." Julie gave him a fond look. "So now, my lovely Lilia, you know more about me than anyone on earth, except for dear Carlos."

Later that evening, Carlos sat in the chair beside Julie's bed.

"You have to leave California soon," she said. "But I want you to come back. A worker's visa would take too long. If the MS doesn't kill me, my lungs will."

A lump formed in his throat. "This is a cruel land, Julie. They hate us here."

"Ignore them."

"I can't sneak in again."

She coughed, and he reached for a towel from the bedside table. She hacked, holding her hand just above the bed, the way she did at the dinner table when she had more to say. He cleaned her chin and waited.

"My lawyer found a better way. There's a visa that allows a fiancé into the country. You could return next month."

Fiancé? What would Lilia think? "We get married?"

"You're a darling man, but I wouldn't actually marry you. The visa gives ninety days to think about marriage. We just have to say we're engaged."

He took in a breath, not wanting to deny her.

"You could come, leave, and return again, as long as you're out in ninety days."

More border crossings, more angry looks … "I should think it over."

"Of course."

"They never found out about McDougall, you're sure?"

"He must be buried deep out there."

If they learned about the deputy's death, wouldn't they rather accuse a Mexican than a rich invalid? But they hadn't in twenty-six years, why should they now?

Julie nodded off, and Carlos headed for the casita. Not likely he'd face this journey again for Julie. But for his beautiful Lilia, how could he not consider it?

CHAPTER FIFTY

Ivy and Ronald departed for San Francisco, leaving Lilia, Julie, and Carlos to peaceful dinners, speaking Spanish.

Carlos was halfway through his chicken fajitas one evening when the telephone rang. Felicia entered the dining room. "It's for you, Señor Carlos."

If the authorities wanted him, they wouldn't telephone. Still, his stomach turned queasy.

"A woman speaking Spanish," Felicia said.

The maid led him to the kitchen, where a phone hung on the wall.

"*Papá*, it's Rita. Something has happened, and I have to ask." Her voice was trembling.

"Everyone's all right?"

"Yes, *Papá*, but this stranger came … *Papá*, I know it can't be true, but …"

Carlos waited.

"He says he's your son."

"*Dios mío.*" Carlos's breath caught in his throat.

Impossible. He wanted to denounce this deranged person. But then … what about María? That night when they crossed the border. All those other times in the mobile home outside Delano…was it possible? Wouldn't he have known somehow? Wouldn't María have sent word?

He cleared his throat, and when he spoke, his voice cracked. "How old is he? Where is he from?"

"Why are you asking these things? *Papá*, is it possible?"

"Does he come from the North?"

"Yes."

"How old?"

"Twenty-five, he says."

Yes. It was possible.

A son? He couldn't speak for a moment. If Carlos and Isabel's boy had lived, he'd be twenty-three now, a young man, perhaps a university graduate. What would his son look like?

Carlos headed toward the sink, reached the end of the telephone cord, and strode back. "Did he say anything about his mother?"

"*Papá*, you're scaring me. Tell me this can't be true."

"His mother, what's her name?"

Rita bit back a sob. "María. María Ortega. The man calls himself Benito Ortega. But, *Papá*, you and Mom were *married*. I was five."

How did he feel? Appalled. Guilty. Sad. And, yes, he had to admit—intrigued. Impossible to believe, but Carlos already was believing; he had a son in the world after all … a son from María.

"I'm sorry, *hija*, but I spent many months alone up there."

Rita began sobbing in earnest. "How could you?"

"I'm having trouble imagining that, too," he said. "I made mistakes. Rita, if the young man comes back, would you talk to him? Find out everything—when he was born and where."

"*Papá*, this is very hard for me. You're far away, again with that—that *Lilia*. All of a sudden, I don't know you, *Papá*."

He swallowed hard. "It shocks me, too. I'm trying to think. Call back tomorrow, would you? I love you, *hija*."

"I love you, too." The misery in her voice struck him, and he realized something unusual—she hadn't yelled or lectured. She was just heartbroken, which was much worse.

Carlos took long breaths to settle himself. *A son.* What would it mean if it were true? What would the boy want? What could Carlos offer him?

Back at the table he told Lilia and Julie, who smiled her crooked smile. "You *knocked her up*," she said in English.

Lilia had a forkful of pepper in midair, headed for Julie's mouth. She set it back on the plate. "María was fooling around with that Travis fellow. The boy could be his."

The expression *knocked her up* and the name *Travis* turned Carlos's stomach all over again. "Maybe."

"Does this Benito look like you?"

"I don't know."

"Travis was Anglo," Julie said. "So you can probably tell. But if he's your son, you're lucky. You missed diapers, juvenile delinquency, him getting drunk and puking on your rug and telling you to fuck off."

Carlos drank from his glass of wine, thinking of the baby he and Isabel had lost. "A man should have a son. I wish I'd been there for him."

"You're accepting this pretty damned fast," Julie snapped. "You had two children and a loving wife. You sure as hell didn't need a kid in another country."

Carlos shook his head. "He's in Mexico now. I should go."

"No, Carlos!" Lilia said. "Julie went to such trouble to bring you here."

"You don't even know him," Julie said.

Lilia touched Julie's hand. "In Mexican families, men would die for a son. My father, drunk that he was, treated my brother like a king."

Carlos breathed in deep and said, "Isabel and I lost a son."

Julie turned serious. "I'm sorry, Carlos.... All right, it's important to you, but please give me the ten days. Benito can wait for you in Mexico. Even if he can't, we'll bring you back here next month. You can meet him in the US."

He saw panic in her eyes and knew he had to stay.

An hour later, sitting on the chair beside Julie's bed, Carlos said, "I accept your proposal."

He stroked her cheek, and she pressed her face against his hand.

"I feel you." She smiled. "See? I'm still here."

The next night, Rita called back to confirm: Benito's complexion was like his, and he bore a similarity around the eyes.

"I'll be back in five days," Carlos said. "Can he stay that long? Where's he lodging?"

"Señora Ramirez's boardinghouse."

"Can you take him in?"

"Don't ask me that, *Papá.*"

"Then let him into my house. Ask Anita to bring him food."

He heard her crying again.

"I apologize, *hija.* I wish you hadn't found out this way."

"At least *Mamá* never …" He heard the click as Rita hung up.

After Julie fell asleep, Carlos walked out into the balmy night. Moonlight revealed a figure in a white robe on the porch of the artist's cottage—Lilia.

"It's a beautiful full moon," she said. "Put on your robe and walk with me."

251

They strolled barefoot into the orange grove. "You've had a couple of thunderbolts strike you," she said. "First Julie's illness, and now a son." She spread a towel on the dirt and lay on her back. "Rest your head on my stomach."

Carlos did as she asked. Resting that way, he let the air and the moonlight soothe him.

"I'm thinking about that strange ceremony you had with María," she said.

"Don't."

"This is my way to say something without making too much of it. I'll speak to the moon, and you listen." Lilia took a breath. "I swear to the moon that I love Carlos very much."

Her words sent a shiver through him.

"I inform the moon that I want to be with Carlos whenever he's near, to lie with him and love him. I hope he'll want me, too."

His heart beat fast. "Lilia."

"You don't have to respond."

"I want to. I love you, too."

"Speak to the moon."

"Moon in the sky, I'm falling in love with this delightful woman." He lay, feeling the glow of love and the tickle of the breeze. "Do we have more to our relationship than lovemaking?"

"For one thing, you're very kind," she said. "You treat me like a special flower and flatter me every day."

"And you?"

"I don't have much to offer. I'll try to be good to you."

"I'm older."

"Sexier than men my age. You've made me feel freer than I ever did."

"Your talk with the man in the moon … was that some sort of commitment?"

"When I make a commitment, a priest and Our Lord will watch over us."

"I told Julie that I'll apply for the marriage visa."

"That will delight her."

"And you?"

"Did you hear what I said to the moon?"

CHAPTER FIFTY-ONE

Carlos and Julie signed the application for a marriage visa. Her attorney promised to expedite.

Lilia drove him to Los Angeles, where he took a plane to Guadalajara. He wasn't scared, soaring so far above the land and sea. His heart was occupied with emptiness for missing Lilia and for Julie's tragedy. As the plane descended, his thoughts shifted to his two waiting daughters—and maybe a son. He'd risked thoughtlessly with unprotected sex, but now he hoped ... hoped what? That this man, who might be his boy, would embrace him?

Walking with his daughters from the airport, Rita handed him her keys. "I'm too upset to drive."

Anita asked, "Is it true, *Papá*?"

"I don't know if he's my son."

"But he could be? That's what I'm asking. Did you ... with a woman up north?"

"I admitted it to your sister," he said. "He's staying in my house?"

Rita slapped the air with her hand. "Yes, *Papá*, as you requested. Did you love this whore in California?"

"I didn't think of her that way.... I'm not saying what I did was right."

Anita stopped in the middle of the parking lot. "I haven't

hugged you yet." She wrapped her arms around Carlos and squeezed.

Rita watched with hands on hips and an angry glare. "I won't hug you, not yet, maybe not again."

"She doesn't mean that." Anita held out her hand for the keys. "I'll drive."

Carlos took the front passenger seat with Rita behind.

"I've been thinking," Anita said. "How exciting it must be for this new brother of ours to live in San Francisco, USA."

Carlos didn't want her holding romantic notions about California. "I was there once and didn't like it."

Anita handed money to the parking lot attendant. A gate rose to let them through. "This new girlfriend you have, *Papá*, so pretty."

"Anita, how could you?" Rita demanded.

Anita touched Carlos's leg. "Not so horrible for him to have some comfort all those months away. And now Lilia's bringing him back to life."

"The world is crazy, my sister and father possessed by demons." Rita began sobbing, at first softly and then louder, finally wailing. Carlos reached toward her, and she cuffed his hand away. "This Benito thinks you're a devil, too. He was disgusted to learn you had *Mamá* and us girls."

"He's handsome, like you, *Papá*," Anita said.

Rita smacked the back of her sister's seat. "Santa María, this grows more ridiculous every minute."

Carlos kept his mouth shut, fearing that any response would precipitate another cascade of inhuman shrieks.

Anita glanced at him as she drove. "If you're nervous about facing him, I could come with you, *Papá*."

"Thank you, *hija*, but no. There are things I must explain to him and things I'll tell you in time. These conversations must be separate, because … you've been shocked in different ways."

"Benito's a bit *antipático*," Anita said. "I brought him groceries and he barely spoke to me."

"What do you expect?" Rita asked. "He just learned his father is a wild dog."

Carlos winced at the insult. "We must give him time, daughters."

"Stop moaning, sister," Anita said. "If he wronged anyone, it was *Mamá*, and she wasn't hurt, not at all."

"You know nothing," Rita spat. "You aren't married. You've never valued family the way I do."

"I care about my father more than about some old mischief he got into."

"You should live on the other side, where they share your immorality."

"I hear it's an exciting place." Anita winked at Carlos and dropped the subject.

CHAPTER FIFTY-TWO

When Carlos arrived home, he found the young man standing in the kitchen doorway. He wore a red T-shirt and baggy khaki pants and a hostile expression. In Benito, Carlos saw not his own face, but María's fine features and noble posture. Still, from his darker complexion and the timing of his birth, there could be little doubt.

Carlos offered his hand, but Benito ignored it. He retreated into the kitchen and tossed a picture onto the table. "My mother, and the man—my father—looks like you."

Carlos took in the image of María standing with him by their trailer in the cotton fields. A strange mixture of nostalgia and regret cascaded through him. "María's your mother?"

"You don't deny it?"

"If you're my son, I welcome it."

Benito glowered and slapped him. "You abandoned us all these years and then welcome me?"

Carlos stepped back, holding his stinging cheek, prepared to fend off another blow. "I knew nothing of you until my daughter called."

Benito stood rigid, clasping and unclasping his fists. "It wouldn't have been hard to find out."

How much should he tell the young man, who no doubt revered his mother? "When I left, things weren't good between us."

"Mother told me they beat you and you disappeared. She said you were deeply in love, and she was afraid they'd killed you."

Carlos felt sweat running down his forehead. He flicked the switch over the counter, turning on the overhead fan. "True enough. Except she saw me alive the day after the beating."

Benito's eyes bulged as he sucked in a breath. "Then why take off to Mexico, where, it turns out, you had another wife and daughters?"

"Your mother knew about them, too."

Benito stepped close and spat on Carlos's chest. "*Bastard. Liar.*" He turned and swept the dish drainer off the counter. Glasses shattered, silverware clattering on the tile floor.

Carlos struggled to stay calm as Benito faced him again. "She told me you were a hero, striving for workers' rights."

"I was a simple man, not a reformer."

"You joined César Chávez in the strikes. You led the men."

"No, *hijo.*" He felt a flicker of old guilt. His work back then had hindered the laborers' cause. "The union didn't want wetbacks. I crossed the picket lines to work for a better life."

"Lying!"

Carlos shook his head. "The money went to plant my orchard here in Mexico, to support *this* family." Carlos gestured around the room. "María hated it, but she knew."

"Shut *up.*" Benito took a cup from the counter and smashed it on the floor, shards bouncing off the cabinets, one striking Carlos in the ankle. "I waited here five days to see you, but you're nothing."

Carlos looked his son square on. "María came here once to find me. You can ask my cousin Rafael."

"I'm getting out of here." Benito headed for the door.

"We should talk," Carlos said. "If you're hungry, I can fry some eggs."

Benito charged back. "Fuck the eggs." He stopped so close Carlos felt his breath on his face. "You call my mother a liar. You insult me."

"I didn't mean to—"

"Prove it. Show me this Rafael."

"He's up north this time of year, at a packing plant near Oxnard."

Benito sneered. "You tell me to ask this guy and then say he's gone."

"If you wait a month, I'll go north and introduce you."

"Screw you. I'm leaving." Benito pushed him aside and retrieved his suitcase from the guest room.

Carlos waited by the door. "Would you shake my hand? I have a son I've never touched."

"Ha." Benito stepped around him and grasped the doorknob. "I slapped you, remember?"

What would keep Benito here a few more minutes? "I met him."

"Who?"

"César Chávez. He gave me food when I was injured."

Benito looked incredulous. "But you didn't work with him."

"No. I told you."

"I should respect you for that, eating César's food?"

Carlos sighed. "Never mind. I shouldn't have mentioned it."

"Yeah, you shouldn't have done a lot of things."

"But if you stay a while—"

Benito stalked out, leaving the door open.

Carlos opened a beer and sat in the living room, thinking about what he and María had wrought. He'd always thought they'd hurt only themselves. But they'd hurt this son, too, a son who had apparently idolized his memory. Learning of his mother's deceit would only deepen the wound.

One beer led to three and then Carlos forced himself to take a long walk.

CHAPTER FIFTY-THREE

July 1994, San Francisco

Benito went from the airport to see Carlos's cousin in Oxnard, and from there, by train to San Francisco. He beat three hard knocks on his mother's door and kicked it once.

She opened it, took one look at him, and retreated to the kitchen.

"We have to talk," he said.

She opened the refrigerator and closed it again without taking anything out. "How are your summer classes?"

"I didn't enroll."

Finally, she faced him. "Benito, I told you!"

He looked her straight on. "I met him."

A wary look crept into her eyes. "Who?"

"My father, down in Michoacán. His name's Carlos, not Luis."

She turned her back on him, leaning on the counter, gazing out the kitchen window. "Luis disappeared. This must be someone else."

"I met his cousin, Rafael, in Oxnard. I've been in Mexico and Oxnard these two weeks, not at the lousy university." He moved around beside her.

She stood there, fingernails tapping the counter, her lips tight, wrinkles showing at the sides of her mouth, still not looking at him.

"I went to find this hero you told me about, but he's a snake who had another wife. His cousin says you knew."

She spoke in a near whisper. "He used the name Luis because he was avoiding the police. They faked charges against him."

"I met two of his daughters, both older than me. He says you knew about them. Did you?"

"I … He and I loved each other." She finally turned toward him but avoided his eyes. "We pledged our love in a ceremony, but we couldn't be wed in the church."

"Because he was *already married*. He was never in César's union."

She sighed and reached for his hand. "You were young and needed a hero. I gave you a father who stood up for his people."

He ignored her touch. "Not bothering to mention that I'm a bastard. You knew he had a family. You went to the town where he lived."

"I'm not a saint, Benito, but I've tried to raise and support you." The usual tears dripped from her chin—pathetic—easy to ignore now. "You were my baby."

"I preached at a rally about my father, friend of the great Chávez."

"You grew up with principles. Not a bad thing, but you've gone too far." She raised her eyes again and looked at him, beseeching. "Maybe now you'll stop with this cause and finish college."

He clenched a fist, almost tempted to punch her. "*Lies.* I've preached lies. And you—" he could not reconcile the mother who'd raised him with the lying whore who'd birthed him. Or his coward of a father, who'd wanted to embrace him.

That evening, when Benito told Juan that he wouldn't speak at rallies anymore, Juan argued for one long, annoying hour, then stormed out. The next day he returned with a new task. "You're Catholic right?"

Benito nodded.

"Some priests down in Los Angeles support us. They're working on Cardinal Mahoney. You'll line up priests here in the Bay Area to preach our cause."

"Okay, but I have to go somewhere first."

CHAPTER FIFTY-FOUR

Carlos was so lonely. Missing Isabel, as always, longing for Lilia, avoiding Rita and her anger, amazed that he had a son, ashamed he'd had no part in raising him. He felt the humiliation of Benito spitting on him every night as he tried to sleep. He deserved that, and more.

A few weeks after Benito left, there was a knock on his door. Carlos opened it to find his son. "Why did you leave my mother?"

"Come in." Carlos felt a flicker of hope even as Benito's tone rebuked him. "I told you, we weren't getting along."

"Why?"

"That was between us." Carlos gestured to a chair in the living room. "Would you like a beer?"

Benito picked up the picture of Carlos and Isabel. "My mother's never had a romance, never looked at a man, so I know she didn't cheat on you." He held the photograph out to Carlos.

Carlos stepped close and grasped the picture. Benito held on for a moment, locking eyes with him. When he let go, Carlos set it on the sofa, out of Benito's reach.

Would it help to tell his son the truth? No, he'd done enough damage. Maligning María would only double the young man's pain.

Benito gave him a hard stare. "You need to answer me."

"I won't."

"I talked with your cousin, and with my mother. You haven't lied, but you haven't said enough."

Carlos shook his head slowly.

"Maybe you're not the devil I thought." Benito swallowed hard. "Can I stay and learn about you?"

The lad's anger would dissipate as they spent time together, maybe discussed history, attended a *fútbol* game in Guadalajara, went fishing together.... "My fondest wish, *hijo*."

For several days, Benito accompanied Carlos to the orchard. He helped with the sheep, lopped unwanted branches from fruit trees, checked the irrigation pipes. Benito gave little speeches about Anglo racists, Proposition 187 and the benefits of migrants to California. Sometimes Carlos supported Benito's arguments. Other times, he stayed silent or reminisced about working in the fields.

He wanted Benito to feel the peace and hospitality of Mexico, to appreciate life in this slow, rural atmosphere. They explored the village and shopped for groceries. Benito observed but commented little—his eyes lingering on an abandoned truck painted with graffiti, a fallen-down shack, a drunken man sleeping in a doorway. Things that Carlos would prefer he pass by. Carlos encouraged him to see the good, the simple, honest life here.

As days passed, Benito spoke less and moped more. "It's all different than I thought," he said one day. "I had this dream that I'd find my father's brothers and sisters—my aunts and uncles. They'd say you'd been a hero of the people, working with César but that you'd disappeared, or maybe your body had been returned for burial. Or you'd been crippled by your beating, and I'd find you still alive."

"So I shocked you."

"Yeah, a big fucking shock."

Silence again.

The next day in the orchard, Benito did little work, gazing off into the distance, eyes narrowed, as if he were about to cry.

Carlos tried to imagine how would he have felt if, instead of losing his father to an accident, he'd only known an empty place occupied by tales of "a hero of the workers," and then in reality, he'd found a fellow with another family who'd abandoned his mother.

One Saturday Rita's husband took their children for the afternoon, and Rita made lunch for Anita, Carlos, and their new half brother. She set the table with her good dishes, pale brown with yellow roses painted on them. She shot angry glances at Carlos as she served *chile verde*, rice and beans.

Anita overcame the silence with questions about California. Rita refocused her scowl on her sister.

Benito smiled for a change as he answered.

"They make exciting movies there." Anita beamed at their guest.

Carlos shook his head. "There's nothing real in them, daughter."

Anita ignored the comment. "I saw one from your city, San Francisco."

"Which one?" Benito asked. "They've made several."

"It was very dramatic, with the cable cars and the Golden Gate Bridge, young lovers. Such a romantic place."

Carlos saw Rita's jaw tighten.

Benito nodded. "My mom lives in San Francisco. I'm across the bay in Berkeley."

"But you go to the city to see her?" Anita asked.

Benito was about to answer, but Rita stood. "How does it feel to be the son of a San Francisco whore?"

"Rita!" Carlos shouted.

Benito jumped up, threw his napkin on the table, and glared at her. "My mother was faithful." He jabbed an accusatory finger toward Carlos. "He's the fucking whore." Benito charged out and didn't return that night or on Sunday.

On Monday morning, Carlos found Benito in the orchard, dirty and disheveled. "You slept out here?"

"Staying under your roof, I might have killed you."

Carlos looked for Benito's ironic grin, but found none. They went to work pruning branches, and Carlos asked, "Have you had many girlfriends, *hijo*?"

Benito gave him a funny look. "A couple."

"A good-looking fellow, like you. I bet you've had many."

Benito didn't answer.

"It's hard to understand women, son. Maybe you've noticed."

"My mother or *mujeres* in general?"

"I didn't know what María wanted, and she let me believe ..."

Benito dropped the clippers onto the ground and gaped. "What, that she was a slut?"

"The opposite. She seemed as wholesome as a nun."

Benito pursed his lips, his eyes hostile. "But she wasn't?"

Carlos didn't mean to, but he shook his head.

"She raised me, dedicated her life to sending me through school."

"That's all you need to know, *hijo*."

"Don't call me that."

Benito grabbed his clippers and moved to another tree, snapping off twigs and heaving them off to the side. After work, he took a long walk, returned after dark and went to his room.

On Tuesday, Carlos drove him to Lake Pátzcuaro, where they rented a boat, rowed out, and dropped lines into the water. Benito sat on the center seat, with Carlos facing from the bow.

"I wanted you to see how pretty this is," Carlos said.

Benito scanned the mountains.

"Because I hope you'll visit me sometimes."

Benito turned away, silent. Then his line jerked, and he reeled in a fish.

"Throw it back," Carlos said.

His son gave him a suspicious glance.

"Polluted."

Benito snorted, twisted the hook out of the fish's mouth, and tossed it away.

"It was my fault," Carlos said. "I regret it. I didn't tell your mother I was married right away."

"I thought you were speaking of the fish."

Carlos glanced at his son, hoping for a smile that wasn't there. "María and I met at a dance, and she was so good looking.... I don't know why she chose me. She learned I was married soon enough. I guess it only took one look for each of us to capture the other."

"Comparing my mother to the fish?"

Carlos would have laughed, but the boy was grim faced. "I didn't mean—"

"That she had a hook in you … that she was polluted?"

Carlos felt a nibble on his line, but he ignored it. "Maybe we were both polluted. Maybe we're all polluted, swimming in the lake of human failings. Look, Benito …"

Benito reeled in his line and dropped the pole into the boat. "And your hook in me, what of that?"

"I didn't know you existed."

"You cast the line when you *fucked* my mother." Benito had that fierce look again.

Carlos pulled in his pole, ready to defend himself or jump overboard if his son decided to attack.

"Here's your hook." Benito hitched a finger inside his lower lip for a moment. "I longed to have a dad all my life, to be like my friends, to know who I was … to be proud. I lectured at a rally about my heroic father."

Carlos shook his head. "Maybe we all have barbs in each other—fathers and sons, daughters, brothers and sisters. When my girls cry, my heart falls into my stomach. If Rita's ashamed, I feel guilty."

"I've seen you now. You're not a hero. I've seen this land where you live."

"I hope you like it."

Benito swung his arm across the panorama. "This beauty isn't Mexico. Mexico is dirt streets and ten people in a room with falling-down walls, coyotes who suck the blood out of their fellow men to sneak them into California."

Carlos tensed. "This *is* Mexico; these mountains, the old beliefs, simple ranchers—your heritage—more real than your Hollywood, your Disneyland."

"Mexico is a man who came north, planted sperm, and ran away."

"I'm sorry. I'd like to know you better if you give me a chance."

Benito jammed the oars into the oarlocks and rowed to shore.

Back in the truck, Benito looked out the window, silent for a while, as Carlos drove. Then he blurted, "I thought I needed you, but I don't."

Carlos slowed as they approached a village. "I apologize, son. I didn't mean to insult your mother."

Benito kept looking ahead. "Let me out up here."

"But—"

"*Let me out.* I'll find my way home."

"Your suitcase, your clothes. We can pick them up, and I'll take you to the airport if you wish."

"Keep the goddamned things. Keep it all. Just *stop*, now."

He pulled the truck over, and Benito jumped out. Carlos climbed out, too, and followed. "Let me drive you. I'll take you wherever you want. We don't have to talk if you don't want to."

"Get away, damn you." Benito waved a hand back behind him.

Carlos returned to his truck and waited there until a bus came and his son departed.

Back in town, he bought two liters of beer, took them to his property, and sat in the dirt outside the sheep pen, speaking sorrowfully to the animals between gulps of beer. "What I did when I was young, I thought it would be all right. I thought … I don't know what. It makes no sense now. How could I not end up being hurt, and María as well? But now, this innocent, Benito. There's no excuse."

He slept outside the sheep pen and woke to the mocking *baas* of his beasts.

CHAPTER FIFTY-FIVE

After Benito left, Carlos hiked in the countryside for two days, returning home at night, exhausted but sleeping little. The third morning, Rita banged on his door. "Your whore's coming." She delivered the announcement accompanied by a jug of lemonade, which she shoved into his arms, her scowl so puckery it looked like she'd sucked lemons herself. "This is from Anita, not me." Her expression amused Carlos, which told him he was recovering from his sorrow over Benito's angry departure.

He finally slept that night. The next day, his ninety-day betrothal visa arrived in the hands of a lovely courier. He and Lilia spent four days together before flying to California—days of love and lust, hugs and sweet smiles, including a night at Freddie's hotel by the lake—and one long, tearful talk about how Benito had rejected him.

Back in Santa Lucia, Julie coughed more and spoke less. He stayed a week, flew home for a several days to tend his orchard, and then returned to California. Now a brace had been attached to the wheelchair, supporting her head and neck. She could barely raise the fingers of her good hand.

But he was living for weeks at a time with Lilia. She accompanied him home to Mexico for several days at the end of August. They roasted a chicken one night, made enchiladas another, and dined with Rita and her family—yes, Rita hosted them to dinner, though the service was less than civil.

After dinner that evening, he walked Lilia back to his house and returned alone. He asked Rita to step out onto the front porch. "Accept her, *hija*. Treat her nicely. I want to marry her."

Rita went back inside without a word. But two days later, she delivered a box of chocolates and a cold bottle of wine to his door. "Not from me. Anita asked me to bring them."

Lilia invited her in, and Rita spent an hour in his kitchen. The three of them consumed chocolate and alcohol but spoke little. Still, the fact that she stayed seemed hopeful.

Lilia retrieved the picture of Isabel and Carlos from the living room and set it on the table. She raised her glass. "To Isabel. Your mother ... your wife. I know she was a wonderful lady."

Carlos saw Rita's face twist into one of her furies. His stomach twisted, too. But her anger dissolved to tears, and she left without a word.

Later, in bed, Carlos lay on his side watching Lilia. "I'm going to ask you something. You should tell me to go to hell, but I hope you make the wrong decision."

She laughed nervously.

"What I told the moon is true, *querida*. You're very dear to me. I can't imagine not seeing you for even a day after the visa expires."

She touched his cheek, looking wistful.

"You're beautiful, and you could have any man. I'm forty-nine years old."

"Is this a very long question?" she asked.

"Not long, but tricky. If you lived in Mexico, I'd propose marriage."

"If you lived in the United States, I'd say yes."

"It's not fair to ask you to give up your culture and your friends, is it?"

"My teaching, too."

He'd hoped she'd say it was worth the sacrifice. "There are schools in Mexico that could use a beautiful English teacher."

"My grandparents struggled to bring us a better life in the United States."

"Bad memories in the North … and danger. I have my orchard and my daughters. Up there, I'd be dependent on you and Julie."

She shook her head and lowered her eyes. "You won't be climbing a ladder to pick plums forever."

"I have grandchildren to assist." He slipped a hand under her chin to raise her face to him. "Maybe more children, if you say yes."

"You told me it would be the wrong decision. Maybe that's true. And we can't leave Julie alone."

Seeing her sad eyes, Carlos felt sick in his heart.

"I go back to teaching soon," she said. "I have long vacations. If you moved to California, we could spend the summer here."

"Your *Estados Unidos* is passing a law to say they hate us."

She sighed. "Let's just make love and leave things as they are."

But they didn't make love that evening.

CHAPTER FIFTY-SIX

Carlos accompanied her back to Santa Lucia. Lilia resumed teaching. They ate most dinners with Julie, Ivy, and Ronald.

Strolling together in the avocado grove one afternoon, he said, "I want to be with you, but my visa's almost over." She didn't respond. "I can't stay here illegal and resented. I hated that."

"You could be legal. Just marry me or someone. Marry Julie."

Her words wounded him. "Or Felicia the cook."

She grimaced. "Don't be an ass."

Later, in the salon, with Julie facing him in her wheelchair, he explained his dilemma.

He expected a wisecrack, but she looked serious. "You *should* marry me, Carlos."

"What?"

"Not just so you can keep visiting us." She paused for a breath. "I've made a decision, something I've thought about for a while. I want to tell the truth about McDougall." Another pause. "Tell the police and newspapers what a scumbag he was so they quit the hero-worship crap."

Carlos felt panic rise in him. "No, Julie. You'll get in trouble. And I—"

She raised a finger that trembled just above the arm of the wheelchair. "I'm sick of this, and I can do something about it."

She began coughing. The coughs went on, and her face grew red. Carlos picked up a towel to clean her, feeling helpless.

"Thanks." Julie gave him a weak smile. "I'm going to die soon from pneumonia in my lungs and a body too immobile to fight it. I'll tell the newspapers that McDougall was a pile of crud. Then they'll stop treating him like some phony saint."

"Why would they print it?"

She glanced at herself. "I'm pathetic, so they'll write about me, and McDougall is still a big story." She kept her eyes on Carlos, assessing. "I'm going to confess to homicide. The police will come."

Carlos felt his pulse pounding in his throat. "You should leave the deputy buried as he is."

"Proposition 187 is about slandering Mexicans. These articles about McDougall slander you, too."

"You said the crime was unsolved, and I was safe. Now—"

"I'll confess that I killed the son of a bitch because he was beating a man to death. I don't have to name you. But," she acknowledged, "if the police follow up, they'll find their way to that bar in Delano."

Suddenly, it was hard for him to breathe, like he was back in the cotton field, terrified, desperate to crawl away and hide.

She raised that finger again, and took a moment to catch her breath. "We'll protect you. My lawyer says even if I confess, they'll investigate. They'll want witnesses. But you won't be a witness. Listen, in California, a man can't testify against his wife, and she can't testify against him."

Shock on top of fear. They'd joked about the fiancé visa, but now Julie really wanted marriage?

"If they brought me back here, they could do anything. They could dump me in a ravine out in the desert."

"They'll have no grounds to extradite you from Mexico. It was self-defense. There's no body, and I won't admit you were there." Another long pause. "My lawyer knows an attorney in Mexico who'll keep you safe."

He paced the length of the room. "If you tell this story, I can never come back here."

"I'm sorry, but I have to do this." She sighed. "You're only coming for Lilia anyway. She and I have long talks about you." A few coughs. "You both want to marry, but also to keep your country. If you can't return here, Lilia will have to move to Mexico."

"Or give me up." The words stung him.

"I'm sorry, Carlos. I just can't let this go."

A phony visa, a phony marriage, a return home to drinking every Sunday night in a cantina and commiserating with his sheep…. *No.* Lilia had proved there was life after Isabel. He wouldn't relinquish so easily to the bottle this time.

Carlos fretted on the casita porch as Julie told Lilia her plans. Lilia came stalking across the yard and dropped a paper sack on the table. "Our lunch," she said, and banged down a bottle of water. "I was shouting at Julie just now. I can't believe she wants to confess murder."

"I know. It's a terrible idea."

"If she implicates you, you can never come back."

"You're right," he said.

Lilia's voice broke. "And now she wants to marry you."

"Only to protect me. And …"

"And she doesn't have long to live. I know." Lilia picked up the lunch bag and dropped it back on the table. "After I yelled at Julie, I kicked the bedroom wall over and over. She knows what this will do to us."

"Julie has a strong determination and won't give in." He shook his head. "If it's true love between you and me, we'll find a way."

"You mean, I'll come to Mexico. I'm not hungry. You eat my food." She opened the screen door, but let it slam shut again without entering.

"How terrible would it be?" he asked.

"I can't hate you and I can't hate Julie. But maybe it is just sex with us, Carlos, like you said."

"And I'm too old for you."

She punched him in the arm. "You're not all that much older. If you weren't such a damned kind man that I've fallen for and who keeps giving me praise I don't deserve ..."

Two days later, a package arrived for Julie. It was a videotape from a television station. Lilia set it up in the living room. Julie rolled in so the three of them could watch together. On the screen, a news piece: *Missing but not forgotten.*

"My God," Carlos said.

Grinning at them from the TV was Deputy Billy McDougall, in his twenties, wearing a crisp beige uniform. Then another image, of him throwing a football with a little boy.

"I feel ill," Carlos said, his heart beating hard. "That man wanted to kill me."

"*Sick son of a bitch,*" Julie said.

A blond newswoman interviewed McDougall's former partner, gray-haired now. He'd been thirty the night McDougall disappeared. "Billy and I were patrolling for gangs that night in Santa Lucia. We got called to help a woman who'd been injured. She was burned and needed treatment. Billy, he didn't want to get drawn away." The partner's voice broke. "So I took the woman to the clinic. Billy used his personal vehicle to go stake out a lot where the Mexican gangs sold drugs. He'd always been dedicated like that, Billy, taking his own car, putting in extra time. He planned to go home when his shift ended at midnight." The partner swallowed, looked down at his hands, and took a few breaths. "Home to his beautiful family ... That's the last I saw of him. He was taken down by those gangbangers, no doubt about it. We just never found him."

Lilia muted the television.

Julie was breathing hard, her eyes fixed on the television. "See how they lie for each other? Now you understand? McDougall was a thug, willing to kill for my father. His partner had to know." She began to cough, and the coughing went on.

Carlos glanced from Julie to the TV, where other police were speaking with the reporter. He felt as helpless to control her coughing as he did to change what had happened in 1968, as he did to keep Julie from dying.

Finally Lilia said, "It was twenty-six years ago. Why speak up now?"

"Because seeing Carlos reminds me. Because I have nothing to lose anymore."

"He'll have to leave the country," Lilia said.

"I don't have much time to put that bastard in his place."

Lilia clicked the sound back on, and the newswoman said, "An American hero and a dark mystery. If you have information about those events twenty-five years ago, contact the county sheriff's office. Help put this hero to rest."

Lilia barely spoke with Carlos that night, and when she finally did, she shouted. "You wanted this. You've found a reason to avoid California."

"I didn't, I swear," he said. "Julie's plan scares me to death."

By morning, Lilia had decided he wasn't to blame, but for the next three days, she continued to argue with Julie. One night, she asked Carlos, "How do you stay mad at your friend who's helpless and going to die?"

"You can't. You love and comfort her."

She gave him a sideways half smile. "You're going to marry her."

"I am."

And so it was.

That Saturday at lunch, Felicia served salads all around.

Julie jiggled a finger, and everyone looked at her. "I have an announcement," she said. "Carlos and I plan to marry."

Ivy's mouth dropped open, and Ronald blurted, "No."

Julie smirked. "This worries you, brother-in-law? You see a future where a Mexican tells you how to grow strawberries?" She paused between sentences. "Carlos does know more about crops than you."

"You're out of your mind," Ronald shouted. "You conniving wetback son of a bitch."

Carlos tried to let the fury bounce off him, glad he wouldn't be dealing with this *idiota* much longer.

Ronald pounded his fist on the table. "We'll contest this. We'll have you deported."

"No need," Julie said. "My lawyer has a solution." They waited as Lilia gave her a sip of water. "The ranch is worth about ten million. Give me two, and I'll sign it over."

"Leave it all to your sister," Ronald growled. "It is the goddamned *Booker* Ranch."

Ivy set a hand on Ronald's wrist. "You're using His name in vain, dear." She turned to Julie. "What's the rest of the deal?"

"That's all," Julie said.

Ronald glared at Carlos.

"I go back Mexico," he said.

Ivy eyed her husband. "Two million's a bargain."

Ronald seemed to be calming down. "We'll have complete control?"

"You two will own it, unless Ivy comes to her senses and divorces you."

Ivy smiled. "We'll write you a check, sister."

CHAPTER FIFTY-SEVEN

The living room was decorated in yellow roses and white ribbons. Lilia and Ivy wore pink satin. Julie wheeled in wearing a pearly white nightgown and a lacy veil. Benito hadn't answered Carlos's invitation, but his cousin Rafael arrived in a tuxedo.

Felicia snapped photos as Julie's attorney, Malcolm Honeywell, took his place by the big windows that faced out to the grove. Honeywell—tall, bald but for a fringe of gray hair around the edges—took wire frame glasses from his dark grey suit jacket and slipped them on. "Julie, Carlos, I'm happy you invited me to perform your nuptials. Please bear with me; it's only my second ceremony." He looked at a pad of paper in his hand. "Dearly beloved..."

There was a bang, and they all turned toward the front door to see Ronald stomping out.

Ivy laughed. "Guess he couldn't take it."

The wedding proceeded nicely without Ronald nor any mention of God.

That afternoon, Carlos sat in a wicker chair on the front porch, Julie beside him in her wheelchair.

"When will you contact the newspapers?" he asked.

"Soon." She smiled. "They could take a picture of my handsome lover for the article."

He shook his head. "This is a terrible idea. They still might come for me."

"That Mexican attorney we hired is a hot tamale." She chuckled. "The police won't come for you, but there will be a surprise in a few months. I'm leaving you and Lilia something from my estate. Felicia, too—one of those presents from God you talk about."

He looked over the avocado trees to the hills where they'd shared that secret spot. "You're the gift, not your money."

"Not this way," she said. "You don't want me like this."

As Julie fell asleep, he listened to her raspy inhalations and gentle releases. There was desperation in those labored breaths, and in the person who listened. It reminded him of the last days with Isabel, yearning for her to go on, praying for a merciful end.

She woke, and after a minute she said, "Do you still believe in heaven?"

"Like the summer sky, my beliefs hide behind clouds and contradictions."

Her chin quivered. "Falling into nothingness would be okay. Or evaporating into the clouds to fall in another storm."

"I love you, Julie. We're the closest friends."

"I'm jealous of Lilia."

"Do you think she'll marry me?"

"My corpse isn't even cold." She did her best to give one of her wide, lovely smiles, but her lips failed to cooperate.

A day after Carlos returned home to Mexico, Julie's Mexican attorney arrived in a black business suit. "Juan Rodriguez, at your service," he said with a smile.

Over coffee in the living room, he explained, "If the *Norte* police want to find you, I will know." He winked. "You and I have friends in high places."

Carlos, nervous, asked, "Can they return me to California?"

"If they try, we will know. We have friends, señor. That's all that matters. You will not see me again unless you need my help. For this I receive a nice retainer from your friend, Señorita Booker."

Despite the lawyer's confidence, sounds in the street at night unnerved Carlos. When would Rodriguez return? When might North American police arrive, accompanied by corrupt local officials and some extradition order?

CHAPTER FIFTY-EIGHT

December 1994, Michoacán, two months
after leaving California

Carlos managed to ignore the cantina and stopped complaining to his sheep. He pruned his peach trees more than they needed in order to keep busy and sometimes watched foolish TV shows. He went to dinners at Rita's house and lunches with Anita, attended dances every Saturday night in a nearby town, even went to a group for widows and widowers arranged by the church—but only once. None of it excited him, but at least he was out with people.

Letters came from Lilia, who was still teaching kindergarten and attending to Julie evenings and weekends. Had Julie taken her story to the newspapers? If she had, Lilia didn't mention it, only said that Julie's condition was grave. The doctor urged her to enter a hospice facility. She refused.

No lawyer came by, no *Norte* police with orders to abduct him.

Returning from the orchard one afternoon in December, he found a note from Rita taped on his door: *Lilia's here. Come right away*.

He knew as he strode to his daughter's house. He knew as he faced Lilia in Rita's doorway and saw her tears.

"Julie died two nights ago," she said. "I held her hand, and she asked me if I'd marry you."

He would ask Lilia what she'd answered, but this wasn't the moment. "Come home with me."

In his living room, Lilia kissed him. "Julie sent this kiss for you."

He wanted another kiss but needed to know. "Did she tell her story to the newspapers?"

"Julie went to the local editor. He promised to investigate, but he turned out to be one of Ronald's clients." Lilia sighed. "Ronald's attorney showed up at the house that next day, calling Julie a delusional cripple and threatening a libel suit. The editor called to say he wouldn't pursue it."

"What about the police?" Carlos asked.

"She called the chief, and guess what? He's another of Ronald's cronies. He sent some guy in a fancy suit. Felicia and I stood guard while he spoke to her."

Carlos gestured and Lilia followed him to the kitchen. He poured two glasses of lemonade but neither of them drank. "You thought this guy would harm her?"

"We could have stopped him if we had to."

"You and your karate."

Lilia laughed. "He never said, but we think he came from some police union. Told her how McDougall's wife was getting the pension of a man who died on duty and using the money to care for her sick mother. If he'd gone off to Delano that night instead of chasing gangs in Santa Lucia, there'd be no pension—the wife would be broke."

"So Julie let it go?"

Lilia nodded. "She could sympathize with a woman caring for her mom."

"She died without that peace she wanted." Julie had never gotten what she desired, had she? That world travel, the freedom and adventures. She'd been brash and bold, but she'd sacrificed for her mother again and again. Now she'd given up the justice she'd craved to benefit a stranger. Good people did that, didn't they?

Carlos had never been fearless like that. His wishes had been simple—a little ranch and every day with his family. His desires had been fulfilled thanks to money from Julie and her mother. But he'd lost his father and Roberto and then Isabel. He'd lost his faith.

"Julie had other forms of peace." Lilia ran a hand up his chest. "Now you can come back to Santa Lucia with me."

He blew out a breath. "You think I dare?"

"The editor and police chief won't pursue the case."

"There was no case when Julie's father and that deputy beat me half to death."

Lilia surprised him by smiling then. "Yeah, I know. Do you still want me?"

"I want you here with me."

She gave a subtle nod.

"I would have bought a ring, but I thought you wouldn't ..."

She put a finger to his lips to quiet him. "You're supposed to kneel or something."

His heart began pounding as he knelt. "Will you—"

"I have conditions," she said.

He waited.

"I want children."

"Of course."

"I'm a North American. I don't want a houseful. Two would be good, and we have to do it soon. I'm not getting younger."

"Perfect, but one will be a son."

She laughed. "You can ask God for that gift."

"I will."

Lilia smiled down at him. "I'll stay home with them until our youngest is two, then go to work. But our kids will never stay with a stranger."

"They'll come to the orchard with me, or my daughters will care for them. When my sheep give me the day off, I'll make enchiladas for us."

"And you'll never play in some other woman's bed?"

Her voice sounded lighthearted, but her questioning eyes told him otherwise. Carlos and María had wounded Benito so badly. They'd hurt each other, too, and Isabel, by the secrets she could only have guessed at. Now he saw that he'd hurt Lilia, as well, disappointed her by his actions twenty-six years before they'd even met. "Definitely not."

She nodded, and he said, "I love you very much. Will you marry me?"

She raised a finger. "One more. We'll be married in your church here, by that priest you told me about."

"Padre Miguel." He nodded. "Retired, but I know where to find him."

"Rita can be my maid of honor." Lilia said.

"If she refuses, Anita would proudly stand with you."

She laughed then. "I'd love to marry you."

CHAPTER FIFTY-NINE

February 1995, Morelia, Mexico

Eight years back, the church had retired Miguel to this rectory near Morelia, too far for frequent visits to his old village, but he'd stayed in touch with Carlos Montoya. When Miguel read a good book, he'd send Carlos a note, and Carlos would do the same. Carlos visited sometimes to drink beer and talk about books and local news.

Then the visits ceased. Carlos sent no notes, read no books, stayed away. His wife, Isabel, was dying. Miguel prayed for her and for him—the first infant he'd held in holy water, the boy with a nimble mind but wayward spirit.

It had been three years with no contact, which meant that Carlos had gone back to hating God. Now a message: *I'd like to come see you. Would you be available to provide spiritual guidance for a companion and me?*

"Spiritual" couldn't mean what Miguel wished for, not coming from Carlos—but what of the companion? He sent word that he'd welcome a visit.

So now, Miguel fastened the top button of his black shirt and slipped in the white collar. Down in the living room, he found Carlos standing by a window, and nearby a beautiful woman seated on the beige sofa. She wore a white blouse and black skirt and looked quite pleased and comfortable.

He approached her. "I'm Padre Miguel." He saw out of the corner of his eye Carlos moving toward him.

She smiled. "I'm Lilia."

Carlos embraced him. "Miguel, so good to see you."

He sat in an armchair as Carlos joined Lilia on the sofa. The housemother set tea and biscuits on a coffee table between them. Miguel looked from one to the other, not knowing their relationship—but knowing perfectly—and unable to keep from grinning. "Your note spoke of spiritual guidance."

"Don't get excited, Padre." Carlos held the woman's hand.

Lilia beamed at Carlos. "Some men are slow, but he's making progress, Padre."

"Obstinate," Miguel said. "Argumentative."

Carlos chuckled. "Sorry. I was angry back then. You lent me those books about Protestants and Hindus, which made it clear that everything's unclear."

"I prayed you'd return to Mother Church."

"My friend Julie was a bad influence," Lilia said. "Carlos questioned but never abandoned God."

Miguel harrumphed. "Questioned *me* rather severely."

"Life challenged my Carlos," Lilia said. "And he doubted."

"And you two are …?"

She looked calmly at Miguel. "Lovers. The most perfect lovers."

Carlos blushed. "Do you speak this way to your priest in California?"

Miguel laughed. "Then you're a believer?"

"I am," she said.

Miguel dabbed butter onto his biscuit and waved it at Carlos. "Think you'll ever convert him?"

She smiled a free, happy smile, shaking her head.

"If you plan to marry in the church, Carlos, you know what this means?"

"You'll insist we raise our children *Católico.*"

"Otherwise it's the town hall," Miguel said. "That wouldn't please your bride."

"I won't lie to my children."

"But allow them to see what the church offers?" Miguel asked.

Carlos nodded. "This beautiful señorita gives up a great deal to be with me. She restores my gratitude for life. Yes, Padre, I'll even attend church sometimes with my family. Our children will talk to their priest, perhaps as I spoke to you ..."

Miguel snorted. "They'd better show more respect."

"They'll be free to believe if they choose, and freedom is a blessing."

Miguel raised his teacup. "A toast to pious offspring."

CHAPTER SIXTY

January 1997, San Francisco

His mother opened the door and Benito stepped in. "You haven't come in a while," she said.

"Busy defending our people."

She led him to the kitchen, recently painted a cheerful yellow, new food processor on the counter. She cut a slice of cake and set it on the table. "Tea?"

"Sure."

She put a cup of water in the microwave. "How's the job at that union?"

"Not a union, like the one you pretended my father was in." Rats. He'd promised himself to stop bringing up the old deceits. "Sorry, Mom."

She shook her head. "I always forget the name of your employer."

"Immigrants to Citizens Union. I'm busy with a case—the government's trying to deport a woman whose twelve-year-old is a natural-born citizen. We're going to court."

"Horrible. I hear about something like that, and it makes me imagine, what if it was me and you?" Tears welled in her eyes.

Benito looked away for a moment. His mother did love him, he was sure. Had loved him even as she'd lied. "We're together, Mom, aren't we?"

She smiled. "And you're studying to become one of their attorneys."

"I won't advance at the ICU without that law degree."

"I had to beg you to attend classes at Berkeley, but now you're making me so proud with all your success."

The truth was that after Proposition 187 passed, and after going to Mexico and coming home so disillusioned—with his mother, with his mythical father, with any notion of truth or honor—college work had become Benito's salvation. Then this job came along, giving him a real way to help his people.

"Lots of things are turning around," he said. "Now that the court has struck down most of Proposition 187, public opinion is changing. Californians are starting to care about the men and women who harvest their vegetables. That's progress."

But not enough, Benito knew. Politicians would return to defaming "illegal aliens" to rally scared and bigoted voters. They always did, the shitheads who ran this country.

"And your friend, Juan—is he still working with you?"

"Yeah, Mom, and he's engaged."

She gave him a sideways glance.

"I see that look. I'm still dating Olivia."

"And?"

"Maybe we will and maybe we won't."

The question she didn't ask, the elephant in the apartment: *Any word from your father?* Benito thought of him as his "bio-father"—a man who could never be his Papa after all those years apart. Sad, really. Thinking about it emptied Benito's heart.

All he would say, if she did ask, was, *He's probably still alive down in Mexico with his new wife.* If only he'd never gone to Mexico to find him. Then there wouldn't be this irreconcilable void between him and his mom.

He swallowed his resentment and said, "Mom, I still love you, you know."

She flashed a smile at him, the happiest he'd seen in a while.

CHAPTER SIXTY-ONE

2004, Michoacán

Carlos drove to the orchard accompanied by his black cat, Curioso, and a thermos of coffee. Turning down the driveway toward his plum trees, he thanked God for this bounty, and he thanked Isabel for being his faithful partner and lover. He never came to the orchard without speaking to her, and he believed she heard.

Even if she couldn't, even if this world was all there was, he had reason to be grateful. Fifty-nine years of good health—more years than many men—a generous accumulation. So many hours, so many minutes!

Life might have been more fair if he and his father had shared equally—each living to forty-seven. Or Carlos could have died when Isabel did, and his father could have had ten more years with his wife and children. Would God have been offended by such a merciful trade? But then Carlos would never have met Lilia.

He settled on the grass as the cat chased birds and butterflies. Lilia had given him this kitten a year before, and he'd objected. "I know," she'd said. "That other one Anita gave you …" She hadn't continued with, *when Isabel was dying*, but she'd added, "We'll keep this one healthy to grow old with you."

Curioso amused and inspired—fearlessly attacking larger cats, stalking squirrels like a panther, batting scraps of fabric across the floor. Maturing fast, gaining strength and calmness, but retaining a playfulness, an absurd boldness, an unpretentious share of life. Cats spoke more truths than any priest.

Those gifts from God, now he saw them differently—paradoxical absurdities, frivolities like the cat, beauty, the miracle of life's unfolding in his children, his trees laden with fruit—served up in abundance from God or from a very creative evolution, who could say? Life was the gift—the sun's warmth, his lovely Lilia, his children, living from nature's bounty, his grief over Isabel and their lost son faded to tender remembrance. Lilia had been able to provide only one child, their precious Julia, not all they'd wished for but an incredible blessing.

And faith? He might have realized sooner that religion was not a search for truth but for comfort. Padre Miguel's books should have showed him that—so many beliefs, each worshipped confidently, fervently, fanatically. One displayed open whimsy— the playful Hindu gods with elephant heads, blue-faced deities, and writhing snakes. Now that Miguel was gone, Carlos regretted tormenting his friend, but they'd made their peace.

The guilt that nagged was Benito, growing with no *papá* and rejecting Carlos after those two brief visits. This remorse springing from the other—María and his foolish rejection of birth control— unforgivable to have blamed his failures on God or on Mexican male culture. Unforgivable to imagine that his actions hurt no one because he was so far from Isabel, to have risked diseases he might have brought her, risked her faith in him.

He'd been foolish, selfish, blind to overlook the way God (or nature) had created humans, needy and jealous—the way a woman like María would react, the way they'd both thoughtlessly created a troubled son. Did God judge him for this? No need. He judged himself.

He bore this painful regret—and, too, a growing worry. At the farmers' cooperative and, from time to time, on the television news, Carlos heard about the expanding marijuana trade in Michoacán—heroin, cocaine, other drugs, too, cooked in a laboratory, public officials bribed. Marijuana and opium poppies had always been local crops, often cultivated by the same ranchers who grew vegetables, hence the common belief that cooperation between *policía* and *narcos* promoted peace and prosperity.

Lilia would watch his face when these television stories appeared, and he'd pretend not to worry. "That's far from here," he'd say, or "We won't go down there."

A few secret murders and a few not-so secret, but all these troubles were farther south. Carlos used Lilia's computer to check—there'd been murders in Santa Lucia, as many as six one year.

He had brought her to this land, and it was no worse than her previous home. They were safe, safe and prosperous.

Two nights later

After little Julia went to bed, Lilia sat across his lap on the sofa. She wasn't as slim as nine years ago; giving birth had seen to that, but could she really be approaching fifty? Still far more attractive than he deserved—from God's hand to his.

"My life is marvelous," she said, gazing into his eyes. "I love teaching dear little children, and I always wanted a cook."

"My *chile rellenos* are excellent, aren't they?"

"I'm not sure they're yours. Julia claims she does all the work."

He laughed. "A good worker, like her mom. If I leave a block of cheese lying around, she'll shred it. In the orchard, Julia's begun to pick more fruit than she eats. I taught her some religion today, too."

Lilia frowned. "Aztec sacrifices?"

"As we pruned the branches from a mango tree, Julia and I admired the way buds had formed on those twigs."

"Oh?"

"Little miracles. Later, we lay on the hillside pretending we were drops of water in a stream. We looked for animal shapes in the clouds and talked about what a gift it is to feel the air filling us and flowing out. We found many ways to say the word 'glorious': marvelous, superb, wondrous …'"

"I think of Julie, too, but you know what?" Lilia sighed. "I'm happier here with you than I ever thought I could be."

ACKNOWLEDGMENTS

I am grateful to my editor, Rebecca Mahoney, who guided me through several iterations of *Carlos*. It was very rough in the beginning, and Rebecca was patient, insightful, and thoughtful. It's a much better book than I could have produced without her;

To my wife, Marguerite, who played a similar role, sharing the women's point of view, a counselor's insight, persistence in the face of my stubbornness and mostly agreeing with Rebecca in a helpful way;

To Kristin Bryant who designed this gorgeous cover, as well as the cover for my previous novel, *Soul of Toledo*;

And to Dr. Bill Garlington of the Osher Lifelong Learning Institute, California State University Channel Islands for introducing an array of beliefs and ideas and detailing philosophers from Thomas Aquinas to Akbar, Mughal emperor of India.

ABOUT THE AUTHOR

Edward D. Webster's wide-ranging interests have led him to diverse careers from teaching Navajo students to managing regulatory compliance to helping establish a center for abused children.

Photo by: Patsy Wright

He is the author of an eclectic collection of books as well as articles appearing in publications from *The Boston Globe to Your Cat* magazine. His writing has been honored by the Colorado Independent Publishers Association, the Foreword Indies, the Boomer Times, and Ed's favorite: Hackwriters.com, among others.

Ed admits to a fascination with unique, quirky, and bizarre human behavior, and he doesn't exempt himself from the mix. His acclaimed memoir, *A Year of Sundays (Taking the Plunge and our Cat to Explore Europe)* shares the eccentric tale of his yearlong adventure in Europe with his spirited, blind wife, Marguerite, and their headstrong, deaf, elderly cat, Felicia.

In his historical novel, *Soul of Toledo*, about Spain in the 1440s, the diabolical nature of mankind stands out as madmen take over the city of Toledo and torture suspected Jews thirty years before the Spanish Inquisition.

Webster also likes to tinker by putting strange characters together to see what they'll do with/to each other. In his novel *The Gentle Bomber's Melody*, a nutty woman, bearing a stolen baby, lands on the doorstep of a fugitive bomber hiding from the FBI. The result: irresistible insanity.

From the happily unusual of *A Year of Sundays* to the cruelly perverse in *Soul of Toledo*, Webster shines a light on offbeat aspects of human nature.

In his latest novel, *Carlos Crosses the Line*, Webster casts his eye in new directions: the 1960s, the immigration quagmire, free love, the validity of borders between people and countries, the question of what to believe if you don't accept your culture's traditional values.

Webster lives in Southern California with his divine wife and two amazing cats.

See Ed's website, www.edwardwebster.com,

And his Facebook page, www.facebook.com/edwebauthor, for more information.

CPSIA information can be obtained
at www.ICGtesting.com
Printed in the USA
FSHW012105291220
77246FS

9 780997 032024